the MYSTERY *of the* INVISIBLE HAND

a **HENRY SPEARMAN** *mystery*

PRINCETON UNIVERSITY PRESS
Princeton and Oxford

MARSHALL
JEVONS

the MYSTERY

of the

Invisible

Hand

COPYRIGHT © 2014 BY PRINCETON UNIVERSITY PRESS
Published by Princeton University Press
41 William Street, Princeton, New Jersey 08540
In the United Kingdom: Princeton University Press
6 Oxford Street, Woodstock, Oxfordshire OX20 1TW

press.princeton.edu

Cover illustration and design by Chris Ferrante

The Mystery of the Invisible Hand is fiction, and all the characters and adventures are imaginary. Any resemblance to actual persons, living or dead, is purely coincidental.

Library of Congress Cataloging-in-Publication Data

Jevons, Marshall, author.
    The mystery of the invisible hand : a Henry Spearman mystery / Marshall Jevons.
        pages cm
Summary: "Henry Spearman, the balding economics professor with a knack for solving crimes, returns in The Mystery of the Invisible Hand—a clever whodunit of campus intrigue, stolen art, and murder. Having just won the Nobel Prize, Spearman accepts an invitation to lecture at Monte Vista University. He arrives in the wake of a puzzling art heist with plans to teach a course on art and economics—only to be faced with the alleged suicide of womanizing artist-in-residence Tristan Wheeler. When it becomes clear that Wheeler had serious enemies and a murderer is in their midst, Henry Spearman is on the case. Was Wheeler killed by a jilted lover, a cuckolded husband, or a beleaguered assistant? Could there have been a connection between Wheeler's marketability and his death? From the Monte Vista campus in San Antonio to the halls of Sotheby's in New York, Spearman traces the connections between economics and the art world, finding his clues in monopolies and the Coase conjecture, auction theory, and the work of Adam Smith. What are the parallels between a firm's capital and an art museum's collection? What does the market say about art's authenticity versus its availability? And what is the mysterious "death effect" that lies at the heart of the case? Spearman must rely on his savviest economic insights to clear up this artful mystery and pin down a killer"—Provided by publisher.
    ISBN 978-0-691-16313-0 (hardback)
    1. Spearman, Henry (Fictitious character)—Fiction. 2. Economists—United States—Fiction. I. Title.
    PS3560.E88M97 2014
    813'.54—dc23
        2014012109

British Library Cataloging-in-Publication Data is available

This book has been composed in Sabon Next LT Pro with Trade Gothic LT Std and Yesteryear for display

Printed on acid-free paper. ∞

Printed in the United States of America

10 9 8 7 6 5 4 3 2 1

for **WILLIAM BREIT**
il miglior fabbro

An economist by training thinks of himself as the guardian of rationality, the ascriber of rationality to others, and the prescriber of rationality to the social world.

—KENNETH ARROW

FLASH-FORWARD

The streets were dark with something more than night.
—RAYMOND CHANDLER

The house was finally quiet. Outside, the black cloak of darkness was just beginning to lift. The change could be seen coming through the crossbars of the skylight. Dawn wasn't far off. But there was still enough time to be sure of things. "More haste, less speed," wasn't that the way it went?

It hadn't been as hard as expected. After clearing the room they'd been able to move the body and chair into the bathroom with nary a trace left for the police. It had been a good idea to arrange for the extra help, even if it took some arm-twisting. Of course, now there was a witness . . . no question about that. Well—all in good time.

The toughest part had been the hoisting. He'd actually awakened enough to struggle. But together they'd got him just high enough to avoid the kicking and flailing, and the spasmodic legs were connecting with nothing but air.

The gurgling and the jerking soon slowed, like a wind up toy beginning to run down. The eyes had bulged, the arms fell and hung limply. And still the murderer had waited, well after the breathing had stopped, well after the furtive accomplice had slipped out into the night. Nothing was going to go wrong this time.

A chiming clock from somewhere within the house broke the spell. Five times the lonely sound echoed in the darkness. Time to go. Careful fingers pulled out a note and held it up to a pocket LED. Its signature passing inspection, the piece of paper was accordingly placed on the vanity, propped up against a glass and toothbrush that would never be used again.

On the way out the dead man's body was bumped. It began to swing slowly, freely. . . .

Freely! From some nether region a dry chuckle emerged. Swinging freely—an apt epitaph. Too bad it couldn't be shared with anyone. The chuckle turned into a laugh which ended only as the front doorknob turned, and the figure melted into the outer shadows.

It had been a productive night.

the MYSTERY *of the* INVISIBLE HAND

1

SPEARMAN MEETS THE KING

The ideas of economists and political philosophers, both when they are right and when they are wrong, are more powerful than is commonly understood. Indeed, the world is ruled by little else. Practical men, who believe themselves to be quite exempt from any intellectual influences, are usually the slaves of some defunct economist.
—JOHN MAYNARD KEYNES

On this particular cold December evening, Henry Spearman was an example of how "clothes make the man"—or in his case how they didn't. The tails of his morning coat hung just a few inches off the ground. Instead of elongating his silhouette, the garment made him look cherubic. But he was not worried about his clothes. He was worried about protocol. Tonight he would meet the king.

The setting was Blå Hallen, the "Blue Room" of the Stockholm City Hall, and Spearman was about to receive the Nobel Prize in economics. His day had already been memorable: a tour of historic landmarks and Swedish architecture followed that evening by the Nobel banquet. Sixty-five tables had been prepared for the Swedish royal family, the prize winners, the special invitees and

1

guests. The tables were blanketed with Swedish linen from Ekelund—supplier to the royal family for over three centuries—and set with Rörstrand porcelain china and Orrefors glassware that glinted and sparkled in the muted light. The fare was Scandinavian, salmon, lobster, and wild game; the table conversation eclectic; the entertainment top notch. Now came the time for the presentation and Spearman recounted in his mind the protocol expected of him. While honors and distinctions had come his way before, this was the academy's big kahuna. Even the name— "Nobel"—lent luster to the award. The cachet of the prize would not be the same if it were, say, the "Jones Prize."

It would be idle to contend that the Nobel had come as a complete surprise. Now in his fifties, Spearman was a heavy hitter in the world of books and ideas. His teachers first spotted his brilliance when he was an undergraduate at Columbia. During graduate school the faculty had recognized him as a rising star. An invitation to join the Department of Economics at Harvard signaled that the academic marketplace agreed. He did not disappoint. Spearman quickly brought more prestige to what was already a prestigious department.

When Spearman's Nobel award was first announced, Harvard's public relations department went into high gear. While some universities battled it out on the football field, Harvard battled its Ivy League counterparts by its faculty winning academic prizes. Winning a bowl game landed a school in the sports section of a newspaper. But a Nobel Prize was front-page stuff, and often above the fold. In the field of economics, the University of Chicago was home to more Nobel Prize winners than any other school. Spearman's prize would help Harvard chip away at Chicago's market share.

At the award ceremony, Henry's wife Pidge was radiant in a pale blue linen gown that accented her buxom figure. Seated next to Pidge was the couple's daughter Patricia. She had left her veterinary practice to be in Stockholm during the awards week. "The animals will have to wait," she laughed.

When the presenter asked the recipient in economics "to step forward to receive his Nobel Prize from the hands of his majesty the king," Spearman rose, walked to the center of the stage, shook hands with royalty, and made the bows that the recipients had been instructed to perform after receiving the prize. For the first time in his life, trumpets from the Royal Orchestra heralded his work as an economist. Also for the first time in his life, Spearman became a million dollars richer in one fell swoop.

On the return flight to Boston's Logan airport, Spearman thought back to his roots. His parents had come to the United States just ahead of the Hitler juggernaut. They were almost penniless. Henry was brought up above his father's tailor shop in Brooklyn. For twenty years, that was his world. Now he had been feted by royalty on the continent from which his parents had escaped with their lives. Moreover, his name had been joined to those of

Akerlof
Arrow
Becker
Buchanan
Coase

Friedman
Hayek
Kahneman
Lucas
Nash
Schultz
Sen
Smith
Solow
Stigler
Stiglitz
Tobin
Vickrey

and other luminaries in the field of economics. He knew his life would never be the same.

It wasn't.

2

A NOBEL INVITATION

Money . . . is the centre around which economic science clusters; this is so, not because money or material wealth is regarded as the main aim of human effort, nor even as affording the main subject-matter for the study of the economist: but because in this world of ours it is the one convenient means of measuring human motive on the large scale.

—ALFRED MARSHALL

"So how much would it cost?" the trustee asked.

"I think it would be expensive," the president responded.

Charlotte Quinn was in the first year of her presidency at Monte Vista University. This was only her second meeting with the school's Board of Trustees. She was still learning what stirred the cocoa of the trustees who had the sole authority to hire and fire her, and who could make her life as president easy or hard.

"Charlotte, that's not an answer to my question," Annelle Cubbage replied. "I don't see why students at Monte Vista University shouldn't be taught by the best there is. And if Nobel Prize winners are the best, then we should have them on campus for our students to learn from."

The other members of the board had left President Quinn to fend for herself. Annelle Cubbage was blunt, like most wealthy Texas ranchers. But she did not fit the TV stereotype of the rich Texan. First, she was a woman. Second, she was a patron of the arts. Yet Cubbage could shoot grouse with the best of the Texas hunting fraternity and could distinguish a Browning over-and-under shotgun from a Merkel at ten paces. "And I never shot a politician," she liked to brag, "tempting as the opportunity might be." When a certain vice president of the United States from Wyoming accidentally shot his companion while grouse hunting in Texas, Cubbage told a television reporter that "people from Wyoming never could shoot straight. You want a good huntin' partner, you hunt with a Texan." Annelle Cubbage definitely fit the don't-mess-with-Texas mold.

"The problem is that we're a teaching university," President Quinn explained. "People who win Nobel Prizes are at major research universities—the Chicagos, the Harvards, the Stanfords. Our focus is on undergraduates, not graduate students. So I'm not sure whether we could make it attractive for a Nobel Prize winner to join the faculty at Monte Vista."

"Doesn't that depend upon how much you pay 'em?" Cubbage asked. "Don't tell me winnin' a Nobel Prize means you don't care about money anymore."

Annelle Cubbage was accustomed to being blunt about money. While the Board of Trustees of Monte Vista University had several wealthy members, Cubbage played in a different league. Most people who thought of themselves as well-to-do measured their net worth in millions.

In her league, the metric was "units." A unit was a hundred million. Annelle Cubbage had multiple units.

Born in Troup, Texas, which her great-grandfather had settled, Cubbage might have been expected to center her life in Houston or Dallas. But instead she had a ranch in the Hill Country outside San Antonio and an apartment on Central Park in New York. Both cities knew her as a patron of the arts.

Charlotte Quinn knew there was a fine line between a trustee who micromanaged the institution and a trustee who rubber-stamped decisions by the administration. The problem was recognizing where to draw the line. Quinn was not sure where the line came down when adding a Nobel laureate to the faculty. Recruiting individual professors was not a board matter. But funding a new position for a distinguished professor of Nobel Prize stature meant spending a lot of money. Anything that involved a lot of money was a matter for the board.

Recalling the old adage that "he who pays the piper calls the tune," President Quinn decided it was prudent to keep the discussion going. Accordingly, she sat silently with the rest of the trustees as Cubbage continued to press her conviction that if Monte Vista students were going to be the best, they needed to be exposed to the best.

Herbert Abraham, the lone faculty member seated at the conference table, waited for a pause. "May I make a suggestion?" he asked. Normally, Abraham would have put his hand up to be called upon by the chair of the board before he would speak. But the silent interval emboldened him to interject. "Why not bring a Nobel laureate to campus just for a semester . . . as a distinguished visiting professor? Offer them a furnished house near campus, have them teach just one course—and make it anything they want to teach. That way they'll have plenty of time to do research, give talks, and pursue other endeavors."

Abraham was a professor of economics at Monte Vista University and served as the faculty representative on the board. He was in his early sixties. At board meetings, he was always the best dressed, always sat ramrod straight in his chair, and always showed a mastery of the contents of the board notebook that some trustees had only skimmed the night before. To top it off, Abraham possessed none of the conventional faculty haughtiness toward the well-to-do. When he saw that his idea seemed to catch the board's attention, he knew he was on a roll.

"If we went ahead with this, I'd suggest we require the Nobel Prize winner to give one, maybe two, public lectures during the semester in residence." Abraham paused. "And, of course, having a Nobel laureate would be great PR for the school." He looked down the conference table to Annelle Cubbage.

Cubbage did not wait long. "Well, I've already paid for an artist-in-residence. So I'll come back to my original question to President Quinn. Maybe you can answer it, Professor. How much would it cost to bring in one of these Nobel Prize winners?"

"Depends on the field," Abraham responded. "A Nobel Prize winner in physics will cost us more than a Nobel Prize winner in literature. In my field of economics, I suspect we would have to pay two hundred to two hundred fifty thousand for the semester, if the school throws in a furnished home."

"You see, Charlotte, there is an answer to my question," Annelle Cubbage announced. She paused, looked at Professor Abraham and added, "I think it would be worth every penny."

•

And so it came to pass, in late May, in the state of Texas, that Annelle Cubbage parted with one tenth of a unit to endow the "Cubbage Visiting Nobel Professorship."

Professor Abraham used his influence to recommend a professor in his field of economics. "Why not?" he thought to himself. "I came up with the idea. And I think I know just the right person for Monte Vista."

In early August, the first recipient of Annelle Cubbage's largesse was announced as Henry Spearman, professor of economics at Harvard University, and a freshly minted Nobel laureate. Time of the appointment: the following spring semester, January through May.

3

NO COASE FOR CONCERN

TUESDAY AFTERNOON, NOVEMBER 15TH

"That is another of your odd notions," said the Prefect, who had a fashion of calling everything "odd" that was beyond his comprehension, and thus lived amid an absolute legion of "oddities."

—EDGAR ALLAN POE

Blake Bailey scanned the crowd in the hallway and then, spying Professor Henry Spearman down the corridor, made a beeline for him. Bailey's long red hair stuck out on all sides of his Boston Red Sox cap. Black horn rimmed glasses, if anything, made his hair color more vivid. When Bailey caught up with the famous economist, who was in animated palaver with a colleague, he was breathless. It was noon at Harvard Hall, one of the main classroom buildings. Much of the time the hallways and stairs of this building were unoccupied. But at this time of the day, hungry and noisy students were filing out the classroom doors after being released by their instructors.

"Professor Spearman, I'm sorry to interrupt, but I have to ask you something."

"Oh?" said Spearman. His frown quickly morphed into an expectant gaze when he recognized that the brash inquisitor was from the intermediate price theory class he'd just finished teaching. He smiled inwardly. Blake was one of those students, common in every class and on any subject, whose silence before the bell was inversely proportional to the deluge of questions afterward.

Before Blake could pose his question, Spearman held up one hand, and pointed to his colleague with the other, "Mr. Bailey, have you met Dr. Henderson Ross in the psychology department?"

Twenty-five years earlier Spearman and Ross both had begun their academic careers at Harvard. They had become friends even though they were a study in contrast. Ross was tall with bushy black hair. Spearman was short and bald. Ross wore contacts; Spearman preferred glasses. Ross dressed like a hippie: jeans and a collarless shirt were the norm, and he carried a canvas book bag. Save for his age, he might have come straight from a college protest forty years earlier. Spearman on the other hand was only twenty years out of style. Decidedly preppy, he wore khakis, a button-down shirt, a rep tie, and a blazer—with an attaché case to hold his class material. What bound the two professors together was their survival of Harvard's tenure process. The handful of soldiers who endured a death march often became fast friends, regardless of race, color, or creed. The handful of professors who survived the tenure process at elite universities often shared a similar bond.

"Hey, how ya doin'?" Blake responded, glancing at Ross after Spearman's introduction.

"I'm fine. How are you?"

"Uh, okay I guess," as he turned his face in Spearman's direction. Momentarily Bailey wondered what it might mean when a psychologist asks, "how are you?" *Wouldn't that be a deep and complex question to answer?* But the young undergraduate realized that to ask Ross what he really meant would divert his inquiry of Spearman.

"Professor Spearman, I'm confused over the lecture you gave last week. You know, the one about real estate developers? I think you ended by saying that even if a person owned all the land in the United States he wouldn't be able to charge a monopoly price for it. Is that right?"

At this point in the conversation, Ross's expression became one of sympathy for the inquisitive youth. The eminent psychologist patted the boy on the back and smiled at his colleague. "Henry, put this young man out of his misery and straighten him out on the matter. It's clear he didn't hear you right. I've always maintained that you let too many students in your courses; this is what happens. One thing we know in psychology is that smaller classes make for better teaching stimuli."

Spearman smiled broadly. "There is nothing wrong with Mr. Bailey's hearing, notwithstanding the class size. That is *precisely* what I said. If you owned all the land, you would be rich as Rockefeller. No doubt about that. But you couldn't charge a monopoly price for any one parcel of it."

"Come now, Henry. That sounds like sophistry."

"No, no," Spearman replied. "Let me put the matter a little differently by asking both of you a question. Assume someone owned all the land in the United States. Would either of you buy any of it as an investment, even a few acres, without a guarantee from the monopolist that additional quantities of the land would not be sold at lower prices?

"Of course not!" Spearman exclaimed, answering his own question. "How else could you protect the value of your investment? At the very least you would insist that the seller buy it back from you at the price you paid, if more land were going to go on the market at a lower price. Or you would insist that any additional land the monopolist offered would be used for some noncommercial purpose—like a public park—that wouldn't affect your investment. Otherwise," he paused, making sure he had the attention of both his listeners, "you, or any other rational economic agent, would never buy any land. So, Mr. Bailey: as I said in class, the market disciplines even someone who owns *all* the land. It was an economist named Coase who first made the point. It's now called the Coase conjecture."

Spearman looked expectantly for dawning comprehension on their faces. He was disappointed. Continuing, he put a hand on the young student's shoulder. "My point in class, Mr. Bailey, was simply this. Assume you sell a durable good, one that's impervious to change from time or the elements. And you face buyers who can defer their purchases. Then *time itself* becomes a substitute—like an invisible competitor who depresses the price of the durable good. So even if you were the *only* seller of a durable good, if you can't credibly commit to not lowering prices in the future, you can't exercise monopoly power."

Spearman waited for a response from his listeners. None was forthcoming. The psychologist looked in the direction of Blake Bailey. "You see, young man, it's Professor Spearman's ability to give answers like the one you just heard that has endeared him to generations of students and made the rest of us on the faculty green with envy. Some of us even wonder at times if Spearman may be right. Or does he just lean right?"

Spearman smiled at Ross's good-natured jab. He knew the two of them saw the world through different lens. But Spearman was perpetually optimistic that in the market-place of ideas, the economic way of thinking would eventually hold the dominant market share. Ross, on the other hand, feared that Spearman might be right, even if his economics was wrong.

•

Henderson Ross had observed Spearman even more closely after his friend returned from Stockholm with the Nobel medal and prize money in hand. As a psychologist, Ross knew that "colleague envy" had never been analyzed by Sigmund Freud. Freud's theory of envy was centered elsewhere, somewhere south of the human heart. But Ross, a keen observer of university life, thought that "colleague envy" might be a reliable indicator of scholarly accomplishment. And he also knew that his good friend Henry now lived in its glare.

The two professors and the student ended their confab with pleasantries and went their separate ways. On non–class days, Spearman was known as a stimulating raconteur and table companion at Harvard's faculty club. But after teaching a midmorning class, he retired to his office in the Littauer Center where he ate lunch alone. He found teaching to be exhausting, and this was especially so if the class had gone well. It took far more energy to teach a good class than a bad one.

There was another reason Spearman did not socialize after teaching a class. Over the years, he had learned that the best time to assess how a class had gone was right after teaching the material. His colleagues who waited months, even a year, before revising a lecture were making a mistake, Spearman thought. What went right and what went wrong would be long forgotten by then.

Ross knew of Spearman's obsession about improving his teaching and had once asked him, "Henry, what would it take for you to file a lecture away, right after you had given it in class, fully satisfied that it could not be improved upon?" Henry laughed at the question and responded with a twinkle in his eye. "A great lecture, one that needs no revision, is when the students carry you out of the building on their shoulders and parade you around the campus." Ross's reply was dry. "Well by that standard, most of us only give a couple great lectures each year."

As he ate a light lunch, Spearman picked up the *Boston Globe* that had been left on his desk. Because he was an economist, his students expected him to be up on the news even if they were not. In the second section, a headline caught his attention:

TEXAS ART CRIME

SAN ANTONIO, TX (AP) State and local police searched the home of prominent San Antonio physician and art collector Dr. Raul Ramos on November 14 as they investigated the break-in and theft of five paintings by acclaimed local artist Tristan Wheeler. Included in the theft was Wheeler's "A Portrait in Blue," which according to the artist signified his "final break from the capitalist confinement of contemporary art" and was the first of his subsequent paintings to garner national attention.

Authorities responded to a call from the Oakmont Avenue residence just before 3 a.m. CST. The call was reportedly placed by a live-in maid who had been awakened by noises coming from the living room where the paintings were located. Officers who searched the home did not comment to reporters on the details of the case.

Ramos is a well-known patron of the San Antonio art community, and frequently hosts benefits to support the city's art museums. Lewis Martin of the Travis Museum of Art in San Antonio told reporters that a guest at one of these events might have hired professionals to steal them. When informed of this statement Ramos admitted the possibility, saying that he doubted the paintings would be found. "I don't think I'll get them back. They will probably wind up in a private collection where nobody else ever sees them." Dr. Ramos said the impact of his loss was compounded because the works had not been insured. The physician added that the theft did not destroy his desire to rebuild his collection. A one million dollar reward has been offered for the return of his paintings.

Most experts believe that speed in such cases is of paramount importance. "It's vital that cases involving the theft of art be solved quickly. Once the art is gone for awhile, it is usually gone for good," Sidnee Van Pelt, security chief of the Fogg Museum of Art at Harvard University and an authority on art theft, told the *Boston Globe*.

•

Spearman punched the intercom button on his phone to call for Gloria Winters, his longtime administrative assistant. When she entered his office he handed her the page from the newspaper and pointed to the article he had just read. "Gloria, would you clip this and file it please?"

"And how do you want it filed?" Winters asked.

Spearman placed his hand to his chin, narrowed his eyes, and thought for a moment. "Please put it in the box of material we're sending to San Antonio. And label it *the barking dog* file."

4

INVESTIGATION OF A THEFT

TUESDAY AFTERNOON, NOVEMBER 15TH

Look at everything upside down. Take absolutely nothing
for granted.

—DICK FRANCIS

"So let me get this straight, you *did* hear or you did *not*
hear anyone upstairs? I don't understand which it is." Detective Fritz Siegfried was interviewing Rosie Segura at the
San Antonio police station. He had wedged himself into
his office chair and the effect was an imposing one. When
he cocked his arms and put his elbows on the desktop, the
burly officer's biceps bulged like grapefruits.

He looked at the diminutive housekeeper skeptically.
His officers had interviewed her at the Ramos home when
they first arrived to investigate the theft. Siegfried knew
that most Latinos in San Antonio were law-abiding citizens. But there were several inconsistencies in Rosie's
story that he was determined to track down himself.

"I said I did hear, but then I didn't hear, then I heard
again. When I heard again, that's when I went upstairs—
with my scissors—to see what I heard." Rosie looked plead-
ingly into Siegfried's face. She had nothing to fear about
deportation. But Rosie depended on having a good job

for the money she sent to family members in Mexico who in turn relied on her income. While politicians debated the immigration issue, for her the debate was not about public policy. It was about economic survival.

"And when you say you went upstairs, did you see anyone—like the person you said you heard?"

"No, I didn't see no one."

"What time was it when you went upstairs?" The question had already been asked, but Siegfried wasn't satisfied. Because criminals lied so often about their conduct, contradictions in their story often told him more than the stories themselves.

"I told you, it was about two thirty a.m. I keep a clock by my bed. I looked at it when I heard the noises and woke up."

"So you heard a noise, someone was upstairs, but you can't tell me who it was. Is that what you're saying?"

"I can't tell you who it was because I never saw no one. When I got upstairs, nobody was there, at least in the dining room and the living room. And the kitchen—the kitchen is the first room you come to when you come upstairs."

"Did you look in any of the closets on the main floor? Or just the dining room and living room?"

"No way was I 'bout to look in any closets. After I got upstairs, I got a kitchen knife, but I still didn't want to find no one hiding in a closet. When I looked in the dining room and the living room, that's when I called to Dr. Ramos and he called 911."

"Ms. Segura," the detective asked, changing his tone from sternness to that of a kindly grandfather, "if you didn't see anyone, how did you know someone had been there?"

"Because the paintings were gone. *That's* why." Rosie looked at the detective as though he were a dull child. "I said that yesterday to the police. I know enough to know that paintings don't just walk out the house by themselves. *Somebody* had to be upstairs. Whoever it was, that's who I heard."

"If paintings don't walk out by themselves, then someone took 'em. It could be your boss, but you said he was in bed when you called him, is that right?"

"Yes, he was in his bedroom."

"How long did you say you've worked for Dr. Ramos?"

"For almost seven years," Rosie said, perplexed by the question.

"Then if it wasn't your boss who took the paintings, I guess it could have been you. You knew they were there. You've been working for your boss for plenty of time to know every nook and cranny in the house. You probably know places in the house that Dr. Ramos doesn't even know about."

Rosie visibly recoiled when Detective Siegfried suggested that she might be the thief. "No, no, you don't understand. I care for Dr. Ramos. I work hard for him. I would never steal from Dr. Ramos. All these years, not a penny did I steal. You think I now would steal his paintings?" Rosie's eyes were again pleading.

"But if you didn't do it, and Dr. Ramos didn't steal his own paintings, how could anyone else do it? Your boss said the doors were locked when he got up. My men couldn't find any evidence of a window being broken or jimmied. Was there anyone else in the house that night? Any family?"

"We were the only ones. My boss, he's divorced. He's got two children, but they're all grown up. The boy, he lives in Austin, the girl she lives somewhere up north—Milwaukee, the last I heard Dr. Ramos say."

Detective Siegfried leaned back in his chair and thought. If Rosie were going to steal from her boss, why artwork? As a housekeeper, she was unlikely to know how to fence high-valued paintings. And why wake up her boss? Unless this itself was a ploy to throw off the police . . . ?

On the other hand, and in detective work there always was another hand, Siegfried knew that some criminals were successful simply because the crime was so unlikely. Rosie could have bided her time, avoided the more obvious temptations to steal petty cash from her boss, and gone for the big score: the most valuable assets in the house. In addition, Dr. Ramos entertained frequently, and the social events in the Ramos home were connected to the art community. Rosie may have made contacts—or even been contacted—by someone who with her help could get the paintings out of the house and then lucratively dispose of them. Siegfried wondered if a situation requiring a large influx of cash—medical, maybe?—had suddenly arisen in Rosie's family. If so, the desire to help might outweigh her loyalty to her employer.

Rosie would bear more watching.

●

The officer first on the scene had interviewed Dr. Ramos and then released him to go to the hospital, where a full docket of surgeries awaited. Siegfried was not thrilled with this decision. He knew that the more time elapsed before witnesses were questioned, the more they forgot—or the more they could dissemble. But the work of a surgeon could not always be pushed around. To accommodate Ramos, Siegfried had agreed to postpone his questioning until the following afternoon.

"I don't think Rosie would take anything from me, Detective." The surgeon smiled. The two men were seated in the small office that Santa Rosa hospital provided surgeons for postop administrative work. "She's worked for me for years—never complained about her work—seems very devoted to me. I can't say she liked my wife too much. Both of my children adored Rosie. Of course they should've. She picked up after them and cooked anything for them they wanted. She's a great cook, but then what *ama de casa* isn't?" Dr. Ramos was still dressed in his green surgical scrubs as he spoke about his housekeeper with the detective.

Siegfried offered no response to any of Ramos's observations. "Let's review the statement you gave to Officer McKinney yesterday. McKinney and her partner got to your home at two forty-five. You told her that your housekeeper, that would be Ms. Segura, awakened you at around two thirty on an intercom system that goes to your bedroom from the kitchen, is that correct?"

Ramos nodded.

"And when you came downstairs she showed you that the paintings were gone, correct?"

Again Ramos nodded, impatiently. Like most surgeons, Ramos believed himself to be the smartest guy in the room. "That's when I called 911. Rosie said she tried, but the line was dead. But someone had left a phone off the hook upstairs."

"And you're sure the paintings were there when you went to bed?" Siegfried asked.

"Absolutely. You see, Detective, yesterday evening I hosted a little fund-raiser for the Travis Museum of Art. I invited Lewis Martin, the curator, to make some remarks that were designed to pick the pockets—and the purses—of my guests. Lewis is always clever in how he does this. He talks about an artist, and before some people even know it, they've parted with a few thousand bucks to support the arts." Ramos chuckled. "He's always been especially enamored with Wheeler's work. I think he was envious that I owned more Wheelers than any other private collector. Last night Lewis lingered lovingly on every last detail of every last splash. Oh yes, they were there."

"Sunday's event, doctor . . . was that kind of thing a regular occurrence in your home?" Siegfried took notes while Ramos spoke.

"Not every week, mind you, but it wasn't unusual either. I invite people to my home, I line up someone to make a presentation, and I spend a couple thousand bucks or so to have the event catered. I'm on the board of the Travis, so I take the cost off my taxes. And who knows? Someday when my guests need surgery, they might think of me." Ramos smiled, as if to congratulate himself on the optimality of it all.

Siegfried found himself wondering if this was why the police department was underfunded. The rich people in town always had a way to get out of paying taxes. But he brought his thoughts back into focus. "Let me ask you a few questions about who was there that evening. You said about twenty guests. Was Ms. Segura there too?"

"Yes, Rosie was there. She doesn't do the catering, but she knows the house and provides backup for just about anything that might happen—a server doesn't show up, a guest calls in who can't find the house, that kind of thing. It wasn't a sit-down dinner party, but nobody goes home hungry from a Ramos party."

"Would you have a guest list?"

"I don't have one at the hospital. But Rosie would have one, as would Lewis. For an event like this, even though I'm the host, he's more responsible than I am for assembling the guest list."

"If you could get me a copy of the list, I'd like to see it. You say every one of these people would have seen the missing paintings. When did the last guest leave?"

"Most of my guests know that I have to get up early. When I try to get them out the door, I often joke with them: 'Remember, I have to be *sharp* in the morning.' Some get the pun, others don't. But I think everyone was out of the house by ten p.m. Lewis was the last to leave. He usually stays until the end to thank me and tell me how he thought it went. 'How it went,' to Martin, means how much money he raised for the Travis. People think museums are rich or somehow run themselves. That's not true. According to Lewis, the Travis is always broke."

Siegfried did not let the travails of the museum distract him. "When your guests left the house, did they all go out the front door?"

"Oh yes, they always leave that way, because their cars are in front. The house has a large circular driveway with a small lot to one side. One of the catering staff usually helps everyone park in front."

"Would you have seen all your guests leave?" Siegfried was trying to learn whether he would need to interview each of the guests who were at the Ramos home. He did not relish the prospect.

Ramos thought before answering. "I stand at the front door and try to say good night and thank everyone for coming and, you know, tell them 'I hope you had a good time.' I don't check them off a guest list when they leave, mind you, but I think I saw everyone out the door. I certainly can't recall that not being the case last night."

"Is there any way a guest could have left your house carrying the paintings with them?"

"There's a kitchen door and a back door. The caterers would come and go through the kitchen. Rosie keeps the back door bolted. The front door—no way. If someone tried to walk by me at the front door carrying five Tristan Wheeler paintings that had been on my living room wall, I think I would have asked them, 'Did you mistake those for your coat?' or something more direct."

"So if the guests can't get by you with the paintings, what about Mr. Martin, from the museum? Would he have been able to remove the paintings from your home that evening?"

"What would he do with them? Hang them on the wall at the Travis, where I'd spot them at the next board meeting?" Ramos imagined his reaction at going to the special collections wing of the museum and seeing all five of his Wheeler paintings hanging there.

"Among all the others in your house that night, that leaves the caterers. Do you recall how many there were?"

"Sure, I always use The Red Carpet. They do a nice job for events that size. That night, they had three staff there. Three good people can handle a group of twenty nicely."

"Were the staff members ones that you had used before?"

"Yes, that's one of the reasons I like The Red Carpet. They know me and how I like to throw a party. Just about always I know the staff they send: Alfredo, Suzanne, and Ruthie—those are the three who were there."

Siegfried consulted his notes. "Dr. Ramos, I have one other question. You told Officer McKinney that the paintings were not insured. Is that right?"

"That's correct."

"Why?"

"In hindsight, that appears to be a mistake, doesn't it? They used to be. But I was trying to save on that expense. And when I first started collecting Wheeler paintings, I didn't anticipate they'd go up in value so much. I'm sure you observe this in your line of work as I do in mine, Detective. We all learn from our mistakes, don't we?"

Siegfried left Dr. Ramos to do whatever surgeons did the rest of the day after they operated. He did not know. What Siegfried did know is that Dr. Ramos once had five priceless Wheeler paintings.

Now someone else did.

5

VISITING PROFESSOR

And thus I clothe my naked villainy.... And seem a saint,
when most I play the devil.

—WILLIAM SHAKESPEARE

As she made her way across campus to the Art Department's building, Jennifer Kim hunched her shoulders to
ward off the chill in the air. True, Monte Vista was not the
rainy, blustery campus that Berkeley could sometimes be
in December—but the nights could prove chilly enough,
and the quick temperature drop after sundown had
caught her by surprise. *Then again*, she thought, *I could be
at some school in New England trudging through two feet of
snow right now.*

At the building's entrance she paused and looked back
across campus. Clusters of students, some in animated conversation with each other, others absorbed in cell phone
conversations, were crisscrossing the grounds on their way
to dorms, or the student center, or the fitness complex, or
the library. In the evening light Jennifer recognized only
a couple students as her own. The scene reminded her of
her undergraduate years when most evenings she would
be making her way to one campus building or another,

engaged in the delicate balancing act of studying versus hanging out with friends. For her, studying usually won out. She had no regrets. She smiled. *No, I'm good.*

Kim had been teaching economics just a little over a year, but that was long enough for her to appreciate Monte Vista's focus on undergraduates. Her economics students had career aspirations in consulting, banking, business, and government. Many of them were interested in the why of economics in addition to the how. She liked that. Her best students, she thought, were as good as those at Berkeley. Teaching at Monte Vista had its rewards beyond the paycheck. After only one year, she recognized that the school fit her personality.

And it had introduced her to Tristan Wheeler.

At the thought of the artist Jennifer's pulse quickened slightly. This in itself wasn't unusual—he'd produced a similar response that first shared evening in his studio, a few weeks after her arrival. But these days, the quickening pulse he provoked was no longer always pleasant.

Her footsteps echoed down the steps to his campus office, as memories of their "whirlwind friendship"—Tristan's initial naming—replayed involuntarily. At first there were discussions on art and literature, color and expression, passion and truth. What was the place of each in society? What was the value of art and literature? And what was the artist's responsibility and the writer's obligation to make what they create available to each and all?

As the fall semester went by, Jennifer and Tristan would go for an evening stroll along San Antonio's River Walk. On occasion, they would go into the Hill Country outside the city limits. What was it he said, when dawn arrived after that first all-nighter? *Tous les beaux esprits se rencontrent*. She smiled at the memory. And then there were the evenings in his "creative cocoon," with Tristan sipping scotch and teasing her for drinking only coffee—as he showed her paintings destined someday for museums and private collections.

Was she his muse? she wondered. Perhaps. She'd provided inspiration, insights, even served as his "emotional center"—again, his expression—as other women came and went.

Ugh. Jennifer grimaced as she navigated the hallway. Perhaps Tristan couldn't help being attractive to women. That's what she'd told herself at first, anyway. Artists were like that, right? But the emotional scenes, the gossip, the claims of sacrifices and broken promises . . . they were clouding his vision. Not to mention the fact that the university had started to take note. Then there were the calls—asking her to come over and help him "put back the pieces." Here she was, doing it again.

This most recent breakup had been worse than usual, his melancholia and frustration noticeably deeper, or she would have refused his plea. She had told herself to draw a line. But now it was happening again. He needed her. And his birds had gone missing too . . . maybe the two truest friends he had, besides herself.

Well, as soon as this blows past, no more postponing a discussion of the future, she promised herself. *This is it.*

At the far end of the hall an office light was on. The door was cracked, and Jennifer could pick out Wheeler's voice on the phone. She stuck her head inside and waved hesitantly.

The artist didn't notice at first. "What? What? . . . Yes—it's all still on, everything exactly as we agreed two weeks ago. The whole East Coast schmeer: Boston, New York, Philly, D.C., and then over to Atlanta. Then Birmingham, I want to include Birmingham, and then Chicago before we break camp and I head back here."

Wheeler looked up, saw Jennifer, and motioned her inside. "Right. Well—it's his loss, Dave. I can't be everywhere. No. If he wants to jump on the bandwagon he's gonna to have to catch it at a station. Later." Wheeler hung up the phone and grinned. "*Viva la revolución*! Looks like it's all a go. Which means that *I'm* all a go. Wheels up tomorrow morning at seven. Wanna come?"

Jennifer smiled tightly. "C'mon Tris, you know I have classes to teach and papers to grade. Let's just get something to eat at Paesanos. Maybe we can talk about. . . ."

But Wheeler already had lost eye contact. Brusquely shoving papers and materials into his briefcase, he stood and looked over her shoulder, running one hand through his disheveled curly hair while the other closed the clasps on the briefcase. "Sorry kiddo. No can do tonight." He shot her a sideways glance. "More phone calls to make, more interviews to set up. Give me a rain check this time?"

"Tris, you called me and set this up, remember?" Kim's temperature started to rise over Wheeler's indifferent reception. "Give you a rain check? I left *my* work behind, I gave up *my* time to come over here—because *you* said we needed to talk."

The artist shrugged. "Did I do that? Life's been crazy, Jen. What makes it crazy is because life's gotten bigger than my life. I'm on to something bigger than myself—and bigger than us. But duty calls and I gotta go." He moved around the desk and took a step toward the door, to be stopped by Jennifer's hand on his shoulder.

She continued, her voice hardening a little. "You said you needed to talk about Jocelyn. Just like you once needed to talk about Joanna—and I listened. Just like you needed to talk about Linus Torvalds and Linux and open software. I came running." At this point Jennifer and Tristan were face-to-face, but with very different expressions. Her words confirmed the look of hurt on her face. His silence underscored the look of diffidence on his.

"I wonder now if my mistake was to come running every time, Tris. And another thing," Kim continued, without giving Wheeler a chance to respond, "I've been combing lost and founds and calling the pet shelter for days, searching for any notice of your birds. I've sent you daily updates. It'd be nice to get some kind of acknowledgment."

"Fine. *Thanks*. That enough for you?" retorted Wheeler. "Don't you get that I'm busy? I've been calling art departments and columnists and airlines. I've run my attorney into the ground. NPR wants to interview me; Lewis Martin's going to New York to talk about an exhibit at MoMA and I haven't finished a speech I'm giving on Free Art. Tomorrow night, mind you." He snorted in disgust. "What do you want, a medal? Tears of gratitude? My God, Jen, you're getting as possessive and peevish as all the rest."

Jennifer flushed indignantly. "Like all the rest? The rest of what? The rest of the women you cajole into your studio with promises of lessons? Lessons in what? About making art free or free sex?" She knew this remark would hit the artist below the belt, and she relished every syllable. The irony that only minutes before she'd been smiling at the thought of sharing just such an evening was sadly lost.

Her voice began to shake. "You think you're the only person who has to balance a schedule and make appointments? But you're not, not by a long shot. A few of us mere mortals have to. . . ."

"Never mind what I think," Wheeler interrupted hotly. "Don't you understand it's not about what I think? It's about what I know. I know the Free Art campaign is going to revolutionize the world of art. I also know to get there will mean a lot of work and a lot of travel, and it's going require sacrifices, not just on my part but on the part of everyone *intelligent* enough to see the score." Kim gasped at this last remark, but Wheeler continued unheeding. "I thought you were one of the smart ones, Jen. I thought you could see that helping might mean having to take a back seat at times. I guess I was wrong."

"Just . . . just hold on." Kim took a deep breath, turned, and swallowed. Forcing herself to appear calm, she endeavored to ratchet down the intensity of the conversation. "Tris, you've heard me say that art can touch people's inner lives, giving them eyes to see the beauty that's around them. That's what art is for. But you've. . . ." She looked away from Wheeler and over to his desk, covered with flyers and drafts of talks yet to be given. Then she looked back at the artist. "The galleries and museums are not exploiting art. You've become the exploiter. It is no longer about art. You've become blind to the fact that it's now all about you."

Wheeler's demeanor, once angry, was now patronizing. "Don't think so Jen," he said coolly. "We once had something special going, you and I. But you've fallen back to where you were when we first met, while I've moved on. You think art is something that people buy at an antique store and use to cheer up a cloudy day. Art ought to change lives and change society. I want to loosen chains, not decorate a hallway."

"Loosen chains?" Kim responded, her voice rising again. "Like the chains you loosed at Monte Vista? In the San Antonio community? All the marriages you helped loosen? The women you used when they were looking for something, anything beyond themselves? You must mean *loose change*, because that's what you treated them like, you...."

"Enough," interposed Wheeler sharply. "Don't give me any of that stuff about the sanctity of marriage. Isn't how I live just a variation on the economics you teach? Free markets in action?" Tristan smiled at Jennifer. "It's a voluntary transaction. Demand and supply, it seems to me. I demand and they supply. Or is it the other way around? They demand and I supply? That's how markets work, isn't it?"

Before Kim—open-mouthed and reeling in anger—could respond, Wheeler's cell phone rang. He pulled it out and flipped it open. "Yes? Yes, this is Tristan. You have? Hey, that's great! Just behind the dining hall? Sure, I'll be there momentarily."

Wheeler snapped the phone shut and looked at Kim, who was breathing heavily, her cheeks flushed and her hands clenched. He smiled paternally. "You look upset. Don't be. I forgive you. In fact, I'm in your debt. That was a campus cop saying that he thought he'd found my birds behind the dining hall. Why they flew back there I've no idea . . . but I'm guessing he got my number from one of the flyers you distributed."

Wheeler moved back to his desk, pulled a piece of paper out of his top drawer, and dropped it on the desk before her. "This is a note I've been meaning to give you for some time. Our talk just now didn't catch me by surprise. I had a chance to think about where our relationship was going a few weeks ago, and I wrote this. Seems prescient now. Not a bad *forecast* is how you might put it." He made his way around Jennifer and out the door, looking back as he paused in the hallway. "It's a short note of gratitude, for all you did for me and for the birds this past year. I thought you might like to have it in writing."

As a tear began to trace its way down Kim's cheek Wheeler smiled. "Hey, none of that. This is what you were looking for, isn't it? A thank-you note? An expression of gratitude?" He turned and left.

She stood alone in the room for perhaps a minute. A tiny gasp of breath, then another, then another broke the silence. Taking the sheet of stationery in her hands, she paused to look at the artistic stylization, with the unmistakable Wheeler signature at the bottom.

Jennifer was about to crumple the paper and throw it in the trash. Then she stopped. Taking a deeper breath, she put the paper inside her handbag. She then turned out the light and made her way back up the stairs, and out into the darkness.

6

WEST TO TEXAS

The degree of utility varies with the quantity of commodity, and ultimately decreases as that quantity increases.
—WILLIAM STANLEY JEVONS

The visibility was less than a mile when the Boeing 737 landed in the city that was famous for Davy Crockett, Tim Duncan, and the River Walk, if not necessarily in that order. Henry and Pidge Spearman had just flown to San Antonio from Boston to take up residence at Monte Vista University, named after the historic neighborhood in which the school was located. Herbert Abraham met them at baggage claim.

"Nothing very fancy this evening," Abraham announced to the Spearmans as he pulled into a Bill Miller Bar-B-Q a short distance from the airport. "That'll happen Friday night when the two of you are scheduled to dine at what some of us on the faculty call 'the presidential palace.' That's where President Quinn lives. But I'm sure you weren't fed much on the plane coming in and we can't have you go hungry your first night here. So I'll introduce you to Texas barbeque, if you haven't had it before."

It was only five thirty, so Abraham was able to park right at the entrance. "We've had guests from Kansas and North Carolina, where they think they know barbeque, tell us that Texas barbeque is the best. Of course that just feeds the Texan's prejudice that we're the best at everything."

"But didn't Texans lose at the Alamo?" Spearman asked, trying to appear serious even as his teasing showed through.

"That is something of a sore spot," Herbert said, as they walked into the restaurant. "We prefer to focus on the bravery of the Alamo's defenders rather than their win-loss record. But let me give you some friendly advice: when you give your public lecture, I would advise you not to make fun of the battle cry: 'Remember the Alamo.'"

Herbert and Henry both chuckled.

After polishing off their dinner, it took only five minutes for the Spearmans to be driven to the Monte Vista University guesthouse on Oakmont Court. The house was one that the school had purchased in the 1960s and substantially renovated. Usually it was made available to short-term visitors to the school, such as a visiting lecturer, or a prospective donor being wined and dined by the administration before being asked to make a major gift. Now the Spearmans would call it home for a semester.

"I hope you'll be comfortable here. It's as nice a place as the university has to offer. Somewhere between Buckingham Palace and a Holiday Inn, as far as the amenities go." Herbert Abraham smiled as he lugged the suitcases into the foyer. Pidge and Henry followed, carrying the lighter bags.

Comfortable indeed. The home was a spacious, Spanish-style residence with a sunken living room, a luxurious master bedroom, and a high-ceilinged library. This being Texas, the computer hardware in the house was all Dell. The interior designer being an audio aficionado, the sound system was all Bang & Olufsen. There was a Florida room on the home's east side and a large patio off the back. The house had enough bedrooms to accommodate an extended family.

"Do you think we can get by here for a few months, Pidge?"

"I'm afraid I might never find you," Pidge quipped.

As Abraham walked to the front door he turned and bowed ever so slightly. "Just a few last details. We're giving you a couple days by yourselves to get settled in. Henry, I'll plan to come by at ten o'clock on Thursday morning to walk with you to the campus. From then on, we'll be riding you like rented mule," he said with a grin. "Most of my colleagues will be back from semester break so I've arranged for you to meet them. Then I'll show you around the school and we'll visit a couple on-campus administrative offices. I'm sorry to report that HR requires even Nobel laureates to fill out forms and papers." He smiled and shrugged: *Hey, what can you do?*

He also informed Pidge that on Thursday morning Madelyn Howell, the provost's wife, would come by the Oakmont House to show her around the city and host her for lunch. Howell did this for all new faculty spouses. In addition to being kind, her hospitality put the provost in a favorable light as the school's chief academic officer.

Finally, Abraham reminded the two one last time about the dinner in their honor on Friday evening. "My sample size is small, but every time I've been at the president's house, the attire is dress-up. And of course, the two of you will be the center of attraction." Abraham knew that Pidge and Henry would welcome being left alone without a host hovering about. He bid them good night, and quietly closed the door.

As Henry unpacked his suitcase, he thought about how lucky he was to be married to Pidge. She had been raised in an academic home and had met Henry when both of them were students at Columbia University. They were married the year Henry completed his doctoral studies. Her appearance had changed little over the past thirty years. The same light complexion, the same chestnut hair, and the soft brown eyes that attracted him to her many years ago, attracted him still. Only the lines at the corner of her eyes and the set of her chin signaled advancing years. She was taller than he, but if that mattered she never mentioned it.

"Here we are in Texas. Did you have any idea how our lives would change after you won the prize?" Henry reflected on her question. He did not need to guess, because Harvard was home to other Nobel laureates. "I knew my ideas would get more attention. What I never anticipated was the number of requests for my time."

Spearman was beseeched to consult with governments, to lecture at conferences, to speak at universities, to serve on boards, and to advise foundations and think tanks. Almost every day, he was called upon by journalists who sought his opinions. A number of Spearman's colleagues at Harvard were academic jet-setters who employed agents to book their speaking engagements. Prior to receiving the Nobel Prize, Henry had never gone this route. But now he had an agent to sort through requests and to negotiate fees and honoraria.

"And I'll never understand why people think the Nobel Prize makes someone an instant expert on everything," Henry continued. "Laureates in medicine get asked their opinions about the federal deficit and I'm asked about a cure for the common cold." Spearman shrugged his shoulders.

Even after winning the prize, Spearman continued to be dedicated to his students at Harvard. He was puzzled as to why the academic buzzword for teaching classes at the college or university level was the professor's "load." Henry also did not understand why some of his senior colleagues in the Department of Economics were bored with teaching. "It's the law of diminishing marginal utility," they would tell him. "After you've taught the same course eight or nine times, the extra utility from teaching it again gets pretty small, maybe negative." Spearman thought his colleagues failed to realize that while the course was the same, the students were always new each semester. Unlike most academic rock stars, he wanted to teach undergraduate courses. Consequently, the fact that the Cubbage Visiting Nobel Professorship required him to teach a course—any course he wanted—appealed to him. Spearman decided the topic would be something new. It would involve art.

7

AN ALL-NIGHTER

TUESDAY, JANUARY 10TH

Curious things, habits. People themselves never knew they had them.

—AGATHA CHRISTIE

For professors who take teaching seriously, what occurs in class is only the visible part of the course—the tip of the iceberg, as it were. The preparation of the course syllabus, the composition of the lecture notes, and the rehearsing for class actually consume more time than the class itself. Spearman was once asked by his brother-in-law how long it took him to prepare a lecture. "Twenty-five years and three hours" was his response.

Because he had never taught a course on art and economics before, Spearman felt even more pressure to be prepared for the first day of class. He knew that initial impressions were of paramount importance in the classroom. A poorly prepared teacher would have a difficult time regrouping. As he began the process, Henry took comfort in the fact that one of the greatest economic theorists of the twentieth century, Professor Abba Lerner, had been so worried about running out of material on his first day of teaching that he overprepared—so much so that the material he had assembled for the first day lasted him for the entire semester. *That's a comfort*, Spearman thought. Not that he expected this to happen. But better safe than sorry, he thought, at least so long as the costs of being safe did not exceed the benefits one enjoyed.

Spearman had started brainstorming about how the new art and economics course should be taught as soon as he finished breakfast. Straight lecture? No, this was too small a class. Socratic dialogue? No, too risky in a new teaching environment. Break-out groups? Maybe, but not for the entire course. Eventually a strategy took shape in Henry's mind, and he began the task of embedding it into a syllabus.

The study on the second floor of the Oakmont House was perfect for Spearman's endeavors. In front of the desk, French doors opened to a small deck, which in turn overlooked a lawn populated with several live oaks. At the property border ran a tall hedge that gave him privacy and reduced distractions. But the best part of the room was its size. It was large, with plenty of open space, and Henry used most of it. He was a pacer. After about thirty minutes at the computer, he would pace the room for thirty minutes. Sometimes he went back and forth behind the desk. Sometimes he walked the perimeter of the room ... but he would always return to and sit back down at the keyboard. After a while, he would be up and pacing yet again.

His daughter Patricia used to observe her father's work habits because he had so often worked at home. When she was in high school, she teased him by saying that he had the *opposite* of ADD. "You don't have an attention *deficit* disorder, you devote too much attention to pushing economics into every nook and cranny of life." Later, after taking an economics course at Swarthmore, she had a different perspective on her father's work ethic. She would tell him, "Poppa, for you, work is a consumption good."

●

This particular day, Spearman's work would consume him from morning to night, his only breaks coming at mealtimes, his only distraction coming from a social event going on next door.

It was the wee hours of the morning before he shut down his computer, rose, stretched, and walked out onto the deck. The night air was cool but not uncomfortable. He had heard the song about the stars at night being oh so bright, deep in the heart of Texas. Tonight they were not. Only a distant streetlight on Oakmont Court thwarted the night's efforts to enshroud the neighborhood in complete darkness. From somewhere an alarm clock faintly jangled. Two bedroom lights blinked on in the homes of neighbors. And a barely visible silhouette moved across a far lawn. Perhaps newspaper deliverers or milkmen were out, Spearman thought—if milkmen even plied their trade any longer. He yawned contentedly and headed back inside to bed.

It had been a productive night.

8

THE ARTIST HAS A VISITOR

WEDNESDAY MORNING, JANUARY 11TH

Art in the blood is liable to take the strangest forms.
—SIR ARTHUR CONAN DOYLE

Sean Daniels glanced at his watch: five minutes past nine. He pedaled a little faster. Tristan Wheeler would be expecting him to arrive by nine fifteen and he didn't want to be tardy. Lately Wheeler's moods had been mercurial, having something of a grab-bag quality about them. They ranged from ebullient to morose, with an occasional stop at suspicious. Yesterday he had alluded to someone being out to get him. "Microsoft types," he told Sean. The biker snorted. *Yeah, right.* Perhaps, Sean reasoned, such parabolic swings were part of the price to be paid for artistic genius. *Well, it is what it is,* he thought. So long as Wheeler was Monte Vista's artist-in-residence, and Sean wanted to keep his job, he would have to get used to it.

When the university's Department of Art had first offered Sean a job as assistant to Wheeler, he felt fortunate, even though he had some qualms about accepting the position. Daniels had once hoped to be a painter and had majored in art when he was an undergraduate at Monte Vista. But there were obstacles. The first was financial. His father had abandoned his mother when he was six years old. His mom could not afford to pay for tuition, room, and board at Monte Vista where her son wanted to study. So Sean worked his way through college waiting on tables in various San Antonio restaurants and picking up odd jobs here and there. While wealthier classmates who also were art majors logged many hours in the studio, Sean was taking orders and bussing tables.

The second obstacle was his mother. She wanted her son to get what she called a "good job" upon graduation. By that, Sean knew his mom meant steady work at high pay. "Why not be an accountant or engineer?" she asked. "You could do that." Often she tried to tease him into changing his major. "You know what the difference between an artist and a twenty-inch pizza is, don't you?" she would say. Sean knew the answer. "Sure, mom. A twenty-inch pizza can feed a family of four."

In his senior year, Monte Vista offered Sean a work-study position that paid his tuition and put him in close touch with the art faculty. But even with the encouragement of his professors and the high grades he received in his major, Sean was honest enough with himself to realize that he could never compete with the great painters whose work he had studied in art history classes. Lack of desire to be a great painter was not the obstacle; lack of talent was.

Upon graduation, he had stayed on at Monte Vista as an assistant in the Art Department, eventually being assigned to help Tristan Wheeler. One of the perks that Wheeler enjoyed as the artist-in-residence was an assistant to aid in whatever tasks he wanted done.

Sean's initial reluctance to accept the position came from his realization that much of the time he would have to perform menial tasks: sweeping the studio, shopping for supplies, preparing canvases, and running various errands for Wheeler. The job would even involve cleaning a large birdcage that housed two parrots. However, once Sean began working for Wheeler, he was charmed by the artist's personality. That first year his boss was upbeat and conversational, at times even brilliantly witty. Sean realized that even if he could not be transformed into a painter of great reputation, he might make other connections to the world of art by working for Wheeler and staying at Monte Vista.

Perhaps someday Sean could own a gallery and represent famous artists, or promote the careers of artists as yet undiscovered. He had also entertained the prospect of being a museum curator and using his position to enhance the public's appreciation for the visual arts. "I wouldn't just hang a bunch of paintings on walls and hope people stopped in," he thought to himself. But for now Sean had cast his lot with Tristan Wheeler, telling his mom, "Hey, the pay isn't bad; the hours are even better."

The benefactor behind Sean's generous salary—and the temporary placation of his mother—was Annelle Cubbage. The maverick trustee had become convinced that Monte Vista needed an artist-in-residence, and had refused to take no for an answer. "Writers-in-residence are common as dirt," she had told administration. "We need an artist here, not so much to teach as to inspire."

Cubbage not only provided the funds for this to happen, she provided the artist. Through her New York connections, she had learned of Tristan Wheeler and thought he was an American master as yet undiscovered. He also had another attribute: he was not wedded to the New York art scene. In fact he wanted out. Lots of freedom, an attractive base salary, an opportunity to lease a house near campus with its own studio—and Wheeler was incentivized to go west.

Wheeler's initial work at Monte Vista was representational and demonstrated his virtuosity as a painter. During this phase of his career, Wheeler painted with great technical facility and speed. He did not reach for the palette so much as stab at it. Annelle Cubbage's forecast soon proved to be accurate. Wheeler's paintings began to sell. Galleries priced his paintings in the two to five thousand dollar range. Because of his speed with a brush, the prices were multiplied by a higher-than-average volume of output. Even though Wheeler's income in those days was nontrivial, he always suspected it was the gallery owners who were getting rich off his creative labors.

•

When he was in his early thirties Wheeler reached a crossroads, a psychological crisis that began when he became convinced that his work was conventional, and not the breakthrough to which he aspired. Pablo Picasso and Jackson Pollock: these two iconic artists were acknowledged to be the most influential painters of the twentieth century (Andy Warhol, the intelligentsia placed in a separate silo). Between Picasso and Pollock, Wheeler picked Pollock. Despite protests from both Cubbage and several gallery owners, he put aside his paints for a year to enter the artistic mind-set of this genius of the abstract. Wheeler came out a different artist.

Pollock was a painter who did not paint. He dripped or poured paint into interlacing lines punctuated by pools of color. In so doing, Pollock found himself at the forefront of the avant-garde who brought something radically new to painting. Pollock had created a norm for other artists to go beyond: to spin subtler variations on new ways of viewing the world.

In response to his yearlong immersion in Pollock's art, Wheeler abandoned the paradigm where paint reflected reality, choosing instead a style where paint reflected only color itself. While Pollock constrained himself to the use of gravity to apply paint, Wheeler combined dripping and pouring with the use of spray paint apparatus. His execution of art became a blend of human labor and capital equipment.

The second stage of Wheeler's artistic relaunch began when his desire to bring art to the public and bypass the middlemen—the galleries, or "plantation owners," as he referred to them—led him to wade into the world of computers and printers. Hardware and software, operating systems, APIs and middleware, lasers and inkjets and dot-matrices—initially these concepts made no more sense to him than a Pollock painting to the uninitiated. But Wheeler's insatiable drive to push past boundaries made him a quick study. As he explored the possibilities of the Internet, as he grappled with the transfer and digital fabrication of images, his philosophical bent quickly identified the good guys and the bad guys in the industry.

Bill Gates he saw as a high tech robber baron whose Microsoft could, with impunity, destroy firms like Netscape and Caldera. On the side of the angels was Linus Torvalds, whose pioneering of Linux open-source software offered a way around Microsoft, and gave hope for all the "little guy" programmers. Wheeler viewed Torvalds as a fellow revolutionary who showed the way, and his take on art was reconfigured accordingly. Just as Torvalds had argued that information should be free, so Wheeler now championed the free exchange and distribution of art. All that remained was a way to marry the medium with the Internet. Then, he triumphantly pointed out, artists would have the horses as well as the cart.

From his freshman year at Monte Vista to now, Sean had enjoyed a front-row seat to Wheeler's rising prominence in modern art and his "Free Art" campaign. While fascinated by Wheeler's view of the artistic endeavor as a vast platform or operating system straining to be free, he wasn't quite sure what to make of the artist's fixation against profits. Nonetheless, Sean was captivated by his employer's astonishing lucidity of mind and powers of persuasion.

Sean also observed firsthand that the life of an artist could involve long hours of work. Wheeler often painted much of the day and late into the night, occasionally locking himself into his studio for days. The artist once told Sean that his two African greys were all the company he needed when he was painting. Yet in cleaning up Sean had seen evidence that the pet birds, Canvas and Frame, were not the only ones to stay the night with Wheeler or accompany him during one of his breaks.

It was only in the past few weeks that Wheeler had demonstrated an explosive temper. Sean had found almost-completed paintings on the floor, the surfaces slashed and the frames broken. While kneeling over to clean up the mess he asked Wheeler what was wrong. Wheeler glared down without responding, and then knocked over a canister of brushes. Sean wondered if his boss had gone berserk. Or was this some kind of artistic license? "As long as you're down there you can pick those up too," Wheeler had snapped, pointing to the items he had just thrown on the floor.

Initially angry at these episodes, the young assistant had nevertheless refrained from responding in kind. There were, he knew, extenuating circumstances—both extenuating and bizarre. Wheeler's two parrots had suddenly disappeared from the studio, only later to be found dead and disfigured behind the school's dining hall. Sean understood what a tragedy this was for his emotionally sensitive boss. It couldn't have been pleasant for the birds either.

•

Sean thrust his chin forward and pedaled his bike even faster. He took the corner into the driveway of Wheeler's house at a forty-five-degree angle. Propping his bike against the house, he walked to the side door and knocked. There was no answer. This was not out of the ordinary. Unlike other members of the faculty whose classes met each week on a particular day and at a given time, art teachers met their students episodically. And Wheeler almost never met his students in his studio at home, preferring instead to teach them in his Coppock Hall studio on campus. For those occasions when Wheeler was away, Daniels had a key that would get him inside. There he always would find a beautifully handwritten note by Wheeler listing the tasks the artist expected his assistant to perform. Wheeler crafted all his notes in black ink using a Montblanc 149 fountain pen. When Sean admitted never having seen a fountain pen before, much less one of the Montblanc brand, Wheeler gently admonished him. "That's a weakness. A Montblanc is a work of art that makes *more* art."

Sean viewed the notes that Wheeler wrote as little works of art and he kept them as mementoes of his time working for his boss. Who knew? They might be worth a lot of money someday. What had once been a Picasso doodle on a sheet of paper now could command thousands of dollars in the art market.

Sean knocked again, just to be sure that no one was in, or against the chance Wheeler had not heard him the first time. Still no reply. Daniels used his key to get inside. Of late, Wheeler had not always responded to visitors at his front door. Nervously he voiced a greeting: "Hello, Tris . . . good morning . . . it's me, Sean." No response. His voice echoed off the terra cotta walls and the inlaid timbers of the open ceiling. He walked down the hallway and into the studio.

Squashed tubes of paint of various colors—burnt umber, bright yellows and greens littered the floor. A half-filled canvas occupied a large easel in the middle of the room. Sean glanced over at the cot against the wall, in which the artist would sometimes sleep when on a painting jag. The sheets were rumpled—evidence of Wheeler at work. There was an aroma of alcohol and the smell of a gas stove—more evidence. Daniels turned and went back into the hall.

"Hello? It's me, Sean. I'm here to check on supplies and clean up a bit. I don't see any note, is there anything else you want me to do for you this morning?"

Again there was no reply. The only response was the chiming of Wheeler's clock. Yet, Daniels couldn't shake the certainty that he wasn't alone in the studio. Then he peered into the small bathroom and flicked on the light. Stunned at what he saw, he fell backward out of the room into the hallway.

For a moment, Sean thought he had just awakened from a nightmare. He felt the urge to be sick. Gathering himself up, he forced himself back into the bathroom and looked at Tristan Wheeler's lifeless body. The artist was hanging from a rope tied around his neck. The chair he'd always sat on in the studio when he painted was now tipped over on the bathroom floor.

Almost against his will, Sean looked up at Wheeler's face. He had never seen a corpse before, but he needed no previous experience to recognize the look of death. Wheeler's face had turned blue and his tongue protruded garishly from his lips. Sean's eyes continued to move upward. The bathroom had a single skylight situated at the top of a twenty-four-inch casing. The casing went from the ceiling of the bathroom to the roof of the house. Two iron rods, crossing and supporting each other, braced the casing about midway up. The rope around Wheeler's neck was tied to the rods at the point where they intersected.

Sean stared at the knot. Then, looking down, he stared at the chair on its side near the sink. He walked over and put the chair aright. Sean was always picking up after his employer. Giving one last look at Wheeler's body, he went back into the studio, and with a trembling hand dialed 911.

He knew this would be the last thing he'd ever do for Tristan Wheeler.

9

THE SCENE OF THE CRIME

The problem with putting two and two together is that
sometimes you get four, and sometimes you get twenty-two.
—DASHIELL HAMMETT

The familiar yellow tape that marked a crime scene encircled the brick residence on Oakmont Court. It had
served as Tristan Wheeler's home and studio during his
years at Monte Vista—now it quartered the team investi-
gating his demise. The police investigation had been under
way for an hour or so, with Detective Sherry Fuller the
homicide officer in charge. Fuller wore wire rim glasses
and had her hair in a bun. She fit the image of a librar-
ian more than a cop. Her appearance led some people to
underestimate her strength, her speed, and her willingness
to use firepower. They made that mistake only once.

Apparent suicides were investigated initially by the San
Antonio Police Department. The Bexar County Medical
Examiner's Office would have the final say as to how the
death had occurred. If the coroner concluded that suicide
was the cause, Homicide stepped aside. Until that happened, Fuller and her colleagues would treat the matter
as though a murder had taken place. If the police were to

stay away until the coroner's report was final, Fuller knew she could not conduct the same kind of crime scene analysis. Time had a way of diminishing the supply of clues.

Investigation protocol meant taking lots of photographs of Wheeler's body before it was taken down. The EMT first responders had left the body hanging because by the time they arrived, it was evident he was dead. When there was no hope of resuscitation, their instructions were to leave the scene uncorrupted until the police arrived. Fuller's colleagues took shots of the body, shots of the bathroom where the body had been found, even shots of the casement from which it had been hung. They also checked for fingerprints and bagged other evidence for the crime lab to review. Fuller wanted to know who else might have been in the home that day. This meant checking the inside for clues and checking the outside of the house for possible signs of forced entry. It also meant that Fuller would need to question the neighbors on Oakmont Court as to what they might have seen or heard.

Sherry Fuller had witnessed more than her share of dead bodies. In her line of work it went with the territory. She had spent a decade on the homicide squad, after five years tracking down missing persons. Making it through ten years in the homicide division of a large-city police force was a rite of passage. Most cops washed out before then. Homicide was hard on marriages, hard on staying healthy, hard on being the life of a party; it was hard all the way around. It was hard to come face-to-face with dead people on a regular basis.

Some homicide cops became callous to the sight of a corpse. But they were never the best cops. Fuller's boss had used the word "stoic" to describe the life of a homicide cop, a word she had never heard before. "Be a stoic," he had told her, "it's the only way to stay sane. But don't ever take a dead person for granted. Start doing that and you'll lose your passion to put the bad guys away."

Fuller was a stoic, for the most part. But even after ten years on the job, encountering the bodies of children who had been murdered caused anger to well up in her gut and kept her awake at night. The bodies of people who committed suicide provoked a different reaction. They gave her the creeps. Wheeler's corpse left her with this latter reaction.

If life's that bad, why don't they get help? she said to herself when she came across a case of suicide. To kill yourself seemed to her to be stupid and unnecessary. Whenever Fuller encountered a possible suicide, she found herself hoping she could prove it was actually murder. Murders had motives she could process and there was a culprit to be brought to justice.

That's what happened in Fuller's first investigation of an apparent suicide. The coroner's office initially had told Homicide to stand down. The death had appeared to be self-inflicted. But Fuller thought not, and managed to keep the investigation open. Later she showed to a jury's satisfaction that the husband had killed his wife, but then bungled the suicide note. The word "extinction" on the purported suicide note was spelled as "extinktion." The victim was an English teacher.

By midday, Fuller and her homicide team had dusted Wheeler's house and sent the purported suicide note to the crime lab for analysis. She would get preliminary results on the note's authenticity later. For now she would take on the job of questioning Wheeler's neighbors. Most people didn't like having a nosey neighbor. But police investigators loved them.

Oakmont Court consisted of one long block of homes that dead-ended at the Monte Vista campus. The real estate up and down the block was upscale. Some twenty years earlier the school had begun buying up any properties that came on the market. As a result, the street was now a mixture of privately and university-owned houses. The university real estate came to be occupied by either administrators or components of the school's administrative infrastructure.

Mixed among the school's properties were homes owned by families who liked living in an established neighborhood with proximity to a university. Realtors would point out the easy walk to a cultural or athletic event. They would mention that the students could be noisy at times, but then added that university neighborhoods were safe ones to live in. Realtors would reference the presence of the city police, as well as university security personnel patrolling the neighborhood.

The safety amenity would be a little more difficult for a realtor to argue these days, however. The large limestone home down the street from Wheeler's had itself been encircled by yellow tape not long ago—the scene of a major art theft as yet unsolved. Now another Oakmont Court residence was marked by the familiar plastic tape.

Sherry Fuller stooped under the tape and walked out to the curb for a breath of fresh air and to collect her thoughts. As she turned toward the street, she noticed a movement in the window of the place two doors down.

Could be I'm in luck, she thought. *Maybe there's a nosey neighbor.* As Fuller walked toward the home, the person in the window retreated from sight. Fuller then realized she knew of this place. It had been in the news a couple months ago. Her colleague Fritz Siegfried had worked the case. Then something else clicked. She realized that the items stolen from that house had been paintings of the now-deceased Tristan Wheeler. The detective went up the front walk to see who had been at the window and what she could learn.

The home down the street was, in fact, the residence of Dr. Raul Ramos, and the woman watching from the window was Rosie Segura. Rosie released the curtain and stepped away from the window. Because of his early departure that morning, the housemaid didn't know if Dr. Ramos even knew of Wheeler's death. But she reckoned her boss would be upset when he found out. She did not understand her boss when it came to artists. Dr. Ramos, she had decided, enjoyed the hunt for collectible art—something Rosie knew she could never afford to do. But she couldn't understand why her boss took such a personal interest in the artists themselves. Rosie thought you could have a painting on the wall, enjoy it, but when it came to who painted it? *No le importa a ella para nada.* Rosie even thought it made sense *not* to know the artist.

In all the entertaining that went on in the Ramos home, it fell to Rosie to restore order after the guests had left. And in her experience, it was almost always the artist who caused the most work. Whether it was smoking cigarettes or something worse, drinking too much, offending another guest, or getting sick in the bathroom, Rosie had observed it all—and more. "I never see anything bad from your other guests, just the artists," she had once told her boss.

"But Rosie, the artists are the reason we invite the other guests. You have to understand that they're the light of the world," her boss had replied. She kept her reply to herself, responding instead with silence.

Rosie's thoughts about problem guests had come to an abrupt end when she saw the woman walking toward the home. She knew she'd been spotted. But there was nothing she could do. She was sure that Dr. Ramos would have bid her open the door—especially to a police officer. She did so on the second knock.

Fuller flashed her badge and asked if she could step inside to ask a few questions. The detective's request might as well have been a command. The two women sat down in the living room. Fuller could tell that Rosie was ill at ease. She wondered briefly if the housekeeper was in the country legally, but elected not to go down that road. She wanted Rosie to be comfortable answering her questions. To Fuller, a live-in maid at a neighboring house did not seem likely to have been involved in Wheeler's death. But maybe she had seen something.

The detective began matter-of-factly. "I assume you know about the death of the man down the street. I'm trying to learn what was going on in the neighborhood the day he died. Were you working yesterday and the day before?"

"Yes, I was here. I'm just about always here, unless I'm runnin' errands for Dr. Ramos—like picking up clothes, or food."

"I noticed you looking out the front window. That window gives you a clear shot of the street. Did you see anything different, anyone going in or out of the man's house the last couple days? Any strange cars parked in the driveway or on the street? Anything like that?"

Rosie Segura took time in responding to Fuller's compound question. Fuller welcomed the pause. The detective did not trust quick and facile answers.

"No," Rosie finally concluded.

"Did you know what he looked like?" Fuller asked, expecting an affirmative answer, given how long Rosie had lived in the neighborhood.

"I know what Mr. Wheeler looks like, sure. I know a lot about him."

"You do?" A look of surprise flashed across Fuller's face. The detective had not anticipated that a housekeeper, even one who lived for years in the neighborhood, would know an artist like Wheeler.

"He's been in this house several times. That's how I know the man." Rosie went on to explain that Dr. Ramos often entertained artists in his home, either to promote their work or to help raise money for the San Antonio art scene.

"Am I right, that this is the home where the paintings were stolen last fall?"

"Yes, ma'am," Rosie responded.

"Was Tristan Wheeler here that night?" Fuller was hoping the answer would be yes.

"His art was the reason for that party," Rosie said. "Dr. Ramos, he showed off Wheeler and his paintings by Wheeler. That was the last time he was here. Until the night before last."

"What? The night before last?" Fuller realized that she'd caught her lucky break.

"The night before last he burst right into the middle of another party my boss was giving. He made straight to the bathroom and got sick."

Fuller realized she might be on to something and so pushed for details. "You say Wheeler was sick in the bathroom?"

"That's what I said. And he was lucky to make it there. He came in the front door, really pale like, asked for Dr. Ramos and then pushed through everybody to get to the bathroom in the hall."

"Do you know why he was sick?"

"Dr. Ramos took care of him, told the guests Wheeler had too much to drink, but he'd be fine. The doctor, he walked him back to his house and put him to bed. My boss takes care of his guests. And he liked the dead guy's art."

Fuller's visit with the housekeeper was more informative than she had anticipated. She had thought other neighbors might know something about Wheeler, but a housekeeper detailing the events of his last night alive? This was a gold mine.

"Ms. Segura, I won't take up much more of your time. But I have to ask: I understand that the paintings from this home were never recovered. And I know the paintings that were stolen were by Wheeler. Did he have access to his own paintings the night of the party in his honor?"

"Sure he did. Before the party, my boss and Mr. Martin, they paraded Mr. Wheeler around as much as his paintings."

"Any idea who walked off with the paintings that night? Wheeler maybe? He painted them, after all."

"No way Dr. Ramos would not have allowed that. My boss, he liked the dead guy's art. He liked Mr. Wheeler, don't ask me why. But Dr. Ramos, he was not going to let anyone walk off with his paintings, not even the artist."

•

The day's questioning of residents on Oakmont Court neither supported nor rebutted the theory that Wheeler had been killed by anyone other than himself. No one Fuller questioned could remember any suspicious persons or activity that would differ from normal Oakmont Court goings-on. The two neighboring homes were vacant. The detective returned to Wheeler's house and told her team to button up the place and call it a day. Her next appointment would be at the police station, with Sean Daniels, who was yet to be questioned. Fuller had considered interviewing him at the studio where he had found Wheeler's body. But she had been told that Daniels was distraught. Checking out his story at the police station would allow her to get the interview on tape. Fuller also thought she could read a suspect's true emotions better at the police station than anywhere else.

•

If emotions were like tennis strings, Sean Daniels's were strung at about seventy-five pounds: very taut and ready to snap. His job had ended. The artist he admired and worked for was dead. And now he was at the police station being treated not as the helpful person who first called 911, but as a so-called person of interest. If this was any different from being a suspect, he failed to see the distinction. If that were not enough, his mother had reminded him that she thought all along that he should not have pursued art at Monte Vista University, but something practical like business or engineering.

One of Fuller's jobs was to find out if Daniels's disconsolation was genuine. The other was to find out what he knew. "How did you happen to be going to Wheeler's house at just that time," Fuller began. She took Daniels through a series of questions, many of them repetitive, in order to ask about everything he did that day, why he went to Wheeler's home precisely when he did, why he did not happen to go earlier, why he did not happen to go later. Then Fuller turned to Sean's personal life.

Did he have a police record? Sean's reply was no.

Did he do drugs? Sean hesitated, wondering if the police could ask him this question. He said no.

Was he on any medications? No.

Where did he live? Did he have a car? Did his paycheck come from Monte Vista or Tristan Wheeler? Daniels answered these questions and what seemed like a hundred more.

Fuller then turned to Sean's relationship with Wheeler.

Why did Sean agree to work for Wheeler? Sean's reply: he wanted to learn more about the world of art and he needed the money.

Had he been a student of Wheeler's before he was an employee? The answer was yes.

Were they close? Not really.

Did Sean consider Wheeler to be a friend? Not really.

Were they lovers? Absolutely not.

Was Wheeler hard to work with? Moody? Could he be abrasive? He could be, especially lately.

Did Sean dislike his boss? After a moment, Sean shook his head no.

If the police checked Daniels's apartment, would they find anything that had been taken from Wheeler's house? Sean invited them to do so and told Fuller in no uncertain terms that he was not a thief.

Did Sean ever hear Wheeler talk about killing himself? No.

Did Sean owe his boss any money? None.

Did Wheeler owe Sean any money? Sean replied no. But then, as if on second thought, he paused a moment and stammered, "I mean, not now."

Fuller looked up from her notepad, her eyebrows arching. "What do you mean, not now?"

"He told me I was going to be in his will. Just a couple days ago. But I thought he was kidding—he had a drink in one hand, he was a little blitzed . . . I mean, you know. Crazy." Sean gulped visibly.

Fuller responded to this admission with a barrage of questions, her tone of voice becoming progressively harder. Had he seen the will? Had it ever been mentioned before? Did Wheeler mention where it was kept? Had Sean spoken of this to anyone else? And of course there was the "million-dollar" question. Why had Wheeler out of the blue turned to Daniels—the guy he'd been treating with contempt and ill manners for weeks—and tell him he was leaving him money in his will?

Daniels met all these question with multiple variations of *no, never,* and *I don't know*. His face was ashen, his voice increasingly frantic. Fuller prided herself on the savvy wisdom ten years of experience had given her. She felt she could read the veracity of a suspect better than anyone else in the precinct. Her gut had been telling her that Daniels was speaking the truth. But the sudden appearance of inherited money and a newly altered will flipped the picture that had been developing. They'd now have to find the lawyer and see about getting a copy of the will, and then see if the kid—or anyone else for that matter—had been added. More work. More headaches.

Every permutation about the connection between Daniels and Wheeler was asked. It made Sean's head spin. Fuller sighed, narrowed her eyes, and threw out one last query. "Did you have anything to do with Wheeler's death?"

This appeared to completely unnerve the young man, whose mouth opened and closed without a sound.

Fuller decided it was time to be the good cop. "Look, Sean. I'm sorry about what happened, and that I have to ask you these questions. But it's my job. I know this must be a trying time for you. The death of your boss. The loss of your job." She reached into her pocket and pulled out a card. "Here's my info. You should feel free to call me if you think of anything at all about why your boss would kill himself, or why anyone would want him dead. Oh, and one last thing. Don't go anywhere."

Sean Daniels stumbled out of the police station, got on his bike, and made his way back to his apartment. He tossed the card in the gutter along the way

•

At approximately eight o'clock that evening, an unmarked police car pulled in front of the Ramos home on Oakmont

Court. Sherry Fuller got out. It had been a long day and she was tired. Preliminary reports from her colleagues on the scene had been inconclusive, and the white coats at the lab hadn't finished their analysis of the suicide note. The image of Wheeler's body continued to give her the creeps. She remained ill at ease with the suicide explanation, although there was precious little evidence arguing otherwise. With one possible exception, she reminded herself. That "new" will mentioned by Daniels. A motive might surface when it was located. In the meantime, perhaps Ramos, who was apparently much closer to Wheeler than she'd expected, could shed further light.

Fuller was met at the door by Ramos himself. As the detective was ushered into the living room and directed to a sofa, she saw Rosie watching from the kitchen. Ramos seemed unaware of Rosie's presence—or didn't care.

"What can I do for you, Detective? I'm afraid I wasn't much help when your colleague—Officer Siegfried I believe was his name—was here back in November. Maybe I'm jinxed at helping the police." Fuller was uncertain whether Ramos was serious or was trying to be delicate about the failure on the part of the police to recover his paintings.

Fuller decided to play it cool. She had no grounds to suspect Ramos of committing a crime—if there even was a crime. "I just want to ask you some questions about Tristan Wheeler, Doc. I understand he was a friend of yours." Fuller waited for the response.

"I wouldn't use the word 'friend,' Detective. I admired Wheeler's work enormously. In this regard, I had put my money where my mouth was. I bought his work. But 'friend,' no. I wouldn't use that term. I don't think Tristan would have either."

"But he was more than a neighbor, I gather," Fuller prompted Ramos.

"Tristan was more than a neighbor, yes. You could say that. He was a guest in my home on several occasions, and I knew him, knew his work. I think it could be said that I was one of those who made Tristan better known as an artist. Annelle Cubbage deserves much of the credit for bringing Wheeler to San Antonio, but I think I helped him along a bit afterward." Ramos hoped Fuller would see the false modesty in what he was saying.

"Wheeler was a guest in your home just last night, correct?"

Ramos winced. "Well, yes. I suppose Rosie mentioned his rather dramatic entrance, eh? I was hosting a party to raise funds for the Travis Museum, with a number of VIPs present—financially well off VIPs, if you get my drift. We were right in the middle of cocktails when there was a tremendous bang from the foyer. No sooner had I realized it was the front door slamming open than there he was, lurching right into the room. It's no secret that the man drinks when he paints. Apparently he had been in quite the creative mood, because he was absolutely gassed. He gave me one wild-eyed look and then walked into the bathroom and became ill."

"What did you do?"

"What anyone in my position would have done. I cleaned him up, gave him a mild sedative, and then helped him back across the street to his home, where I tucked him into bed. It only took a few minutes. And I'm glad to say that while virtue is certainly its own reward, there were other recompenses to my good Samaritanship. Several would-be donors were so touched that they wrote checks to Lewis Martin, on the spot! Martin's the curator of the Travis." He smiled. "We took in several thousand dollars, 'not a bad night's haul' as he told me later."

"Did you see anything unusual around his house or the neighborhood yesterday?"

"I'm afraid not. I leave early in the morning when it's still pretty dark."

Fuller went through some of the same questions she'd asked Sean Daniels concerning the connection between Ramos and Wheeler, taking care to drop the ones that had made Sean cringe. But Ramos was asked whether he had any reason to believe Wheeler would commit suicide.

"Well, I was shocked, when I heard the news. I did know that Tristan had been despondent. Many artists get melancholy. My theory is that this stimulates their synapses to be creative. It's no secret that the drinking had increased. Then there was the matter of the dead parrots."

"Dead parrots?" For a moment Fuller paused, completely at sea. *Dead parrots?* Her mind snapped back to college days and Monty Python skits.

"Yes. They were African greys, actually. 'Canvas' and 'Frame,' Tristan called them. Clever, yes? He loved those birds." Ramos shook his head sadly. "When Wheeler painted, it was very dramatic, in case you didn't know. He would not exactly paint with a brush. Well, he used to, but lately he drizzled the paint on the canvas. When he was drizzling Prussian blue, he would call out the color. 'Prussian blue,' he would say. '*Prussian blue, Prussian blue, Scraw!*'

one of the birds would call back. If Wheeler was going to use burnt umber, he'd say burnt umber and damned if one of those birds would not mimic him: '*Burnt umber, burnt umber, get the burnt umber, Scraw!*' "

"What happened to the birds?" Fuller asked.

"They got out of Wheeler's house somehow. They turned up dead in the street, and they'd been mutilated. Whether some animal caught them or whether somebody took 'em, I don't know."

"But nobody in their right mind would kill themselves over the loss of a couple birds," Fuller said.

"Do you have pets, Detective?"

"No, I don't."

"Then perhaps you're in no position to judge." Ramos got up and began to move toward the front door. "Do you have any other questions for me? If not, my day tomorrow begins rather early in the morning, and I need to be sharp."

Fuller left the Ramos home and got into the car. Wheeler's corpse no longer was on her mind. The image of two dead birds had replaced it.

10

SPEARMAN GETS THE NEWS

THURSDAY, JANUARY 12TH

Economics is what economists do.

—JACOB VINER

Early Thursday morning, before he joined Pidge for breakfast, Spearman realized that he should check the mailbox at their new residence. Not many of their friends were aware of the Oakmont Court address and most of Henry's professional correspondence would come to the Economics Department. Still—something might have arrived.

Walking outside, Henry noticed for the first time that the mailbox was built into one of the stone columns that marked the entrance to the front yard. He opened it up and found a couple pieces of junk mail. Did he want to buy aluminum siding? No thanks, not for a brick house that he did not even own. Did he want to carry an American Express credit card? He already was carrying three cards. *"But what's this?"* he wondered, as he saw an aperture located beneath the mailbox itself.

Stacked inside this space were three copies of the *Express-News*, wrapped in thin plastic bags. That day's paper was on the top of the stack. Spearman gathered the newspapers and the mail and went back to the house.

"Hey Pidge, did you order a newspaper?" he called, putting the mail and papers on the dining room table. Her response was negative.

"Well, with all the other things that come with the house, so does the local newspaper," Henry replied. As he glanced at that morning's edition, his attention was drawn to a story on the front page:

LOCAL ARTIST FOUND DEAD

Nationally known artist Tristan Wheeler of San Antonio died of an apparent suicide, according to a spokesperson for Monte Vista University where Wheeler served as artist-in-residence. Police officers reportedly found the 46-year-old Wheeler inside his bathroom Wednesday morning. Officers had entered the home in response to a 911 telephone call from an associate of the artist. The body was taken to the Bexar County Morgue.

Wheeler had moved from New York City to San Antonio in 1991 to join the Monte Vista University faculty. He was considered the leading artist in the San Antonio art community and had gained national attention as a vocal advocate of the "open source art" movement. Lewis Martin, senior curator of the Travis Museum of Art, told the Express-News that "We were shocked and saddened to learn of Tristan Wheeler's death this morning. His departure leaves the art community bereft by the loss of an irreplaceable talent."

Wheeler was born on December 5, 1960 in Sandusky, Ohio. A child prodigy in representational art, he reversed himself at the age of 30. Inspired by the open source software movement, Wheeler challenged others to follow him in changing how art is distributed. As he put it, "if we can have free speech, why not free art?" He believed there should be no distinction between the two.

Annelle Cubbage, a San Antonio art patron and an early collector of Wheeler's work, sponsored the artist's first showing at San Antonio's Travis Museum of Art in 1998. The show drew crowds not only from Texas but much of the Southwest. In 2004 the Museum of Modern Art in New York assembled a comparative collection of Wheeler's earlier work and contemporary work. The Museum's "About Face of Tristan Wheeler" then toured Los Angeles, Miami, and Atlanta before coming back to San Antonio.

Lieutenant Sherry Fuller of the San Antonio Police Department said that Wheeler's death was being investigated by police pending final determination of cause of death. Reports were that the artist had been despondent over the loss of his two pet parrots whose bodies were found near the campus.

Wheeler is survived by his parents, Mr. and Mrs. Clare Wheeler of Shaker Heights, Ohio, a sister Caitlin Huizenga of Muskegon, Michigan, and a brother Oscar of Philadelphia, Pennsylvania. Funeral arrangements are as yet undetermined.

"Anything interesting in the local paper, Henry?" his wife asked.

But Henry did not hear his wife's question. He was trying to recall why he recognized the Wheeler name. Then it came to him. The barking dog folder.

Three loud raps came from the front door, stopping Henry in his tracks. "I'll get it," he said, putting the paper back on the table. Henry had no idea who would be visiting this early in the morning. He did not expect Herbert Abraham until ten; Pidge was not expecting the provost's wife until around that time as well.

Knocking at the Spearman's front door was Detective Fuller. She was not optimistic that her visit to this particular residence would be helpful in her investigation. University security, which had briefed her on the neighborhood, reported that the current occupants of the house had just moved in. But sometimes newcomers paid close attention to their surroundings simply because they were not familiar with them. She also was told the man of the house had just won the Nobel Prize.

Fuller had never met a Nobel laureate. She expected an Einstein type to answer the door: wild gray hair, black piercing eyes, and a look of deadly gravitas on his face. What she found standing in front of her was a short bald man with twinkling eyes and an impish grin. Introductions were made and Fuller's credentials were displayed. "Do you mind if we step inside?" Fuller said. Spearman motioned for the detective to follow him through the foyer and into the living room.

"I suppose you heard what happened down the street?"

"I haven't any idea," Henry replied.

"There was a death in the house two doors down. An artist. He was on the faculty at Monte Vista University."

Spearman put two and two together. "I just read of the death of an artist by the name of Wheeler, a faculty member at Monte Vista. It was in today's paper. I had no idea that he lived down the street. We just moved in Monday evening." Spearman motioned to the dining room table where the newspaper lay open.

Detective Fuller kept her eyes fixed on Spearman and asked whether he had ever met Tristan Wheeler.

"I never did."

"Your wife, maybe?"

"She's upstairs right now so you'll have to ask her. But I don't see how she could. We've been together pretty much the whole time since we arrived."

"I understand you haven't been here long, but your place is just down the street so I need to ask: Did you see anyone coming or going into Wheeler's house since you moved in? Maybe when you were walking to the campus?"

"My wife and I walked over to the campus the evening we unpacked. I guess we walked past the place where Wheeler died. But to answer your question, no."

As Fuller jotted some notes, Spearman said to her, "I know I'm not the one who is supposed to be asking questions. But if I may: you introduced yourself as being from Homicide. Wasn't Wheeler's death supposed to be at his own hands? That's what the newspaper reported. He had been despondent—over the death of some pets. . . ."

Before Spearman could complete his sentence, Fuller replied, "Well, professor, in our line of work, we can't take anything for granted. A person dies; we have to check out why."

"Do *you* think Wheeler killed himself?" As soon as he said this, Spearman had regrets about asking.

"Off the record, Professor, it looks that way. He was an artist, you know. Aren't they all a little bit crazy? I think one of 'em once cut off his ear. And then I think the guy killed himself afterward. I mean, why go to the trouble of cutting off your ear if you're going to kill yourself anyway?"

"That doesn't seem to fit any rational cost-benefit analysis," Spearman responded.

As she walked back to her car, Fuller puzzled over the interview. What Spearman said sounded odd to her ears. Then she remembered something she'd been told when she was a young pup on the force. Armando Gomez, one of her friends who worked campus security at Monte Vista, claimed that half the professors at the school behaved like normal people, but the other half were weird. "Not criminal-weird," he added, "just weird."

Fuller reckoned Spearman might be in the oddball category. Not criminal-oddball. Just oddball.

•

A little before ten, Madelyn Howell arrived to acclimate Pidge to the ways and mores of San Antonio. As soon as the two women pulled out of the driveway, Herbert Abraham arrived to accompany Henry on his own acclimation.

"You look dapper today," Henry said to Abraham. He was staring at the fresh boutonnière on the lapel of Abraham's softly tailored gray suit. "Do you wear a flower every day?"

"Yes, it's my occupational uniform. I'm something of an anachronism. Most of my male colleagues these days don't even wear a coat and tie to teach in. Just this week, the subject of appropriate professional attire came up and one of our assistant professors that I'm taking you to meet, Matt Battles, told me that he could never wear a tie to work. He said he'd be too afraid that he might spill something on it."

"If young Battles is afraid of staining his tie, the solution is simple: he should purchase a more expensive tie."

The fissures on Herbert Abraham's brow revealed his puzzlement. "You mean Matt should wear *inexpensive* ties. Yes, I completely agree with you on that."

"No, he should *not* wear inexpensive ties. Battles should wear the *best* ties he can afford. In that case, he would have a greater incentive not to spill on them. If Battles would put an optimal incentive structure in place, his tie problem would take care of itself."

Abraham's face lit up and he smiled broadly. He was reminded that Spearman was known for finding hidden economic logic in every corner of human behavior.

Spearman grabbed his sport coat and the two men left the guest house for the short walk to campus. At first no words were exchanged. Then Spearman broke the ice. "I read in the paper that a faculty member died yesterday, a young artist."

"Oh yes," Abraham replied. "I was reluctant to raise the unpleasantness. It happened in the house just two doors down from yours. In fact, it is *that* house." Abraham pointed to a Georgian-style brick home as the two men walked up Oakmont to the Monte Vista campus. Everything looked normal about the house: except, of course, for the yellow crime scene tape, a police cruiser in the driveway, and an unmarked van at the curbside.

"Please know, notwithstanding the Wild West's reputation, this occurrence is a bit out of the norm here."

"I'm sure it is," Henry replied. "It must certainly cast a pall over the campus."

"The loss will be felt the most in the Art Department. Wheeler was our artist-in-residence. But he wasn't the sort of colleague that one meets at the faculty club for coffee or lunch. It's unlikely your orbits would have brought the two of you together, even as neighbors."

The two men turned onto the sidewalk that led to Hamermesh Hall, where the Department of Economics was located. "Still, the news was disconcerting for us," Abraham continued. "My wife Jocelyn and I actually own two of his paintings. I'm old-fashioned in my taste for art. I bought the first one years ago when Wheeler was doing landscapes . . . beautiful piece of work. My wife was given the other by Wheeler just after he'd gone hopelessly abstract. I was opposed to Jocelyn accepting it. You and I know there's no such thing as a free lunch—or a free painting that has no strings attached. I barely knew the man and didn't care for him, frankly. Still don't. But it's irrelevant. I couldn't afford one of his paintings today."

Spearman shot a glance at his companion. An odd comment, he thought. The cost of the paintings was not what Abraham paid, but the opportunity foregone of possessing the paintings. Which, according to Abraham's own words, appeared to be very costly.

"Of course, heaven only knows what price a Wheeler will command now," Abraham grunted.

"Heaven is not the only place that knows," Spearman said. "The market for art could tell us as well."

The two men walked in silence into the building that housed the Economics Department. Once inside, Spearman was taken on a tour of faculty offices to meet several members of the department. He was first introduced to Matthew Battles and Jennifer Kim, the two assistant professors of economics. Battles and Kim both greeted

Spearman timidly. From their perspective, having a Nobel laureate in their small department was a mixed blessing. On the one hand, they had to make everyday conversation with one of the profession's superstars. Each of them had studied under famous professors. Kim in fact had a Nobel laureate, George Akerlof, on her dissertation committee at Berkeley. But they were not certain if it was okay to talk about the weather or a basketball game with someone of Spearman's stature.

On the other hand, Battles and Kim knew that having Spearman as a colleague could be a boon to their research agendas. Both asked him if at some point he would sit down with them to discuss their research. Good teaching was expected of assistant professors at Monte Vista University. But gone were the days when good teaching alone would gain tenure for an assistant professor. Battles and Kim knew that they would have to get some things published if they wanted to stay at Monte Vista. Or move up the academic ladder elsewhere.

•

While Herbert Abraham was introducing Henry to his new colleagues, Pidge was on a journey of discovery of her own. Madelyn Howell proved to be a congenial and experienced guide to the San Antonio environs. "You and your husband won't want to go back," she teased. The colors, sights, and smells were startlingly different from the snowbound Cambridge that Pidge had left behind.

The two women were strolling downtown. The sky was azure blue and if the breeze was cool, it nevertheless carried the delicious scent of grilling food. "This is my absolute favorite bookshop in the city," Madelyn said. "Anything you want to learn about the Southwest, you'll find here." After a short time browsing, Pidge left with three books in hand and followed the provost's wife into a small bistro across the street. While considering her lunch options, Howell carried on her description of Monte Vista University without a pause.

"We have a wonderful community at the school. The faculty and staff are all respectable and approachable, and no one has an axe to grind." Howell held her tongue for a few moments. "For the most part that is," she added as she looked at Pidge, winking. "My husband thinks the crown jewel of Monte Vista is the Department of Art. Thanks to donors like Annelle Cubbage and others, we have one of the best programs for our size in the country, and like they say, the best programs attract the best practitioners. In fact, we have one very famous. . . ."

At this point Madelyn did, in fact, pause as an almost imperceptibly sad look passed across her face. "Are you thinking about Tristan Wheeler?" Pidge asked quietly. "Henry told me about his death this morning. I'm so very sorry. It must have come as quite a shock to the community."

"Yes, it has been." Howell looked out the window at the passers-by. "The news broke yesterday afternoon, and by now it's all over the campus. Monte Vista probably is very different from Harvard. Everybody knows everybody, and when something good—or in this case, something bad—happens, it isn't long before we all know it." She looked aside and then put down the menu. For the moment her enthusiasm had vanished.

"Were you acquainted with him?" Pidge added. "I suppose he was well known. . . ." Her voice trailed off.

The face of her companion across the table didn't change. "In one way he was. Actually, in a number of ways." She made a sound that Pidge took to be a sigh. "Tristan had begun to gather quite a bit of national attention, thanks to his Free Art theory. And his art got museum and collector attention. So we had the major art publications knocking on our door, and then the bigger national ones like *Time*, *Newsweek*, even *People*, came calling. Of course it was great publicity for the school."

She stopped as the waitress arrived to take their orders. Then she continued.

"Lewis Martin, the curator for the Travis Museum of Art here in town, was thrilled to receive a number of paintings in Wheeler's new style. The joke is that if the paintings hadn't been donated he would have stolen them himself. But apparently a lot of people feel the same way, as museum attendance shot up. Considering the museum's financial state, that was welcome news." She looked out the window again. "Let's see, what else? Students enjoyed the notoriety he brought to the campus. I'm given to understand 'Free Tristan Wheeler!' tee shirts sold very well at the campus bookstore." She chuckled at the irony. "Enrollment in the art program went up, and that also helped the school."

She then turned back to Pidge with a sad smile. "But his art wasn't the only thing he was well known for. Let's just say that the stereotype of the artist—painting hard, and playing hard—found its realization in Tristan Wheeler. And there are more than a few in our community who won't mourn him too much."

Madelyn Howell looked away, shifted in her seat, and began to stir her iced tea. The spoon made a *clink-clink-clink* sound in the tall glass. The casual chatter and ambient noise of the little bistro seemed to fade into the background. "What do you mean?" Pidge finally asked.

Madelyn decided to lay her cards on the table and then drop the subject. "Tristan Wheeler was a very talented painter," she said. "And he was also a womanizer. I suppose it isn't polite to speak ill of the dead, but the stream of stories beginning to surface about his affairs was becoming increasingly worrisome to my husband as the provost of the school."

Howell lowered her voice. "Thankfully Tristan stopped short of having affairs with students—at least, that we know of. But there was a string of dalliances with faculty members, both single and married, that kept him in hot water and caused the school lots of grief. Women just couldn't seem to resist him. He must have been forty but he looked thirty. Just the opposite of my husband, I have to say, who is sixty but looks seventy. And then the latest rumors, about an affair with Abraham's wife . . . well, enough. It's not going to be an issue any longer. And I for one am glad it's over."

"Abraham's wife? *Herbert* Abraham?" Pidge looked around to be sure her voice had not carried. It hadn't. "He's the nice man who met us at the airport and took us out for dinner when we arrived. He mentioned that his wife was unable to join us at dinner ... oh, my." Pidge felt both sad and stunned. A memory of the nattily dressed older man, a fresh flower in his lapel, went through her mind's eye.

Silence hung at the table, with neither of the two women making eye contact with the other. Madelyn was the first to break the silence. "Herbert is one of the most respected faculty members we have at Monte Vista," she said almost in a whisper. "And we adore Jocelyn. I'm already regretting dropping those names. Sometimes I talk too much, as you may have noticed this morning."

"So let me repeat one thing," Madelyn then said, "and then we'll leave it all behind. This was a rumor. It may have started because of the age difference between Henry and Jocelyn—she's almost twenty-five years younger, after all. And there's no question it was fed by both Tristan's reputation and Jocelyn's love of art. She was carefree enough to have a number of private painting sessions together with Tristan, and, well, as I said, in an intimate community like ours people talk. But Jocelyn maintained nothing happened, Herbert is prepared to believe nothing happened, and now Wheeler's gone. That settles it for me." She placed her hands together, palms up, side by side on the table—and brought them together with a small clap. She then gave a thin smile. "Let's say the book is closed, okay?"

As if at the direction of a stage manager hidden in the wings, the waitress arrived with their orders. The two women began to dig into their food as Madelyn endeavored to give the conversation a lighter tone.

But for Pidge, the carefree atmosphere of the day had changed. From her years as a professor's daughter and now as a faculty spouse, she knew that life in the academy was not always simply academic.

•

Promptly at noon, Abraham brought Spearman to Maguire Hall where the faculty dining area was located. By the time the two men got their food from the serving bar, six other members of the Economics Department were already seated at a large table. As Spearman approached, each of them stood up as if on cue. While he had already met Battles and Kim, the two junior members in the department, the rest of the department was new to him.

Abraham introduced Spearman to Don Compton and Hannah Talsma, the two associate professors in the department. They greeted their new colleague somewhat woodenly. Spearman then walked over to the other side of the table and introduced himself to Chuck Adams and Marco Salvatore who, like Abraham, held the rank of full professor in the department. As Spearman shook hands all around, each one addressed him in a deferential tone as "Professor Spearman" or "Dr. Spearman." Every time this occurred, Spearman requested that he simply be called "Henry." When the introductions were finished, he motioned for them to please be seated.

As Spearman took a chair in the middle of the group, Salvatore said that the other full professor in the department, Rowena Johnson, could not be present and reported that she sent her regrets. "Johnson, the labor economist? I know her work," Spearman responded. "I hope I can meet her later."

"The reason she's not here is because she's being interviewed for a deanship at Washington State."

"For the business school," Spearman hazarded.

"You're right," Abraham said. "It's striking how many economists end up as deans of business schools. You don't see this happen as much in the liberal arts. I suppose that's because economists fit better as deans in business than liberal arts."

"I don't think the skill set of being a good dean varies across different kinds of schools. What you've spotted is really a matter of supply, not demand."

"I don't follow you," Herbert said. The faces at the table turned curiously to Spearman.

"Well, think about it this way. In a college of arts and sciences, economists are relatively well paid. I'm sure that's true at Monte Vista; it's certainly true at Harvard. Economist salaries are well above those of historians, biologists, you name it. But in a business school, the wage differential gets reversed: economists are not paid as much as the accounting and finance faculty. So as a matter of supply, it follows that more economists would pursue deanships in business schools, where they are relatively low wage earners, than in liberal arts colleges, where they are relatively high wage earners. If I'm right, and Johnson gets the offer, Monte Vista probably will have to dig deep to keep her."

At that point, the table fell silent.

Professors are usually eager to profess. But initially the conversation was nonexistent, each person at the table dining quietly. Finally, after everyone in the group had digested several mouthfuls of their lunch, Salvatore broke the conversational ice: "Two of my best students are signed up for your course, Henry. They said they're excited about taking a class with you. But they also said they're worried everything will be over their heads. I understand you're teaching something not in our regular course catalog."

Spearman set his soup spoon down on the table. "At Harvard, when we teach economics, we usually distinguish between the economics of consumption and the economics of investment. You probably do the same at Monte Vista. So we teach our students a theory of consumer behavior, and we try to explain what that has to do with someone buying a six-pack of beer. Then we teach our students a theory of investing, and we try to explain what that has to do with someone acquiring a hundred shares of Intel stock. I want to explore the economics of buying durable goods that have consumption value to some, investment value to others, and for some, both. I'm thinking here of art. So I'm calling the class 'Art and Economics.' We don't offer this as a course in the Econ Department at Harvard either, so I'm using your students as guinea pigs."

Salvatore was the first to respond. "I like the idea of economics plus something else . . . like art. But don't expect a lot of sophistication from the econ students about art. Your class probably will be mostly econ majors, and most of them won't know beans about art. If you get art students, they probably won't be able to handle the econ." Salvatore gestured with his knife and fork in his hands as he spoke. "I've always thought interdisciplinary classes violated Adam Smith's principle of specialization and division of labor—and that was why they don't work very well."

Hannah Talsma towered over Spearman, even while seated. She had been a nationally ranked volleyball player before going to graduate school in economics. The large eyeglasses she wore seemed to make her even taller. She looked down at the professor and said, "I think you'll have a problem defining what's art. Marco and I have had this conversation before. He thinks art began and ended with the Italian Renaissance." She tossed her head back as if to say "he's hopeless." "But I think art isn't just what hangs on museum walls. It's the design of a Fender guitar or a Mustang Fastback."

Abraham chimed in: "Well Henry, to counter my colleagues' negatives, one positive is that you'll find San Antonio rich in art. Dallas and Houston think they're the alpha dogs. But San Antonio is an older city and has a long tradition in the visual arts: two solid museums and a lot of well-known artists call San Antonio home. And we have some well-heeled patrons also." Abraham took a sip of iced tea as he pictured in his mind the feisty Annelle Cubbage at a trustee meeting.

"Actually, you already know of one: Annelle Cubbage by name." Abraham went on. "She's the one who picked up the tab for your being here. And here's another name for you: tomorrow night, when you and your wife have dinner at the president's house, you'll meet Michael Cavanaugh, one of our school's big names. Cavanaugh's an authority on art history, though I should warn you he's a bit of a character."

Professor Adams had eaten his lunch in silence to this point. Now he looked up and down the table at his colleagues and said, "If our guest is going to teach about art, we need to inform him that art is a somewhat delicate matter at Monte Vista because of what happened yesterday. I think we all know what I'm talking about."

Before anyone else could respond, Herbert Abraham said, "Henry is aware of Wheeler's death. He read about it in this morning's paper, *and* he had to walk past the crime scene tape on our way in. The house the university puts him up in is close to Wheeler's."

Adams resumed the conversational lead. "Tristan Wheeler was not only the most famous artist at the school, he was the most well-known member of the Monte Vista faculty." Adams paused. He wanted to say to Spearman, "until you joined us," but he was not sure if this would come off as praise or as being obsequious. Adams let it go at that.

"Does that mean I shouldn't offer a course on art and economics?" Spearman asked, trying to see the connection.

"No, not at all," Adams responded. "But you should be aware of the incident. Wheeler's death has put a shadow over the school, particularly the artsy side of the school, that won't go away soon."

"As Herbert said, I read about Wheeler's death in this morning's paper." Spearman explained. "But it wasn't until my walk to campus that I realized Wheeler and I were neighbors . . . or I suppose, would have been."

"I don't get it," Salvatore interjected. "The guy is famous. He's making tons of money. And then he kills himself? What's with that?" Salvatore was gesturing again with his knife and fork.

"I saw the guy just three days ago, coming out of the library," Battles said between bites from his king-size tuna sandwich. "Of course, we didn't speak. I don't even know the guy to talk to. But he looked fine to me then."

"It just goes to show, you can never tell," Adams continued. "And what about the students who signed up for his classes this semester? What about the people who work for him and help him out? What about the people who like his art? It makes you wonder whether people who commit suicide think through the havoc they cause for others."

Spearman listened to all this without comment as he ate his lunch. Then he looked over at Marco Salvatore, whose original question had begun the discussion. "You should tell your advisees that we'll be concerned with the economics of consuming art, the economics of investing in art, and also the supply of art. And while I suppose the art could be a Fender guitar or a Mustang fastback," he grinned at Talsma—"I plan to hang our analysis on the more conventional visual arts, like paintings." Spearman wondered if there was a pun there but decided probably not. "If students want to look at other markets for art. . . ." Spearman's voice trailed off.

Matthew Battles had almost finished his tuna fish sandwich and was waiting for a time to interject. "When I heard you were coming to Monte Vista and would teach a special topics course, to be honest I hoped you planned to offer a class on economics and sports. Some econ departments offer courses on sports economics. We don't. But our students would love it." Jennifer Kim had a look of shock on her face. She could not imagine herself, or any junior member of the faculty, being so brash as to tell a distinguished professor, in effect, "this is what you *really* should be doing." But Battles was just getting wound up.

"Can you imagine one of our students being able to do a paper on the demand and supply of Spurs basketball?

And get credit for it! In case you don't know, Professor Spearman, the Spurs are *huge* in San Antonio." Battles elongated the word huge. "I mean *h-u-u-u-g-e*." He started to return to his sandwich but then added, "You can't be in San Antonio for long without hearing about the Spurs. They could rename Main Street 'Duncan Street' and nobody would object."

Spearman was left trying to identify who Duncan was. All he could think of was Duncan Black, the British economist who pioneered applying economic analysis to the behavior of committees and elections, what economists now called public choice.

Hannah Talsma piped up, "Matt has a point. I happen to be a baseball fan. But San Antonio is not a baseball town. Everyone here is nuts about the Spurs. A lot of our students who aren't even from Texas become Spurs fans."

Don Compton, who had been silent until now, chimed in. "And the Spurs have been great for the local economy. That could be another angle for a course on sports economics: the whole topic of financing the stadiums." Spearman turned to look at this table companion who only seemed interested in his food until now. "In a lot of cities, the taxpayers who don't like professional sports get gouged, because the local government subsidizes the construction of the stadiums and arenas where the teams play. San Antonio doesn't do that. Here, the city financed the Spurs' stadium by a tax on hotel rooms, so the stadium didn't cost the citizens of San Antonio a thing."

"It cost the city the full value of the stadium," Spearman said in response.

"No, you misunderstand how it was done here." Compton never ever dreamed that someday he might be teaching basic economics to someone like Spearman. He wished his own students were watching. "To pay for the stadium, the city didn't tax local income or property. The tax was on hotel rooms—two dollars per night as I recall—until the stadium money was raised. That's how the city fathers persuaded residents to go along. So only out-of-towners paid the tax." Compton then took a professorial pause as though he were in a seminar. "And I think you'd find this interesting, Henry. The demand for hotels was apparently so inelastic that it hardly affected occupancy rates. So we didn't pay a dime for the stadium. That's what I meant."

"You're missing my point," Spearman replied, looking over his glasses at Compton. "I don't dispute that the city fathers *told* the people of San Antonio that the tax wouldn't cost them anything. But it did nonetheless. If there is one thing we know in economics it's that the cost of something is the alternative opportunity foregone. So the cost of the tax is what the city could have done with the tax money if it had not built a stadium for the Spurs. So whatever the stadium cost . . ." Spearman paused.

"Two hundred million," Battles interjected from the end of the table.

". . . then the cost of the stadium is two hundred million worth of foregone public services," Spearman continued. "These could have been parks, schools, police and fire protection, roads, whatever the city of San Antonio provides."

Battles and Kim, the two most junior economists at the table, listened to the conversation intently. They were both learning one of the first lessons of academic lunch conversation: *watch carefully what you say*. Among professors, there was rarely such a thing as small talk about the weather. Even talking about a basketball stadium could involve intellectual one-upmanship. Don Compton was now glad his students were not present at lunch that day.

Then Jennifer Kim spoke up: "But until the stadium initiative, no one had thought to tax hotel rooms as a source of revenue. Wasn't this a case of 'found money' rather than a cost?" Her voice trailed off at Spearman's smile.

"One thing I've learned," Spearman said, "is never tell a government about some activity it has not yet thought to tax. If you do, it will provoke a cost."

Unlike Battles and Kim, Herbert Abraham was a veteran of faculty table talk. He deftly switched the conversational gears. "Henry, Monte Vista is growing and our department has been given the funds for a junior hire. Hannah and Matt and I interviewed candidates at the American Economic Association meetings last week. So we have a favor to ask. I realize, in asking, that this might not seem like a big deal to you. You have what, thirty, forty colleagues at Harvard? But if Rowena were here, you'd be looking at our whole department. So adding someone is a big deal for us. We'd be grateful if we could get your advice on the candidates we've narrowed it down to."

Spearman said he would be happy to help, though he recognized there were risks involved in doing so. Most professors, Spearman observed, had thin skins and long memories. If he panned a candidate, he wanted his evaluation treated with discretion.

•

That evening he returned home to find Pidge back from her time with the provost's wife. The day had been packed for each of them. Henry had met most of his colleagues, initiated the move into his university office, and taken care of all the HR forms and paperwork. Pidge now reckoned she could find her way around San Antonio, had located the closest branch of their bank, and had found a grocery store that could meet all their household demand for food and drink. After a light dinner, the two of them adjourned to the side porch of their new home. The room was an inviting environment for unwinding from a long day. A ceiling fan softly buzzed as it circulated the evening air.

As Pidge was relating her day's endeavors, her expression suddenly changed. She sighed. "I learned there's friction in the marriage of Herbert Abraham. And it's linked to Tristan Wheeler, the artist who just died. There was talk of an affair between Wheeler and Herbert's wife Jocelyn. I don't know the details, but it apparently led to bad blood between Herbert and Wheeler." Pidge looked out at the shadows on the lawn as the sun began to set. "It made me sad. Herbert Abraham has been so nice to us. Maybe Wheeler's death will cause some good—and his marriage will survive."

As they sat next to each other, Henry thought about Pidge and what she had just said. He realized that economists who modeled marriage using the theory of bilateral monopoly often got it right. But not always. In his case, marriage was a husband and wife having interdependent utility functions: one spouse deriving more utility by increasing the utility of the other.

Spearman put an arm around Pidge. He had long believed that if he could find words that rhymed with interdependent utility functions, he could write an economist's poem about love. But he could never find the words.

11

THE ACADEMICAL VILLAGE

FRIDAY MORNING, JANUARY 13TH

When we strive to solve a scientific problem, is ambition for our own professional status completely overshadowed by our love of knowledge?

—GEORGE J. STIGLER

Jennifer Kim looked directly into Henry Spearman's eyes. As a graduate student, she had experienced professors who—distracted by her good looks—failed to take her seriously. So she had adopted the practice of looking at her mentors straight on. This seemed to deter eye wandering by male faculty.

"Thanks for meeting with me, Dr. Spearman . . . I mean . . . Henry." She paused. "Before we begin, I might as well confess. Calling you 'Henry' is going to be a challenge for me. I hope you can understand that. My parents came to this country from Korea. I grew up being taught to have great respect for anyone older. I never called any adults by their first name. *Never*. Now I'm in a world where people older than I am expect it. And a lot of my students call me by my first name and don't think twice about it."

"I think I understand," Henry said, smiling warmly at Jennifer. "You aren't the first colleague I've had who found using my first name to be difficult. And I'm sure you won't be the last."

"Even your use of the term 'colleague' throws me," she continued. "I'm just out of graduate school. And now you call me a 'colleague.' My parents would be so honored that you even think of me that way. But I can assure you they wouldn't want me calling you 'Henry.' They'd consider that disrespectful. In fact, when I first joined the faculty here, I had a hard time calling Herbert Abraham by his first name. But then one day he told me that if I called him 'Professor Abraham' one more time, he'd call me 'Professor Kim' for the rest of my life!" She laughed nervously.

Spearman and Kim were sitting in the office that Monte Vista had provided for the Cubbage Nobel Prize Chair holder. The room had a polished corporate look to it. There was Herman Miller furniture throughout. In addition to a corner desk with a computer and Aeron chair, the room had a circular beech-wood table and four matching chairs to accommodate visitors.

During his student days, Spearman could not recall ever visiting a faculty office where the professor did not sit behind a desk and he, as a student visitor to the professor's office, did not sit in front of the desk. In those days, the desk served as a physical and a symbolic barrier between teacher and pupil. But in the contemporary academic milieu, students and professors sat more as equals and the office furniture reflected this change in tastes and preferences. Today's students usually sat around a table in their professor's office.

"Jennifer, you probably know of my colleague, Win Li. Talented econometrician. So talented we asked him to join our department when he finished his Ph.D. at Harvard. This meant that for Win, overnight, all his former professors became his colleagues. Win thought he would ease into calling us by our first names. Two years have gone by. He still calls us by our last names. So much time has gone by that poor Win thinks it would be odd to start using our first names. If you aren't careful, you'll end up like him."

"Okay, *Henry*," Jennifer said, smiling broadly as she put emphasis on Spearman's first name.

"Now what would you like to talk about?" Spearman leaned back in his chair.

"When you first met Matt Battles and me, we asked if we could get advice about some research ideas. And you agreed to talk with us. Well . . . I'm here to take you up on your offer." Spearman's eyebrows raised in encouragement.

Kim leaned forward in her chair. "Here's my situation as I see it. I'm at a school that takes teaching seriously. And I want to be a good teacher. But I also enjoy research. My advisors at Berkeley told me that if I ever wanted to leave Monte Vista for a more research-oriented school, I needed to show I can get stuff published. So I'd like your advice on my research strategy."

"When you say you enjoy research, what do you mean by 'enjoy,' if I may ask?"

"When I was an undergraduate, I had a professor who asked me to do some research with him. And it was like a light went on in my head. What's the right word? Epiphany? For the first time, I saw the difference between trying to understand what somebody *else* had done versus doing something new *myself*."

Jennifer's cheeks flushed as she talked about her under-graduate student days. "I used to think education meant learning what was already known. But after that I began to see that education also meant creating something new that wasn't known before." She then paused and began to bite her lip. Her face, animated only a moment earlier, grew sad and reflective. "That's how a friend in the Art Department once described art to me, actually." She looked over at Henry. "You were talking about him at lunch, so I know you heard about his . . . well, his passing."

Spearman nodded. Once again he was reminded how Wheeler's death had set in motion so many emotional responses on the campus, Jennifer Kim's now among them. "I'm sorry," he said.

Kim lowered her head. When she raised it, Spearman saw that her eyes were moist. "That's okay. Thanks for caring." She smiled at Spearman. "When I first got here, Tristan and I were quite close. Not so much anymore. Being close, I learned, meant something different to him than it did to me." She looked out the window and then turned back again. "But that first day when we met he told me about reading *Tristram Shandy*, and how the title character would wind and unwind the same rope. He said he didn't want to be an artist who ended up winding and unwinding the same rope. He said that great art was creating a new rope entirely. I feel the same way about doing economics."

The two were silent. "Strange isn't it? 'Tristan' and 'Tristram.' How many people do you meet with either of those names?" Jennifer spoke almost in a whisper. "And then there's the rope. Tristram Shandy writes about a rope. Tristan Wheeler dies by one. I mean, how bizarre is that?"

Spearman looked quizzically at Jennifer. He decided to change the conversational gears. "We started talking about your research, Jennifer. Let's go back to that. Tell me, what have you done so far?" He leaned back in his chair.

"The usual," Kim replied. "I've mined my dissertation for articles and sent two in. One has been accepted in the *Journal of Law and Economics*, the other has a revise and resubmit from the *Review of Economics and Statistics.*"

"Two publications in good journals. That's a fine start," Spearman said. "You're off and running. Congratulations, Jennifer. I mean that."

Jennifer Kim was flushed with pride. Now she wished that her parents were present, even if they had heard her call Spearman by his first name.

"That's my problem . . . Henry. I know I'm off to a good start. But I'm a little unclear on where to go from here. In grad school, my professors were always tossing off research ideas. Now that I'm a professor, I've got a bunch of ideas. But I'm worried about going off in too many directions."

Spearman smiled warmly at his junior colleague. He had seen the same professional fears and aspirations in his daughter Patricia as she prepared to be a veterinarian. "As you know, the class I'm going to teach this semester is something I'm calling 'Art and Economics.' I'm not sure where the class is going to go. Art is what I picked. It could just as well have been any number of topics." Henry stroked his chin as he thought through what he was about to say. "Let me make a suggestion. I don't know the students at Monte Vista. But you do. I'd like to have you sit in my class as a kibitzer. The students will be relieved to see a familiar face; and as we learn about art and economics, you might pick up some fruitful research ideas."

Spearman paused and looked kindly at Jennifer. "I'll be better off having you in the class, you'll be better off if you get a new research idea, and the students will be better off. So everybody's better off, no one's worse off. Sounds Pareto-optimal to me."

As an economist, Jennifer could not disagree with a move that was Pareto-optimal. She would sit in on the class.

•

As Spearman escorted his young colleague into the hallway, he was surprised to see Detective Fuller and another officer exit the office of Henry Abraham. The professor stood in the office doorway, his face brick red. His expression was less than cordial as he addressed the departing officer. "At least you didn't have me do a perp walk in front of my colleagues," he snarled. "I guess I should be grateful for small favors. But if we have to talk again, I'd prefer it be at my home. I can assure you I can answer any question there that you might put to me here."

Embarrassed, Kim made a beeline for her office. Henry, stunned, continued to observe the scene unfolding before him. Fuller's face was hard, her voice matter-of-fact. "Look, professor, my job is to interview people where I find them. If you like, we can always go downtown. But I can tell you, most people would rather talk to me in their office than at the station."

"I did not propose the alternatives of the police station versus my office. Maybe you didn't hear me: I proposed *my home*—get it, the place where I live."

"Sorry, Prof. If there's a next time, we'll see if your home works."

The detective and her colleague made their way out of the building. Several professors who had been observing this scene from their office doorways retreated into their academic sanctuaries. Only Henry Spearman remained in the hallway, looking at Herbert Abraham.

"Like some company? Or would you rather be alone?" Spearman inquired. "I'm good, either way."

"Why don't you come in," Abraham motioned. "You must wonder what *that* was all about."

"I think I have some idea," Spearman responded after the two were seated. "Campus grapevines are legendary for having low information costs, even before the digital era. Yesterday, Pidge and I became aware that you could—shall I say—restrain your enthusiasm for Tristan Wheeler. We also heard there might be . . . reasons for that."

"You don't have to be delicate with me, Henry. I know what's being said about my marriage. And I think I can guess where that's leading."

"Are there in fact suspicions being raised? I read that his death was considered a suicide." Haltingly, Henry tried to placate his friend, and show that he didn't suspect Abraham of anything. He went on. "I recognized the detective in the hallway. If it's any consolation, you may remember that she also called on me about Wheeler's death. This was just a short time before you picked me up and brought me to the campus yesterday. It's part of their routine."

"But Henry, there's a huge difference. You could never be seen as a suspect. And your encounter wasn't humiliating like mine. Several of my colleagues saw the police come to my office. I honestly expected to be taken out in handcuffs, with the press waiting outside. That didn't happen, thank God. But in an hour, all the faculty will know. Soon, the students will have heard about this." Abraham put his head in his hands. "You know it's suicide; I know it's suicide. But soon the rumors will morph into some grotesque story that I killed Wheeler out of jealousy and somehow made it look like a suicide." He looked up at Spearman. "Or almost worse, that I'm an old man, and I can't handle having a younger wife. Who knows what ugly direction this will take?"

Spearman looked around Abraham's office. It was lined with books and journals, the printed output of thousands of hours of labor by economics scholars. Henry recognized many of the titles. He knew their contents. He knew some of the authors personally. And he realized that pulling any one of them down from the shelf would offer no consolation whatsoever to the person in whose office the books and journals had been carefully assembled.

"I asked Jocelyn recently, 'Are you having an affair with Wheeler?' You know how she replied?" He looked up. His eyes were moist. "She didn't. She said, 'Why do you ask?' Not a 'no' mind you, but a 'why do you ask?' " Abraham spoke as though he'd been pierced by an arrow.

Spearman's mind functioned at full capacity as he tried to think how to help Abraham. He realized that he barely knew his colleague, but he also knew that this was the person whose confidence in Henry as the ideal Nobel laureate had brought him to Monte Vista University. Before he could say anything, Abraham erupted.

"To hell with Wheeler." He looked at his office door to be sure it was closed. "There, I've said it. If there's a hell, I hope he's there. He takes advantage of other men's wives and leaves them to pick up the pieces of the marriage. Personally, I think his art became a scam." Herbert sighed. "I'm sorry Henry. I wanted you to enjoy Monte Vista and for the school to bask in your reputation. Now Wheeler's sullied even that."

Spearman let Abraham be silent for several moments. "Did you and Wheeler have much of a relationship?" he eventually asked.

"If hating his guts is a relationship, I suppose we did. Plus we had a couple rows in which I said some things in front of others that I now regret."

Spearman looked his colleague directly in the eyes. "I've always been one for facing fear, Herbert. Let's say the police reject the suicide angle, and pursue this as a murder case. Did you have a motive?"

"Did *I* have a motive? Sure. People have motives to do all sorts of things. But they don't actually do them—and they don't because the costs exceed the benefits. That decision calculus applies to murder as well. Would there be *benefits* to me if Wheeler were dead? Sure. And they're nontrivial. But the *costs* of my killing him myself are too high to make it worth the candle."

"Do you think murder lends itself to the rational actor model?" Spearman asked.

"You are asking *me* that question?" Abraham said, his eyes fixed on Spearman's face. "You're the great mahatma when it comes to economics. I'm just a mere mortal in the dismal science. You tell me."

12

DINING PROTOCOL IN THE ACADEMY

FRIDAY EVENING, JANUARY 13ᵀᴴ

Economics is the art of putting parameters on our utopias.
—JAMES M. BUCHANAN

It was seven o'clock Friday evening, time for the Spearmans' center-stage appearance at what Herbert Abraham had called the "presidential palace." Henry and Pidge had decided to walk to the president's home because it was only one street over from the guest house in which they resided.

After a short stroll, Henry pulled up. "This must be the place," he said to Pidge.

"How can you tell?"

"Because it is the largest house around. Every school I've ever visited, the president lives in a mansion. In fact, you can count on the president having the biggest house—but only the *second* biggest salary."

Pidge took the bait: "Who makes the most money?"

"The football coach, at least at schools with major athletic programs."

"Why is the football coach paid more than the president?" Pidge asked. Her growing-up experience in a professor's home had always been at private liberal arts colleges where she was pretty sure this wasn't the case.

"Like most things, it's explained by demand and supply," Henry replied. "At every university, there's a demand for one president and one head football coach. But the supply of presidents is greater than the supply of talented coaches. So you end up with a significant wage differential." The couple took a turn toward the house before Henry added, "And remember, when it comes to coaching, there is a quantitative measure of performance. What's the win-loss record? The closest quantitative measure for a president's productivity is the amount of money raised for the school." Pidge had learned while dating Henry that even an evening walk would involve a lesson in economics.

The Spearmans strolled up the walkway of the formidable white stucco home that was capped by a Spanish tile roof. Wrought iron adornments decorated the entrance-way and windows. The centerpiece of the front yard was a giant live oak tree whose lower branches spread out in every direction at angles that defied the laws of physics. President Quinn and her husband met the Spearmans at the front door.

"Welcome, Mrs. Spearman, Professor Spearman, do come in. I'm Charlotte Quinn. This is my husband Nicholas. We are delighted to have you at Monte Vista. You already know Professor Abraham, of course; he and his wife Jocelyn are in the house with the other guests." Both of the Spearmans wondered if meeting Herbert's wife would be unpleasant. "At least they're together," Pidge whispered to her husband, as they followed the president inside.

President Quinn ushered the Spearmans into a spacious living room. At the center of the east wall, two

French doors opened to a piazza whose focal point was a circular stone fountain. The Quinns did most of their entertaining there. This evening, the inner courtyard was set up for both cocktails and dinner.

Pidge noticed that in the president's house all the accoutrements for hosting guests were first-class. The cocktails in the piazza were served in Waterford crystal. The flowers in the hallway and on the table were freshly cut for the occasion. After introductions and pleasantries were exchanged, beverages were consumed, and the guests ushered in to find their places at the table, Pidge further observed that the dishes in front of her were Dresden china. The linen and silver that accompanied the meal also were of the highest quality, and when the dinner wine was served it was at exactly the right temperature.

As any number of previous guests could have testified, Charlotte Quinn had an obvious talent for gracious hospitality. Her guests included notable literary, scientific, and political figures, and Quinn believed that her skill at seating arrangements would assist in the cross-pollination of ideas. This evening the table was set for twelve.

Margaret Mead's *Coming of Age in Samoa* enlightened Pidge's generation about the peculiar folkways and mores of what was then considered a primitive society. In academia, the folkways and mores were just as rigidly adhered to as those of the Micronesians and were just as mysterious to an outside observer. The protocol at academic dinners could supply a cultural anthropologist with enough material for a scholarly book that could bring its author fame if not fortune.

The seating arrangements bore eloquent witness to this fact. The president of the university would always be at the head of the table. Everyone understood that. Greater speculation among the guests was reserved for the question of secondary prominence, determined by who should sit on the president's immediate right. *This* was the place to be coveted. At the president's house this evening, the prohibitive favorite was Henry Spearman, the new Cubbage Visiting Nobel Professor.

Who was seated to the president's left received the next closest attention. A dean or provost on the guest list might expect to be seated there. But a top administrator might be trumped by a member of the school's Board of Trustees, especially if the trustee chaired the board, or was a likely candidate to assume that role in the near future. If a mere professor were chosen over a dean or a provost or a trustee, this would signal that another school was trying to hire that particular professor away. President Quinn would allocate this coveted real estate at the dinner table if she were going all out to retain a valuable member of the faculty. But she would count the cost in doing so.

Tonight, the choice was a no-brainer: Annelle Cubbage, the trustee and donor who made Henry Spearman's presence an economic reality, would be seated on the president's left and across from the Nobel Prize winner. Quinn hoped there would be no friction between the two of them. Like any college or university president, she wanted donors to think their money was being well spent, so they might donate more.

In accord with academic dining protocol, at the other end of the table sat the president's spouse. Who occupied the chairs on either side of the president's spouse also brought strategic considerations into play. These were highly valued by their recipients. It gave them a chance to gain the president's ear, albeit indirectly. A professor always could hope that a congenial conversation with the president's spouse would be passed on to the president and could be career-enhancing.

This evening, Nicholas Quinn's most proximate conversation partners were Pidge Spearman (to his right) and Michael Cavanaugh (to his left). As Pidge was being seated some distance from her husband, she looked quickly out over the long table to give Henry a wave. He returned her wave with a wink, a smile, and a nod of his head.

For dinner, President Quinn and the university's head of food services had selected a minted Mediterranean fruit salad followed by a Frenched rack of lamb and parsleyed new potatoes for the main course. After President Quinn had given the requisite signal, and Pidge was starting to eat her salad, the guest across from her said, "I take it that you are the spouse of the guest of honor? I arrived a bit late for cocktails and so I'm afraid we were not properly introduced. I'm Michael Cavanaugh, Art Department."

"And I'm Pidge Spearman, Henry Spearman is my husband. Nice to meet you."

Pidge noticed that Cavanaugh darted his eyes and gave her a quick glance rather than giving his full attention when he introduced himself. He barely moved his lips when he spoke, giving the impression of a ventriloquist as he threw off a high-pitched chirpy sound followed by a quiet yet distinct belch.

Pidge always felt comfortable around professors—she had grown up among this social tribe after all. She empathized with Cavanaugh, who seemed nervous about being in the president's home. She also knew of the death in his department.

"I was sorry to learn of your colleague's death, Mr. Cavanaugh," Pidge said kindly. "It must be hard for you to be here tonight." She glanced around the room at the sparkling glasses, the starched linens, the prim and unobtrusive wait staff tending each and every need of the chattering guests.

"It is," Cavanaugh responded. "Tristan was a friend as well as the most notable person in our department. I almost didn't show up. In fact I thought of calling the president's office to decline but one of my colleagues said it was important I be here. 'Stiff upper lip,' 'life goes on,' and all that. She also said it might be good for me to be around people."

"I'm glad you came," Pidge said. "It can't be good for you to sit at home, alone." She had guessed that the professor was single. "And of course with a suicide, death is sad, and sudden."

"Oh, it wasn't suicide, Mrs. Spearman. Tristan didn't kill himself. That's what *they* want you to believe."

"Who is 'they'?" Pidge asked. But before he could respond the next course arrived, and following the exchange of dishes Nicholas Quinn had picked up the conversational football.

Seated between Pidge at her end of the table and Annelle Cubbage at the other end were Herbert Abraham, Professor Portman Vines of the Department of Romance Languages, and Jocelyn Abraham. Opposing them, the three guests seated between Henry Spearman and Michael Cavanaugh were Jack Cubbage, Anjali Vitali, and Susan

Rose. Vitali was a senior at Monte Vista majoring in economics and was one of the school's student "emissaries." He was the only student at the dinner. Rose was from Mathematics.

Jack Cubbage had been silent through the first part of the meal, then he looked sideways at Vitali and said, "Don't ever buy a Rolls-Royce, young man. They're too much trouble."

Emissaries at Monte Vista University were chosen because of their clean-cut appearance and their ability to present the university in a positive manner to all types of guests. They were groomed to be welcoming to prospective students and to be winsome to returning alumni and other visitors to campus. But nothing in his training had prepared Vitali for this remark. For that matter, nothing in his background had ever led him to think he might someday have a Rolls-Royce. "Why do you say that, sir?" he finally responded, thinking this was the most diplomatic reply. "Isn't a Rolls-Royce considered a famous automobile?"

"They're a lot of trouble. If you live in San Antonio and your Rolls breaks down, you have to get someone from Houston or Dallas to come fix it. That's a pain in the ass. And they do break down. I can tell you that. If you want something reliable, buy Japanese. Are you Japanese, by the way?"

"No sir, I'm American," Vitali replied. "My parents came here from India."

"Best place in the world to live. America that is. Just don't buy a Rolls-Royce, that's my advice, young man." Jack Cubbage chewed up another mouthful of lamb. "Unless you live in Houston or Dallas, maybe. Then it might be okay."

Anjali pondered his situation. His classmates in high school thought some of the customs his parents brought from India were odd. But surely, he thought to himself, by any metric they were no more odd than the customs of the wealthy Texans he encountered as a student emissary for Monte Vista University. But Anjali did not become a student ambassador for the school by being socially inept. "Good advice, I'm sure," he said to the husband of the university's biggest donor.

At the presidential end of the table, Cubbage and Spearman were engaged in conversation. Henry had moved a floral arrangement that, because of his short stature, blocked his view of the wealthy university trustee who sat across from him. He knew Annelle Cubbage was the money behind the invitation for him to come to Monte Vista as a visiting professor. Spearman was not intimidated by this, but he did not want to appear ungracious either, for he wasn't. "I know my being here is because of your generosity, Ms. Cubbage," Henry said. "I want to thank you."

"Well, let's get a couple things straight between us," Cubbage replied in a voice that most everyone at the table could hear. "First, it's *Annelle*, not 'Ms. Cubbage.' I don't care much for formality, even at a dinner with fancy china. Second, it wasn't my money that got you here. It was my daddy's, bless his heart. And third, I gave the money to bring a Nobel Prize winner to Monte Vista. It wasn't given specifically to bring *you* here." Cubbage then smiled sweetly at Spearman. "But you're kind to say thanks."

Henry Spearman smiled back at Cubbage. "I know you allocate some of the money you invested from your father to benefit the arts." Spearman could be direct as well. "You might be interested to know that the course enabled by your father's wealth is about art and economics."

"That so?" Cubbage gave Spearman a stern look, her eyebrows arching above the lens of her eyeglasses. "Did Charlotte Quinn or Herbert Abraham put you up to that so I'd think my money was well spent?" Cubbage looked at Quinn and then at Abraham.

"I'm afraid the choice was mine alone," Spearman said. "Nobody put me up to it. But I hope you end up being pleased nevertheless, and the students too."

"No need to worry about me. Let's see what the students think at the end of the semester. Isn't customer satisfaction the best indicator, professor?"

"Actually it is," Spearman parried. "But sometimes that metric is hard to measure when it comes to teaching."

"Well, how do you propose to measure it before you go back East?"

Spearman gave an impish smile to President Quinn and then looked back at Cubbage. "I've been asked that question before, Annelle. I think the best measure of excellent teaching is when students carry you around campus on their shoulders on the last day of class." Everyone within earshot laughed, except Cubbage.

"That ever happen, professor?"

"Well, not here yet, but remember I just arrived."

"I hope it does. Remember the deal is you also give a public lecture while you're here. I'm in New York quite a lot, but I'll be sure to be there for your lecture."

"I wouldn't want it any other way, Annelle," Spearman said.

While to observers like Vitali and Rose the repartee between Cubbage and Spearman seemed rough and tumble, neither of them saw it that way. If others at the table saw Cubbage as being caustic, Henry Spearman did not. He liked her directness. In many academic settings, Spearman thought too much scarce time was spent trying to figure out what someone "really meant" by what they said. With people like Cubbage, you could economize on conversational resources.

For Annelle, the conversation persuaded her that her investment in the first Cubbage Visiting Nobel Professorship was a sound one. Despite the external appearance of the conversation, she liked Spearman. But she was not ready to lay those cards on the table just yet.

Their conversation continued over dessert, turning inevitably, if somewhat awkwardly, to the death of Tristan Wheeler. "I know you played a major role in bringing Wheeler to San Antonio and promoting his art. From what I've learned about his reputation and the prominence he brought to Monte Vista, your contribution to the school in this regard probably trumps your funding the Nobel Visiting Professorship." There was a false modesty in Spearman's saying this and Annelle recognized that.

"It hasn't been easy, I'll admit that." Cubbage's voice was lower now. She was not speaking to the whole table. "You pour yourself into trying to help someone, the person's work starts to get known in many places, and then the damn fool kills himself. Maybe I could get it if his art was awful. But I'm from a little town in Texas. Live on a ranch in the Hill Country. And even *I* know his stuff was great."

•

After the dinner party ended and President Quinn had said goodbye to all the guests, the Spearmans retraced their steps back home. They walked hand-in-hand, at first in silence.

"Quite a contrast between Charlotte Quinn and Annelle Cubbage, don't you think?" Henry said.

"Why do you say that, Henry? I could only hear bits and pieces of the conversation."

"Well, the president is so gracious, while Cubbage is so blunt."

"She likes you very much, Henry."

"You mean Quinn?"

"No, Annelle Cubbage."

"Really? How can you tell?"

"A woman knows these things," Pidge responded and held Henry's hand more firmly.

13

A DOCTOR'S HOUSE CALL

Some people think that economists care only about
money. I have heard an unkind critic say that an economist is someone who would sell his grandmother to the
highest bidder. This is quite wrong. An economist, or at
least a good economist, would not sell his grandmother to
the highest bidder unless the highest bid was enough to
compensate him for the loss of his grandmother.

—CARL CHRIST

"Howdy, neighbor!" Dr. Ramos hollered out to Henry
Spearman. "Now I reckon for someone new to Texas that
must sound corny. But that's how people talk in these
parts." Raul Ramos grinned as he walked across the driveway from his house to the front lawn of the Spearman's
residence, pulling a Trek bike alongside him.

"It doesn't sound strange to me at all," Spearman called
back to his next door neighbor. "One of my friends back
home is from Oklahoma, a little town called Woodward
if I have it right. He hasn't been back for years, but over
and again I'll hear him say 'howdy' to me or someone else."
He smiled as he remembered some of Henderson Ross's
other quirks.

"Well, let me clue you in, Oklahoma isn't Texas. Maybe you haven't seen the signs: 'don't mess with Texas.' One of the ways people from the East mess with Texas is to equate us with Oklahoma. The two states are bitter rivals. Not sure why, even though I grew up in Texas. It's just the way it is. The Okies don't think much of us either." By now Spearman's new neighbor was almost face-to-face with him. "But you're probably right—an Okie might say 'howdy' too." It was a Saturday afternoon and the two men encountered each other when Ramos was about to go for a bicycle ride and Spearman was getting ready to walk to his office.

"I'm Raul Ramos and I'm your new neighbor." He pointed back to his house with his thumb. The exterior of the spacious two-story home was dominated by gray-yellow limestone blocks punctuated with small casement windows. "Been in this house for almost fifteen years," Ramos went on, "but I'm not part of the university like most of the neighborhood. I've seen half the houses on the street picked up by the school, including the one you're in. Where you live used to be the Breit place. They sold out years ago, said they didn't like all the students in the neighborhood. But I think this is a great place to live. My two kids grew up on this street and some of the Monte Vista students were like big brothers and sisters to them."

Ramos was wearing a cycling outfit and was half-leaning on his bike while he spoke. At six-two with broad, muscular shoulders, he exceeded Spearman in height and width. Henry was wearing a new polo shirt his daughter had given him as a going-away present for San Antonio. It still showed the creases from its original folding and packaging. Because it was Saturday and not a teaching day,

Henry was going to the office without his usual coat and tie. Neither man had a pending work appointment, which meant the opportunity cost of their taking time to chat was relatively low—so they talked amiably after exchanging handshakes.

"I'm a doctor," Ramos said, "but drop the 'doctor' title and please call me Raul."

"My name is Henry Spearman, but Henry works for me too," Spearman responded. "You say you're not with Monte Vista University?"

"No. The school asked me once to direct its student health program, but my specialty is surgery and I told them they needed someone in internal medicine or family practice. Occasionally, I'll operate on one of the students if an appendix needs to come out, that sort of thing. But that's about it. What brings you to the Lone Star State?"

Ramos actually knew more about Spearman than he was letting on. He had learned from Lewis Martin that his new neighbor was from Harvard; that he had won a Nobel Prize in economics and that his wife was with him; that the couple would be his neighbors for the spring semester; and that, as Martin had told him, landing this guy was a "big deal" for Monte Vista's reputation. But in meeting Spearman personally, Ramos thought it best to start as equals—as if neither knew anything about the other. He reckoned a small amount of dissembling on his part would facilitate getting acquainted and that he would learn, from the horse's mouth so to speak, all about his new neighbor.

"I'm a visiting professor at Monte Vista. My wife Pidge and I plan to be here for the spring semester. Then it's back to New England, where we are less likely to hear 'howdy' and to experience the Texas hospitality we already have enjoyed."

"So it's just the two of you?"

"I'm afraid so. We rattle around in such a large house. Our one child is a veterinarian. We hope she'll visit us while we're here. Your children have left home, you say?"

"They left, and so did my wife, but on very different terms. I have a good relationship with my kids but I'm divorced from their mother. The split was a few years ago. So I live in this big house by myself, except for Rosie Segura, my housekeeper. You'll see Rosie around, I'm sure. She basically runs the place. When I have a social event, I count on her to make it happen. Thanks to Mexico's economy being a basket case, you'll find that Texas has lots of people like Rosie. We'd be in a sad state without the Mexicans who come here to work. I know I'd be lost without her. What do you teach, Henry?" Ramos asked, even though he knew the answer.

"Economics."

Almost before Spearman had completed his one-word response, Ramos said, "I took an economics course in college once. I hated it. I once heard someone define economics as the 'dismal science.' I think whoever said that must have had my economics professor."

Spearman did not know what to make of Ramos's tone, which seemed only half teasing. But he didn't miss a beat in responding: "Actually, Raul, the term 'dismal science' was coined by Carlyle, and he didn't mean that the subject was dismal to learn. Carlyle disliked economics because he saw free markets as a threat to the social structure in

England that kept blacks and others in their place. Carlyle was a bigot who worried that a market economy would reduce the authority of the English ruling class. And history proved his fears to be well founded. Carlyle thought economics was dismal—for him and people who thought the way he did."

"Well the course I took seemed dismal," Ramos replied as he removed his glasses.

"The expression 'dismal science' has had a long shelf life," Spearman conceded. "I get teased about teaching the 'dismal science' all the time. I suppose one reason the term has stuck is because so many people have an experience similar to yours when they take an economics course. Of course," he chuckled, "as an economics professor I like to think my course is different."

"I don't encounter economists very much. Because of my work, I'm around doctors and my patients most of the time," Ramos said. "So let me ask: what do you think the stock market is going to do?"

Spearman looked Ramos straight in the eye, but spoke with a broad smile on his face: "I'll tell you what Raul. Let's make a deal. I won't ask you about my sore back if you don't ask me about the stock market. In addition, I won't ask you about my blood pressure if you don't ask me about interest rates." Before the doctor could respond Henry added the kicker: "Or if we do give each other professional counsel, let's agree that we each expect to be paid for our time."

"Fair enough," Ramos said smiling back at Spearman. "One of the curses of being a doctor is meeting so many people who want me to diagnose whatever ails them right there at a cocktail party. And if I do, and then send them a bill, they get all bent out of shape."

"Actually, you're relatively fortunate. There are *two* curses of being an economist. So people in my field are twice as bad off as you are."

Ramos laughed. "Okay, I'll take the bait. What are they?"

"The first is the same as yours. People always want to know what's going to happen to interest rates or the stock market. They expect us to know the answer, but they never offer to pay for the answer to their question. Where we differ is that when you're introduced as a surgeon, you get respect. When I'm introduced as an economist, people often look for a way to escape!" Spearman smiled. "That's the second curse. Economists don't have a reputation for being the life of the party. In fact, there's an old joke: an accountant is like an economist, except accountants have personality!" Spearman laughed as he spoke with Ramos. He enjoyed poking fun at economists because deep down, he had great confidence in the robust power of economic analysis.

"What kind of economics do you teach, Henry?" There had been no answering smile at Spearman's joke. "All I remember from my class is that there were Keynesians and some other guys and my professor thought the Keynesians won."

Spearman winced. "I'm afraid I don't have a dog in that fight. I try to teach students how to use economic analysis as a lens to view the world around them so as to understand that world in a new way. Actually, this semester I'm teaching a course that's about art. The class is called 'Art and Economics.' "

"You've got to be kidding," Ramos said. "I might have liked economics if it had to do with art. When I'm not doing surgery, I spend a lot of time thinking about art. I'm no authority, mind you. But I enjoy it and I think it's a good investment."

"Well, you're the kind of person I'd like to bring to my class. You could be Economic Exhibit A."

Ramos looked puzzled.

"The economic peg on which my class hangs is that art can be viewed as a consumption good, just like you said, or an investment, just like you said. This semester I'm exploring both of these economic characteristics as applied to art." Henry went on to explain that while art could involve many different kinds of artifacts, the focus of his class was on paintings.

"Huh." Spearman had captured his neighbor's interest. "Do you collect art yourself, Professor?" No longer fiddling with his glasses or asking rote questions, Ramos was now clearly engaged.

"Gracious no. I plan to teach about art, but I don't really own any. Oh, wait a minute, my wife bought a Thomas Kinkade once, for our den. We have friends in Cambridge who tell us that Kinkade 'isn't really an artist,' although I'm not sure why. Some people buy Kinkade's paintings as a consumption good. They enjoy looking at it. Some people buy his art as an investment good—in the hopes it will appreciate in value. So looked at through the lens of economics, Kinkade certainly meets the economic definition of art."

"I probably side with your friends about Kinkade as an artist. He's no Picasso, that's for sure. But let me add a different twist, Henry. In addition to its status as a consumption good and an investment, art is also something that can be stolen. How would that look through your analytical lens? Having art stolen was my sad experience a few months ago. Five of my prize paintings were taken right off the walls of this house." Ramos pointed back to his place of residence. Now it was Henry's turn to feign ignorance. He had been aware of Ramos's "sad experience" since November, and had wondered when—or if—the subject would come up in their conversation.

"I'm sorry to learn of your loss," he said, realizing immediately that his use of the word "loss" suggested that there had been a death in the Ramos family. But for Ramos, the word was not a faux pas.

"It was a horrible loss," Ramos said. "And not just from an aesthetic or financial standpoint. I knew the artist. Personally. His name was Tristan Wheeler, and I was one of the first to be a serious collector of his work. And," he pointed a short distance away, "he lived in that house over there. Right next to me and just two doors down from you." At this point, Ramos asked if he and Spearman could sit down for a spell on the oak bench in Spearman's front yard. Getting permission, the surgeon put his Trek down in the grass.

"I don't want you to think you've moved into a bad neighborhood. But it's bizarre, no question about it. The paintings that were stolen from my house were all by Wheeler. As I said, I knew him, helped promote his work, and we were friends. Not pals, mind you. Tristan was not the kind of person who had 'pals.' But we had a high regard for each other, I think that's fair to say. Then, just as you moved in, Wheeler committed suicide. Not that there's any connection with you're moving here, of course. I didn't mean to suggest that. But it is weird for me to lose my paintings and then lose him, just six weeks later."

Spearman shook his head sadly. "I often tell my students that correlation does not necessarily mean causation. I cannot imagine that there is any connection—or cause and effect—between my coming to Monte Vista and the death of your artist friend. But I am nonetheless sorry for your double loss."

This provoked Spearman to recall something from the article that had stuck in his mind. "How valuable were the paintings?"

"Well, you can't put a price on them. Some things are priceless in the world of art."

"I don't see why that's true," Spearman said, with a puzzled look on his face. "Sotheby's and Christie's put prices on works of art every week. The prices are nothing more than demand and supply in action."

"But the paintings had special value to me because I knew the artist. That's why it's hard for me to put a price on the Wheeler paintings I lost. You can't put a price on that."

"Actually, you can, Raul. If knowing the artist is of value to you as a collector, and not to others who didn't know Wheeler, that simply means you'd pay some premium for Wheeler's work over others who saw the same aesthetic merit and investment potential in the art, and who had the same financial wherewithal as you, but didn't have your connection to the artist. Economists call this difference the 'delta'; it's the price tag that the market places on your personal connection to the artist. So in that sense, we are back to what is the value of the paintings. One way to think of this is what you would be willing to take to part with the paintings."

Ramos had not anticipated that trying to be a friendly to a neighbor would take this conversational turn. He began to look at Spearman with annoyance but was also intrigued by the questions. "I've never given that much thought. The paintings were not for sale."

"Let me ask you this, Raul. Is your house for sale?" Spearman nodded in the direction of the Ramos residence

"No, I told you earlier that I've lived here for almost fifteen years. The house is not for sale. The house you were in was for sale not long ago. That's when Monte Vista bought it. But no, mine's not for sale."

"Would you take five million for your place, cash?"

"Well . . . sure . . . five million, I suppose I'd be crazy not to."

"What about four point nine?"

"Sure, that's almost five million."

"Then we've established that your house is for sale. We simply do not know the exact market price you'd be willing to take for it. It sounds like the price is somewhere south of four point nine million."

"Well, professor, if you define terms that way, every house on Oakmont is for sale." Ramos looked smug, thinking this would befuddle his new neighbor.

"I have no doubt that they are all for sale: every house on the block. The only thing we know is that they are not listed. But from the perspective of economic analysis, that simply means the transaction costs of acquiring these houses probably are higher than the costs of those that are listed with a real estate agent."

"Even the president's house up the street? That's for sale?" Ramos countered weakly. He was now seeing Spearman's point.

"Even the president's house is for sale at the right price, the right price simply being the price at which the market will clear," Spearman replied. "Here's another way to get an estimate of the market price for a product: what was it insured for?" Spearman seemed to recall from the newspaper article that the Wheeler paintings were not insured. He took a stab with the next question: "How much insurance did you have on the Wheeler paintings?"

"I'm afraid I had none," Ramos said. "I used to. But each year seemed a waste. Sounds foolish now, in hindsight. But I suppose if you're a rancher whose horse got away, it doesn't make sense to complain about not locking the barn door."

Before Ramos could continue, Spearman interjected, "You've heard the expression, 'there's no sense crying over spilt milk,' which is a cryptic way of saying 'bygones are bygones.' But if you were to go back to before the bygone had become a bygone, how did you come to choose against insuring the paintings?"

"I just didn't give it much thought, I guess."

"Don't you insure your automobile?"

"Well, yes, but that's different."

"Your life?"

"Of course, I didn't put myself through med school and then not get life insurance."

"I think that makes sense," Spearman countered. "As a surgeon, you have a small fortune invested in your human capital. But why not your art? I understand the Wheeler paintings have a high market value."

"Well, you probably don't know anything about insuring art, Henry, if all you have is a Kinkade painting at home." Ramos's voice took a dismissive tone. "Because the Wheeler paintings are priceless, the insurance company would want a lot of money to insure them at full value."

"Most insurance companies wouldn't want to insure your Wheeler paintings at full value. That leaves you with too little incentive to protect the paintings. What an insurance company wants to do is sell you insurance to reduce the cost of the loss for you, but still leave you with an incentive to protect the asset itself. That's what we call 'moral hazard.' "

Spearman paused, just as he would in the classroom if he were introducing a term that would be new to most students. Then he started up again. "If an insurance company is going to make me whole after my goods are stolen or lost, I don't have as much incentive to lock the door to my house when I leave or keep track of my assets. That's a moral hazard problem. If you had insurance, the company would want to structure the policy so you would have an incentive to secure the paintings—only partially compensating you if there was a loss. Frankly, it would seem to me that as a surgeon who deals in risk all the time, insurance would have been an attractive economic proposition for you."

"You know Professor, I don't want to start off on the wrong foot between us." Spearman noted that Ramos had switched from Henry's first name to his title. "Here in Texas we value being good neighbors. But your trying to put a dollar value on my Wheelers, and trying to put a dollar value on my friendship with Tristan, and then badgering me with questions about my failure to insure the paintings—maybe that's not messing with Texas, but it sure is messing with me. I came out to ride my bike. I think it's time I do just that." Dr. Ramos got up from the bench, put his Trek upright, mounted it, and started toward the road.

As Spearman watched Ramos ride off, he recognized the conversation hadn't ended well. More than once Pidge had tried to explain to her husband that what Henry thought to be perfectly innocent inquiries were received differently by those who did not have the curiosity of an economist. On several social occasions, Spearman had been surprised at how prickly some people were when asked to reveal economic data about themselves. That seemed to hold true for Texans as well.

14

A CONFERENCE OF DETECTIVES

If you're a real top flight detective like me, you'd rather go after an alibi than the truth.

—REX STOUT

Detective Sherry Fuller felt a heavy hand on her shoulder. Turning around, she found herself exchanging sympathetic grins with her colleague Fritz Siegfried. "Still working the Wheeler case, huh? How's it going? From what I heard the guy simply decided to hang it up. Whoops, maybe that's not nice." Fuller's smile vanished but her eyes remained fixed on the older officer. *Obviously not open and shut in her mind*, he thought. Siegfried made a sweeping motion in front of his office door, like a doorman at the Ritz Carlton. "Shall we adjourn to my suite to talk it over?" Without a word Detective Fuller walked past her senior colleague and into his office. He followed, closing the door behind them.

Before he could lower himself into his chair Fuller started up. "Fritz, there's something screwy about this case. I've been going over it in my head, again and again. Things just don't add up." She held out five fingers and began checking them off. "*One*: Wheeler's teaching career was going great guns. Art students wanted to take his class. Non–art students wanted to take his class. Married ladies wanted to take his class. *Two*: he was BMOC at Monte Vista. 'Free Tristan Wheeler' tee shirts and coffee mugs were hot items at the student bookstore. *Three*: journalists were pestering him to talk on that whole open source art thing. *Four*: his paintings were bringing in seriously big bucks—nobody on our salary is ever going to own one. And *five*: he had off-campus speaking engagements that ran through the summer." She paused. "Fritz, that's not 'boo-hoo, I think I'll commit suicide' stuff. That's livin' the dream."

Siegfried leaned back. "What about the birds? What did his assistant say? That Wheeler had been depressed, acting funny because his birds had been kidnapped or something? Sometimes that can get to you. I had a bulldog once. . . ." His voice trailed off.

"Oh, puhleeze." Fuller gave her colleague an exasperated glance before continuing. "And what about the art theft at the Ramos house? That's practically *right across the street*, Fritz. Five Tristan Wheeler paintings get swiped, and then the artist who painted them gets dead a few weeks later. Coincidence? You tell me." It was now Fuller's turn to sit back in the chair.

If Siegfried was willing to concede a connection, it didn't show. "And just why," he asked, "should it be anything else? Paintings get stolen all the time. I learned that in the Wheeler case. It isn't like car thefts, but it happens. And when it does, that doesn't mean the next murder that comes along has anything to do with it. You think a guy swipes the paintings and then kills the artist because he didn't like the colors? C'mon."

Fuller knew her mentor's weak spot: an unsolved crime on his watch. She looked her colleague straight in the eyes. "So, you ever figure the Ramos case out?"

"Well . . . no. Not *yet*." He met her gaze.

"Any suspects? Rosie the housekeeper? Dr. Ramos? The caterers?" She leaned forward and spoke in a stage whisper. "How about super villians, Fritz? You know, I heard the Joker was loose that night." Before he could become riled, Sherry leaned back, smiled, and shook her head. "Fritz, I *read* your reports. There were no clues and there are no leads. Two months go by and no contact from the thieves, which would lead one to think: an inside job. But it *wasn't*." She threw up her hands. "The two most likely suspects—the housekeeper and the doc—washed out right at the start. Rosie is as clean as a newborn babe, and the doc didn't even insure the paintings, so no bucks from that corner and thus no motive. Ever have a case like it?" Fuller paused. "And then the artist's lights go out a couple months later. And where does he live? Right down the street. Doesn't that strike you as odd?"

Siegfried said nothing. It was hard for Fuller to tell whether her colleague's reticence was due to being swayed by her argument—or frustrated by her stubbornness. As they sat looking at each other, a floor fan pushed the day's stale air around the room.

Sherry stood up and glanced out the glass dividing wall that separated them from the rest of the station's first floor. As a homicide cop, she had learned to trust her instincts. Now was one of those times. If she could just persuade someone, maybe buy some time, before the coroner's verdict caused them all to stand down.

"Fritz, there's more. I checked with the suicide note boys, and there's room for doubt there. Take the fact that the thing was laser-printed, with Wheeler's signature at the bottom. Okay, we did find the guy's prints. And the signature was genuine. But I learned that Wheeler usually sent *handwritten* notes to everyone—his dean, his students, his lawyer, his lady friends, even his assistant. The Daniels kid said he had a note about feeding the parrots that was so beautiful he was going to have it framed." She snorted. "You think a guy like that is going to leave this veil of tears without a note they'd want to hang on a wall some place?

"Then there's his will. I talked to his lawyer, Bruce Goolsby—remember him from the Carter case? He shoots straight. So he says when he was first engaged by Wheeler it was for routine legal stuff—contracts for the paintings, figuring out pricing, tax work, some preemptive legal advice about some affairs that got complicated." She chuckled as she saw her colleague's face brighten. "I'll get to *that* in a minute. The point is, Goolsby said Wheeler never wanted to fool around with writing a will. Like most single guys he waved it off, figured he'd live forever. Until two weeks before his death, just a couple days after Christmas, Goolsby's off skiing with his family and he gets a call. *Bang*—Wheeler suddenly wants a will."

She paused for a moment. "And guess who says he's in it?" Siegfried cocked his head to one side, squinted his eyes and made a show of thinking hard. "Let me see . . . hey, I *got* it! The guy who found the body. Am I right?"

"You're as funny as you are smart, Fritz. Yeah, the Daniels kid. Goolsby can't tell us who the beneficiaries in the will are, not yet, not till it's cleared by Probate. But the way the guy's estate has been ballooning the past few months . . . added to the fact that he suddenly, out of nowhere, wants to get his will done . . . don't you think it's worth a look?" Siegfried's response was to slouch deeper into his chair.

She continued. "I'm still trying to figure out Daniels. My gut tells me he's telling the truth. But there's no question he had the means and motive. He had keys to the house. Faculty in the Art Department say the two got along fine for the first years they worked together, but . . . ," she checked her notes, "they *also* testified to a change in the relationship. Wheeler started acting like a jerk around Daniels, treated him like a flunky. Complete about-face from the way things had been before. Add all that to the fact that he's a lot richer if his boss suddenly decides to exit stage left . . . and you got something."

Fuller paused again. "Finally we get to the good stuff." Siegfried grinned, sat back up in his chair, and stretched his hands behind his head. *In police work, there's almost always a good part*, he thought. "Okay Sherry, let me have it. No—wait! Let me guess. Wheeler was an artist, and he had a roving eye. He came on to the ladies. He was a philanderer and all the Monte Vista women fell at his feet like so much cordwood. Am I right?"

"Are you telling this story or am I?" Fuller feigned being put out. "Well, it's not quite *that* over the top. But there's no question that Wheeler made a lot of friends at Monte Vista and that some of those friendships got very friendly. I've interviewed maybe a dozen faculty and staff. And they *all* back it up. When the guy arrived he was a hottie: fame, good looks, talent, money—believe it or not, some women go for those things. He took full advantage and played the field. The faculty started to talk, but it was dismissed. Artists will be artists, that sort of thing.

"But that 'sort of thing' starts to build. Soon it became a topic of gossip around the community. People then started to worry, especially the administration, if this guy's taking advantage of students, which would've been nuclear bad news at a university. Looks like he was smart enough to stay away from the coeds. But all those significant others and spouses were starting to add up.

"Since Wednesday, I've talked to several people who've described how several *other* people would've liked to punch this guy out. Nobody threatened to *kill* him. But they're worth a look see when you have someone die under mysterious circumstances." She paused. "And then there's this."

Fuller pulled a notepad out of her pocket and reviewed a page. "One of the most popular professors at the school is a mild-mannered guy, midfifties, named Herbert Abraham. Head of the Economics Department. No record, not even a parking ticket. Faculty all respect him as do the students. I didn't talk to one person who didn't sing his praises."

She continued. "So it turns out Dr. Abraham is like that guy in the movie, Mr. Chips, who gets married to someone who's a lot younger and gorgeous. Wife's name is Jocelyn, she's twenty years younger and looks like a model. Everyone's wondering how come she married this nice older guy. Everyone thinks it's all charming and sweet until . . . she decides one day that she wants to learn to paint."

Siegfried sighed. He knew what was coming. Sherry continued. "She asks to take some art lessons from Wheeler and he agrees. They begin having private sessions together, first at the campus studio and then later on at Wheeler's place. The sessions get longer and the faculty start to talk, and then, finally, word of this reaches Mr. Chips."

Fuller looked at her notebook again. "Apparently there was a fight between husband and wife at some social event. Nothing came of it. But the next day Abraham runs into Wheeler on campus and the mild-mannered prof goes ballistic. He backs Wheeler into a corner, right there in front of God, faculty, and about fifteen students. Tells him that he's heard the rumors and he wants Wheeler to know he's heard them. Says he's choosing to believe his wife that nothing 'untoward' has happened. But then he adds"—she checked to get it exactly right—"*'if I find any of this to be true you'll regret the day you came here.'* I can't find a witness who doesn't report his saying those words."

Siegfried sighed again and looked over Fuller's shoulders. Outside his office door almost everyone but the night sergeant had gone home or was out on patrol. "Fritz, we gotta keep on this one. This just doesn't smell right."

Siegfried relented. "Okay, Sher. I still wish we had just one piece of solid evidence—the, whaddaya call it, 'piece of resistance.' But I'll talk to Olson tomorrow." The detective pointed to his paunch. "I'll throw what little weight I have around. What are you going to do?"

Fuller walked toward the door, turned and said, "I'm going back to talk to Wheeler's neighbor, a big poobah on campus name of Spearman. From Harvard, if you believe it. I talked to him earlier. He never met Wheeler, but he's been spending time with Abraham. I want to know what he heard and I want to know what he thinks."

"A Harvard prof? C'mon Sherry. All you'll probably get are a bunch of theories."

She smiled as she walked out of the office. Siegfried heard her voice as it echoed back from the empty squad room. "Sometimes theories are good, Fritz. Especially when you don't have all the facts."

15

ART AND ECONOMICS

The application of economics to the arts . . . teaches us almost as much about economics as about the arts.

—MARK BLAUG

Henry Spearman had expected the first day of class to be perfunctory. At Harvard, the initial meeting usually involved handing out the syllabus, discussing course content, and giving out the first assignment before ending class early. But students at Monte Vista University expected classes on the first day of the semester to go the full period. This Tuesday was a different experience for Henry, but he thought to himself, "When in San Antonio, do as the San Antonians do." He walked into the room.

The classroom layout could have been at Harvard, except the furniture was newer and showed less wear. At the front was a table with a portable lectern. On the wall, facing the students' seats, was a whiteboard for the physical presentation. A retractable screen for digital presentation of material hung to one side. Spearman and the students would make use of both. The room had two rows of seats separated by a middle aisle. From the teacher's perspective, one saw four quintets of young men and women.

Henry Spearman stood before the class. He did not begin by giving his name or handing out a syllabus. Instead, he read these words.

> Beauty is truth, truth beauty,
> That is all Ye know of earth,
> And all ye need to know.

Spearman closed the book from which he had been reading. "All of you have heard those words before. You have had to study them. They are from John Keats's 'Ode on a Grecian Urn.' This semester we'll see that these famous words that link beauty with truth present only a half-truth. One may cherish the Grecian urn for its aesthetic properties, and rightly so. But Keats did not appreciate that one can also seek to understand the production and allocation of the urn. Indeed if one of you could uncover the exact urn that inspired Keats to compose his immortal poem, we could study and seek to understand the value of that work of art in economic terms." The twenty students looked at the short, bald, bespectacled professor before them as if he were from a different planet.

At that point, Henry Spearman stated his name, welcomed them to "Art and Economics," and began to hand out the course syllabus. He explained that while his office hours would be henceforth held in the afternoon after class, his public lecture that evening would preclude them on this day. As the twenty students relaxed, Spearman went on to note that economists knew a lot about the production of goods like wheat and steel; they knew a lot about investing in financial capital and human capital;

they knew a lot about trade across national boundaries; they knew a lot about monetary and fiscal policy; they knew a lot about taxes and incentives. But he claimed that when it came to the consumption and production of something like art, an economic barrier was crossed— leading explorers into a relatively undeveloped field. He told the students that his plan for the semester was to challenge them to study the demand and supply of art, and to then test their ideas as to what types of art were chosen to be produced, how this art was allocated to consumers, and what were its subsequent rewards to producers.

At this point Spearman nodded in Jennifer Kim's direction. "Many of you may know my colleague, Professor Kim. She plans to sit in our class. She will not do any of the grading. That's my job. But I'm sure her presence will add to our human capital formation."

Jennifer smiled inwardly. It was beginning to sink in that she really was a faculty member, and not a graduate student masquerading as a professor.

Spearman then made his starting point clear to the class: "I don't know a lot about art. No doubt some of you are more avid consumers than I am. Perhaps a few of you are even producers. And it's likely many of you are wondering what art and economics have in common." Henry smiled at his students. "We'll answer that very question this semester."

A young woman in cowboy attire seated in the front row raised her hand. "My name's Cookie, I compete in rodeos. I think the economics of rodeos is an undeveloped field just like you say art is. Can we study the demand and supply of rodeos in this class?"

Spearman smiled warmly at the student whom, as the semester went on, he came to think of as "Miss Cowgirl." "I've no doubt that the market for rodeos is ripe for economic analysis. However, in this course we won't go along for the ride. I've made an executive decision: our focus will be on art and economics."

As her face fell, Henry held up his hand. "I'll tell you what," he said, "if you come to Harvard someday to do graduate work, I'll encourage you to do research on the economics of rodeos. I'll even lasso some research funds for you. But if you pay attention this semester, the economics you learn will help you someday study the sport you love."

Turning to the whole class, Spearman issued a caveat: "Now let me warn those of you who might be here because you love art. Merely liking an activity is not the same thing as doing economic analysis. It can even be a hindrance. One of the best authorities on the economics of the wine industry is a teetotaler." Spearman paused to let that point sink in, as he walked slowly back and forth. "For that matter, being artistic is not the same as knowing the economics of art. The best clarinetist on the Boston Pops might not understand the economics of the orchestra and actually believe that wage levels of musicians have nothing to do with the sustainability of an orchestra."

Henry pulled himself up and sat on the table in front of the class. His feet dangled above the floor. "Okay, this is an economics class. We think in terms of demand and supply. So let's start with demand, and pool our class knowledge. How does the demand for a painting differ from the demand for a pizza?"

He paused. "Oh, and let's follow Cookie's example, shall we? Please give your name as you begin."

Jennifer Kim got the ball rolling. "Well, for starters, the market demand for pizza is bigger. I've never seen an art gallery with a bunch of delivery cars going around in order to meet demand."

"Lots of demand curves simply appear *ex nihilo* in an economics class," Spearman said. "What would the demand curve for a painting, say by Rembrandt, look like?"

A young man wearing a ball cap and horn-rimmed glasses held up his hand. "Hi, I'm Orley." He smiled sheepishly. "I guess . . . the same as any demand curve. Downward sloping and to the right," he responded. "The lower the price, the greater the quantity demanded. We learned from Dr. Kim, that's the law of demand. Applies to everything. You name it, the price falls, people want more of it."

"Does it?" queried another student. "I'm Donnie. And I know a lot of people go to museums to enjoy art. But they don't actually buy art, like the way you buy pizza. I mean, like, it's totally different."

A young man dressed in an Oxford cloth shirt and Vineyard Vines khakis piped up. Spearman recognized the student from the dinner at President Quinn's home. "Some people don't just look at art, they buy it. For them, a painting is not something they enjoy, the way you enjoy pizza. Instead of buying a painting to look at, they buy it because they hope it will go up in price. Nobody buys a pizza hoping it will be worth more five years later. So buying art can also be like an investment." This led some of his classmates to reflect on what a five-year-old pizza would be like. The young man paused to gather his thoughts. He realized there were *two* professors listening to him, not just one. "I know that's the only reason I'd buy art. If I simply want to see the stuff, I'd just go to a museum." He hastily added, "Oh, I forgot to say, I'm Anjali."

"Thanks, Anjali," Spearman responded from his perch on the table. "Of course, there are different reasons for liking art—just as there are different reasons for liking pizza. Some people want to be surrounded by art. For them, it's a pure consumption good. So put investing aside for a moment. What are the variables that will affect how much consumers will pay for works of art, just to enjoy them?" Before anyone responded, Spearman said, "Let's hear from someone in the second row."

"Kelvin's my name. Income would be another variable," an African American student sitting behind Miss Cowgirl responded. "People with more income will demand more art."

At this point, Spearman jumped down from the table and went to the board, grabbed a marker, printed the word "income" on the board, and underlined it.

"Okay, Kelvin. What else? Anybody?"

"I'm Susan." A second student in the back row had spoken up. "Another factor would be the price—that is, how expensive is the painting." Spearman wrote the word "price" on the board and underlined it.

"What about the price of complements?" Spearman then asked. "Complements supposedly affect demand. What's a complement to a painting? Besides, 'hey good lookin', that is."

This stopped the class for a moment. Then a Latino coed in the second row replied, "How about the frame for a painting? Pissarro thought the frame was almost as important as the painting."

"Good," Spearman replied. "And your name is . . . ?"

"Anita," she replied breaking into a beautiful smile.

"After recording 'price of complements' on the board, Spearman returned his gaze to her and asked, "What about substitutes? The price of substitutes supposedly affects the demand for a good or service. What might be a substitute for a painting?" Spearman turned to the board, stopped, and then turned back to Anita. She paused, and then said, "I guess something like a print, maybe. . . ." Her voice trailed off as a question. "Like, if you really like a painting but you can't afford it because it costs thousands and millions of dollars, you can buy a nice print of it. And that's, like, the substitute."

Anita paused, as if expecting someone to disagree. Another student piped up: "My name's Mark. And I see what she's saying. It's like beer in a way. If you're putting on a party and you can't afford Shiner or Sam Adams, you substitute PBR or Meister Bräu instead."

"I think going to the rodeo could be a substitute for going to the art museum," Cookie piped up. "They're each just forms of entertainment," she continued, as if to underscore her view that art wasn't much different from rodeos.

"Tastes," another student called out. "We're leaving out the most important variable. If you don't like the painting, that will affect your demand for it. If you like it, your demand will be greater. Oh, and my name's Haiyang." Spearman wrote and underlined the word "tastes" on the board. Henry looked back at the student, his face showing approval.

"A pizza would always 'taste' better than a painting," a boy with a Deep South drawl interjected. The class groaned, as did Kim, who nevertheless smiled and added, "Thanks, Pete."

"They say at Harvard that every class has a clown," Spearman replied, with a grin. "Maybe I'll find that's true in Texas as well."

Emboldened by Spearman's jovial expression, Pete added, "What about a *painting* of a *pizza*? I mean a really good painting of a pizza. I'd be willing to pay some serious money for that."

Henry noted a young woman in the back who had not yet spoken. Her hand was up and he pointed at her. "My name's Mary and I think we've missed the most important variable that affects the demand for art, at least high-priced art, and that's the Veblen effect. Veblen argued that some people engaged in what he called 'conspicuous consumption'—conspicuous in that it put the consumers on display more than the object that was purchased. So to Veblen, paying a fortune for a piece of art would be no different than paying a fortune for a Rolls-Royce that you rarely drove, or a yacht that you rarely used. You don't buy it for the utility of consuming it. You buy it for the utility of showing you have it and others don't."

"You make it sound like buying a famous painting is like purchasing the envy of others," Spearman responded.

"I think that's what Veblen was getting at," Mary replied.

"Thomas Carlyle was an Englishman who could restrain his enthusiasm for the subject of economics. He once wrote, 'Teach a parrot the terms supply and demand and you've got an economist.' Clever quip, eh?" Spearman's face had a big grin as he quoted the familiar canard. "But I think we've seen that understanding demand would be outside the comprehension of a parrot, and maybe even beyond that of Carlyle—and we haven't even gotten to supply yet."

As the discussion about demand wound down, Henry asked if there were any questions. "I have one," a young man piped up. "My name's Walter. I'm majoring in art. In our art history classes we're expected to know facts about the art—like who painted it, when or where it was done, or what school of art it represents. In economics, are facts like these important? Or don't we have to know stuff like that?"

"I appreciate the question. I recall when I took an art history class at what might seem to you many years ago, that we had to learn a lot of facts. In economics, we think facts are very important as well, though we usually gussy up the term and call them 'data.' But in economic analysis we're persuaded that facts make no sense or have no relevance apart from their being placed in a theoretical framework." Spearman paused to retrieve a lesson from literature. "One of the most famous professor characters in all of English literature is Professor Gradgrind. Can anyone identify who created this fictional professor?" To a person the students, along with Jennifer Kim, wondered where Spearman was going with this.

"Sure," said Kelvin, after searching his memory banks. "Charles Dickens."

"Can you remember anything about him?"

"Nope, other than he was in *Hard Times*."

"*Hard Times* it was. Here's what caught my attention about Professor Gradgrind. He was the opposite of a good economist. I keep something by Gradgrind in my class notes, lest any of my students at Harvard get carried away by facts alone." Spearman took a brown folio off the table at the front of the room. He read, "*Teach these boys and girls nothing but Facts. Facts alone are wanted in life. Plant nothing else. You can only form the minds of reasoning animals upon Facts: nothing else will ever be of service to them.*' Close quote. As if to emphasize the point, Dickens put a capital 'f' on the word 'facts.'" Spearman closed the covers of the folio.

"Now here's the problem. We could spend hours pulling together fact after fact about a painting to ascertain its value. How much paint went into it, how much did it cost to ship the gold that gilds the frame, what about the wire that is used to hang the painting? How many hours were spent painting the picture, how many hours went into planning the painting, how many hours went into the training that led to the planning that led to the painting? How many brushes were used? How much turpentine? And on and on and on. But economics offers a theory of the value of a painting: it abstracts from all these data points and asks a question that cuts across all these facts: in a market with informed buyers, how much will be paid for the painting?" Spearman decided to take his response further. Before doing so, he sat back on the table again.

"We mentioned Dickens. Who can identify Ezra Pound?"

"The poet?" Anjali asked.

"Yes the poet. And not just any poet. One of the most notorious poets of the twentieth century. The author of *The Cantos*. Some people believe Eliot's *The Wasteland* is a great poem because of Pound's editorial suggestions. Pound was fascinated with economics, one might even say obsessed with the subject. He argued that with an understanding of economics, one should be able to look at a painting and tell something about the rate of interest when it was painted—because the economics of the time would somehow be suffused within that painting. How's that for integrating Art and Economics?" Spearman said with a grin on his face, his dangling feet swinging back and forth.

"Was Pound right about that?" asked Cookie. "Can you really tell the rate of interest by studying a painting?"

"Not at all," Spearman said. "Just because someone believes economics is important doesn't mean that he does good economics. As an economist, Pound was a crackpot. A total crackpot."

Henry noticed that several students seemed taken aback. "I have no idea if your generation reads Sherlock Holmes stories any more. I read them all as a boy. And in his very first outing, Sherlock Holmes told an incredulous Dr. Watson that one could deduce just about anything from the smallest of clues. Sherlock Holmes claimed that from a drop of water the true detective could infer the possibility of the Atlantic Ocean, or of Niagara Falls." Spearman looked directly at Cookie: "That sort of thing works great in fiction, but real life is another matter. Real-world economists often spend hours and hours 'cleaning up the data.'"

"But what about when *you* solved crimes as a professor? Did you learn how to do it by reading Sherlock Holmes?" Cookie asked.

Spearman took a long time to answer this question. "I'm afraid not," Spearman finally said, his face showing signs of discomfort.

A hand shot up, and then another, and yet another. One hand in particular moved up and down, as if to command attention. Spearman sighed as he nodded at the student.

"My name's Dan. Dan the Man," he smiled as Cookie shook her head. "I know this may sound weird, and I hope you don't mind my asking, but I think we all have the same question." Dan looked around at some of his classmates. "A lot of us did some homework on you when we heard you were coming to Monte Vista. Nothing real involved— just Googling you, checking out Wikipedia. And we were wondering about you and solving crimes. We know you solved a murder in the Virgin Islands, a murder at Harvard, and one in England. I think that's so cool. I mean, really cool. But we don't know if it is fair to ask you about this just because we're in your class, and maybe you don't want to tell us about it."

Spearman looked over at Jennifer Kim for guidance, but her face was expressionless. It was true: using economic theory as his guide, Spearman had solved three murder cases. But he always thought that these were minor accomplishments, the result of his being at the right place, observing the right facts, and having the right mode of analysis—in his case, economic reasoning—to make sense of the criminal activity.

"Okay, okay," Spearman announced. "If we have extra time at the end of the semester, I'll try to explain how economic reasoning can facilitate police work. But for now, that's not the task set before us. Understanding the relationship between art and economics is."

•

As the minutes went by in spirited class interaction, Spearman noticed his watch. "Okay, before the figurative bell rings, does everyone see how much we have to learn? What I hope we find, this semester, is that the world of art is also the world of economics. Some of you will be interested in the economics of being an artist, the supply side. Some of you may be interested in the economics of consuming art, the demand side. I hope some of you will be interested in how demand and supply are brought together. If you are wondering what I mean by that, let me toss out a few examples before we are out of time." Spearman gestured with his right hand as though he was actually tossing a ball to a student.

"A man named Joseph Duveen was the greatest dealer the art world has known. He was famous for his observation that 'Europe had plenty of art and America had plenty of money.' Based on this simple observation, Duveen made a fortune as a broker, as a middleman, as an *arbitrageur*—one who brought supply and demand together. I hope some of you will want to study this part of art. Maybe even Duveen himself. He is one of the great examples of the interplay between art and economics. Here's one teaser about Duveen, against the chance you have never heard of him.

"Once, at an auction, he bid seventy-five thousand dollars for a Houdon bust, an unprecedented amount.

Houdon busts had previously been selling for twenty-five thousand. Why did he do that? It turned out he had Houdon busts in inventory. When people saw what Duveen was paying for Houdon busts, they thought they should be buying Houdon. Duveen was happy to oblige them from the inventory he had been quietly building up. Pretty soon, what Duveen paid became the market price." Spearman paused to allow his students to reason through his illustration.

"But Duveen didn't always get it right," Spearman began again. "One of Duveen's failures in the market for art was trying to sell paintings to Henry Ford. Duveen went to Henry Ford's house with a lavish book illustrated with one hundred of the world's great paintings that he presented to Ford. Duveen hoped to entice the great entrepreneur to buy the whole lot. But so the story goes, Ford left Duveen speechless when he thanked him for the book and said, 'What would I want with the originals when the ones in the book are so nice?'"

Spearman was caught up in the game of teaching. He stopped lecturing and started interrogating.

"So who knows the work of Ronald Coase? What's he known for?"

"The Coase theorem," Kelvin said. "He got a Nobel Prize like you."

"He's a big name because of the Coase theorem," Spearman said, hopping down from the table and walking to the front of the classroom. "But he's also known for a conjecture, the Coase conjecture." Spearman took the time to write "Coase theorem" and "Coase conjecture" on the whiteboard. "Most economists are lucky if they have a dog or a cat named after them. Coase got a theorem *and* a conjecture. Almost every econ student learns something about the Coase theorem. In fact, almost every law student has to grasp it just to get through law school. But I want us to think about the Coase conjecture—in terms of art and economics."

Spearman reviewed the conjecture, and then asked, "So if Coase says you can't monopolize a durable good, what's that mean for us in this course?"

Orley spoke up: "Art is a really durable good. Really durable. A washing machine or refrigerator might last fifteen years. And we call that a durable good in economics. But, you know, the *Mona Lisa* is over five hundred years old. That's really durable."

"So what does the Coase conjecture seem to tell us?" Spearman pressed the class.

"That if you owned all the paintings of some artist, you couldn't sell them at a monopoly price?" Anita hazarded.

"Because . . . ?" Spearman said, motioning with his hands to come up with more.

"Because the goods are durable, over time each good competes with itself. So a monopoly seller might get rich selling the paintings of some artist, but not, like monopoly-rich."

"Well played, Anita."

Spearman paused and glanced at his watch, gauging how much more material he could cover. He looked back at his students. "What I hope you come to realize is that just as the lens of the human eye gives us the ability to appreciate art, the lens of economic theory gives us the intellectual ability to understand art."

Spearman walked across the front of the classroom toward the door, thinking as he paced. When he reached the door he turned and retraced his steps to the windows. There he turned and faced the class directly. "My hero in economics is Adam Smith. He made famous the profound economic principle of 'specialization and division of labor.' We are going to adopt this principle. There are twenty of you in this class. I want ten of you in two groups of five to collaborate on a term paper and prepare a class presentation on an economic question primarily involving the *demand* for art. It can be demand for consumption purposes or investment purposes."

Seeing that the class was engaged, Spearman continued. "I want the other ten to form two groups of five and do the same thing with regard to the *supply* of art. How is art produced? What is the nature of the production function? How does it make its way to the market?" Students in the class who feared that a Nobel laureate would be stuffy or unapproachable saw that Spearman was anything but. He was making the classroom sing.

Spearman continued to pace across the front of the classroom. "I'm told that most students here know each other. So here's the deal: by my watch, we have ten minutes left in our class period. Dr. Kim and I are going to leave the room. We're going to let you decide how the class will be divided between demand and supply projects. So after we leave, you're to select some allocation mechanism to determine the ten of you who will specialize in demand and the ten who will specialize in supply, and how the two groups of ten will become four teams of five.

"I'm a free market person generally, so any allocation method you choose is acceptable to me, except one based on physical force. I won't allow that." The students looked closely at Spearman's face to see if he was kidding. Almost all their professors at Monte Vista tilted to the left politically, and could restrain their enthusiasm for free markets. Was this guy—from Harvard of all places—different? They thought Spearman's lips looked serious but his eyes were smiling.

•

As Spearman made his way back to his office after class, the smile in his eyes began to fade. This was not a sign of weariness. Rather, his thoughts were turning to the final preparations for his public lecture that evening. While his students had not carried him out of the classroom, Spearman took comfort knowing that his prep time had paid dividends in his first class. For that success to continue, he reasoned, he'd need about two to three more hours of reviewing his material for that evening's lecture. *Which I believe I just have*, he smiled to himself. His hand turned the knob of the office door and he walked inside.

"Hey, Professor, you busy? Got a couple minutes to talk?"

Momentarily startled, Spearman turned to see Detective Fuller leaning against the opposite wall. He nodded and motioned her to a chair as he began removing books and papers from his briefcase. "I must warn you in advance, Detective. I'm taking your statement that you only need a couple minutes of my time on its face. I have a hot date tonight."

At Fuller's look of surprise, Henry winked. "A hot date with seven hundred people who are coming to hear me give a talk . . . including one very demanding Monte Vista trustee, who wants to know if her money to bring me here was well spent. I still need some prep time to get ready."

Fuller smiled at Spearman as she sat down. "No problem, Prof. I get it. Just wanted to check on a few things we didn't get to on Thursday." She pulled a notepad from her pocket and checked its contents. "You know Herbert Abraham, correct?"

"Yes of course. His office is across the hall. He's really responsible for Monte Vista bringing me here as a visiting professor . . . as I suspect you know."

Fuller's smile tightened a bit as she continued, unfazed. "Did he ever mention anything to you about his relationship with your former neighbor Tristan Wheeler?"

"Yes. Last Friday, after I witnessed your . . . departure from his office, he told me that he'd had an argument with his wife about her relationship with Wheeler. He also told me the unpleasantness continued the next day when he'd confronted Wheeler about it." Spearman stood by his desk and stared at the detective. "His great fear now is of the campus grapevine—that it will generate rumors that will threaten his marriage and even his position at Monte Vista."

"What types of rumors?"

Spearman found himself mildly irritated. It seemed to him that the detective knew the answer to her own question. "Rumors of passion, jealousy. That there might have been infidelity between Wheeler and his wife."

"Do you think there's anything to the rumors?"

"I'm afraid I don't know Herbert's wife well enough to even attempt to answer that question." Henry looked at his watch, and then walked toward the door, signaling that for him the meeting was at a close.

"And now, Detective, I really need to get ready for that date."

16

IT ALL BEGAN WITH ADAM...

It is not from the benevolence of the butcher, the brewer, or the baker, that we expect our dinner, but from their regard to their own interest. We address ourselves, not to their humanity but to their self-love, and never talk to them of our necessities, but of their advantages.

—ADAM SMITH

Spearman cocked an eyebrow as he began his speech. A faint smile played across his lips. "My career as an economist started at Brooklyn College in my freshman year. It all began with a single book."

This is how Spearman began the public lecture that was part of being the Cubbage Visiting Nobel Professor at Monte Vista University. The university's public affairs office had done its job. The place was packed, standing room only. Monte Vista students, faculty, and board members made up the bulk of the audience, but townspeople also were there along with the press. Annelle Cubbage was seated in the second row on the aisle. Anjali Vitali had arrived late because he was assigned to help board members to their seats. As a result, he had to stand against the back wall.

The only problem that Spearman's hosts had not anticipated was his stature (or lack thereof). The imposing walnut podium not only hid Spearman from view because of its width, it almost hid him from view because of its height. People sitting in the front of the sloping auditorium of Mason Hall could see only the top of Spearman's head. But this did not phase Henry. He was accustomed to both the benefits of being short, such as sitting uncramped in an airplane seat, and the costs of being short, such as struggling to get one's luggage into the overhead bin.

He spoke without notes, diving confidently into his lecture. "Many people, I realize, claim that one book brought them to an inflection point in their lives. I have met people who claim it was the Bible. I have a colleague for whom it was Dickens's *A Tale of Two Cities*. I was in school with a friend for whom the book was Jakob Bernoulli's *Ars Conjectandi*. He is now one of the Netherlands' leading statisticians. For many, the pivotal book was Darwin's *The Descent of Man*. They now defend Darwinism with the same zeal that others deny evolution. Incidentally, the pivotal book need not be high-brow. A colleague of mine at Harvard, the well-known psychologist Henderson Ross, swears that his life was changed reading the Hardy Boys series.

"For me, it was a book written some two hundred years ago: *The Wealth of Nations*. I could scarcely sleep for excitement the night after reading Adam Smith for the first time. It seemed to me an incredible achievement to have brought the whole, vast, and seemingly chaotic universe of economic activity to an all-embracing order. To have perceived an *overall* organization, a superarching principle uniting and relating all the elements, had a quality of the miraculous, of genius about it. This gave me, for the first time in my life, a sense of the transcendent power of economic logic as I realized that economic theory might be equipped to decipher the deepest secrets of human behavior. This is how Smith described economics: 'that science which pretends to lay open the concealed connections that unite the various appearances of nature.' Now I must say a word about Adam Smith's use of the word 'pretends.' Smith did not mean 'pretend' in the current sense of the word—to seem or claim to do something which in fact one is *not* doing. In Smith's day, to 'pretend to lay open the concealed connections' was to succeed in doing so."

Spearman explained that when he was an undergraduate student, he was exposed to various disciplines. A course in psychology explained abnormal behavior; one on sociology explained the characteristics of mass culture. The anthropology class he took studied the myths of nonliterate peoples. But questions about human behavior remained unanswered. History professors taught him about the past but did not offer a method for predicting the future. And his political science classes seemed to skirt critical questions—like why people in government were assumed to operate in the public interest, while people in business were assumed to be self-interested.

In his economics classes, however, Spearman found a subject that was concerned with people in the ordinary business of life. It had enabled him to explain behavior that appeared paradoxical. Enlightenment, for him, came through the engine of economic analysis.

To illustrate his point, Spearman shared a story from his childhood days above his father's tailor shop. It had seemed to Henry that his father's personality, when in his place of business, was very different from his personality when he climbed the stairs to their apartment.

When downstairs, the elder Spearman was attentive to the desires of each of his customers. He was friendly, courteous, soft-spoken, and even amusing. Henry had observed his father being full of compliments for his customers. He noticed when his female customers changed their hairstyle, and usually commented appreciatively on the cut or color they had adopted. To his male customers, his father often told funny stories that provoked smiles and sometimes laughter.

But this posed a puzzle. Why did climbing the twenty-four stairs to the apartment above seem to turn his father into a different person?

Spearman grinned broadly as he recounted, "I do not remember my father ever telling a funny story at home. I can still hear my mother kidding him. 'Ben, you never tell a joke up here. But to your customers, you are a regular Jack Benny or Bob Hope.' And if my mother had her hair done on a particular day, she received no comment from my father.

"I do not want to leave the impression that my father did not love us. I always knew that he did. But it was not until I read Adam Smith that I had a plausible explanation for why his second floor personality differed from that on the first floor. The discipline of economics provided the explanation. I learned the most important lesson economics had to convey—that *incentives affect behavior*. Those of you who have studied economics will understand perfectly why my father's motivation differed between the store and the apartment above. The incentive to ensure repeat business, and so feed and clothe his family, outweighed the temptation to allow his weariness to become apparent.

"My study of economics taught me three basic principles. If you know them well, they keep you from muddled thinking.

"The first I mentioned: incentives matter. That principle alone tells us a lot about tax policy. If the government thinks innovation and investment and saving are good things, then taxing these things reduces the incentives people have to innovate, invest, and save.

"The second principle is that the cost of something is the highest valued alternative opportunity foregone. This is a profound principle, perhaps the most important notion in all the social sciences. What we have here is the equivalent of what Isaac Newton was doing in physics.

"Economics is the only social science that has a sure-fire metric for what any good, any service, any activity, or any endeavor costs: it is the highest valued opportunity foregone. And this metric applies not just to items you might buy from a merchant. If you are a student at Monte Vista, ask yourself this question: what is the cost of getting A's in two economics courses you're taking this semester?" Spearman let the question sink in. Some students in the audience were thinking they would have to spend twenty hours a week studying Econ to get straight A's.

"So what's the cost? It isn't the tuition. That's a sunk cost. For some students, the cost might be opportunities foregone in studying another subject, and ending up with a B or C in Organic Chemistry; for others the two A's in Econ might come at the cost of learning ballroom dancing or keeping up with close friends—whatever is the highest valued opportunity foregone, that's the cost."

Spearman stood on his tiptoes to get a better look at his audience. "I notice that students wear jeans as commonly in San Antonio as they do in Cambridge, my hometown. So what's the *cost* of buying a new pair of jeans? To an economist, it is the highest valued opportunity foregone. So we start with the price of the jeans. Once that amount is forked over to the merchant, the student loses the ability to spend that money on something else, that being the *next* highest valued use of those funds. That's the explicit cost of buying the jeans. But if students here are like the ones at Harvard, that's not the full cost. I'm told that students spend time going from store to store, they spend time trying on different brands and sizes of jeans, they incur search costs and transaction costs. These are implicit costs and they are just as real to an economist. For those students who impute a high value to their time, these costs may exceed the explicit cost of the jeans recorded on the price tag."

"The economic theory of cost is simple to state, but it is profound in its implications—and is the most important contribution economics makes to the world of books and ideas. Years after Adam Smith, Robert Frost expressed the same profound principle poetically and more memorably. Perhaps those of you who have never heard of Adam Smith have nevertheless heard, and pondered upon, these words." Spearman gripped each side of the lectern and closed his eyes and solemnly intoned:

Two roads diverged in a wood, and I—
I took the one less traveled by,
And that has made all the difference.

"What was the cost of the road selected? Whatever opportunities that awaited the traveler on the road that was
not chosen. Just as you cannot avoid Newton's law of gravity, you cannot avoid the economic law that every time
you make a choice, you incur a cost."

He paused. "And now we come to the third principle.
The third principle is mysterious. It sounds like the title of
a detective story. It involves the invisible hand." Spearman
took a drink of water from a paper cup and then scanned
the auditorium before speaking. "You have an expression
that is deeply embedded in Texas culture: 'Remember
the Alamo.' I have come from New England with a new
expression: 'Remember the Invisible Hand.' " Spearman
smiled and then he looked very serious. "Now what do I
mean by this? Other authors have used the term 'invisible
hand.' Many of you, I suspect, know the writings of Flan-
nery O'Connor. She used the term 'invisible hand' in her
novel *Wise Blood*. In *Frankenstein*, the creature found his
foodstuffs replenished 'by an invisible hand'—though it
was probably by a peasant family. Nietzsche wrote: 'It is by
invisible hands that we are bent and tortured most.'

"But no one ever used the term with the brilliance of
Adam Smith. Smith understood this principle: that, as if
by an invisible hand, social good would be accomplished
when people are in pursuit of their own self-interest. Later,
as I was starting to understand Smith better, I came across
this anecdote from the writings of Frederic Bastiat, a

French economist who wrote several decades after Smith. I committed this passage to memory, because of the truth that lay within it. Let me recite it to you in English." At this point, Spearman stepped alongside the lectern. For the first time, many in the audience could now see what he looked like. He spoke these words:

> On entering Paris which I had come to visit, I said to myself—Here are a million human beings who would all die in a short time if provision of every kind ceased to flow toward this great metropolis. Imagination is baffled when it tries to appreciate the vast multiplicity of commodities which must enter tomorrow . . . in order to preserve the inhabitants from falling prey to the convulsion, famine, rebellion, and pillage. And yet all sleep at this moment, and their peaceful slumbers are not disturbed for a single instant by the prospect of such a frightful catastrophe.

"Now let's give Bastiat the benefit of the doubt here. He is writing about Paris, after all. Perhaps not everyone was sound asleep during the night time when Bastiat wrote these words." Spearman waited for the appreciative chuckles from the audience.

"But Bastiat taught an important lesson for those who live in economies that are primarily market-oriented. What Bastiat wrote about Paris in 1850 is true for San Antonio today. As I speak these words, and as you sit listening to them, there are thousands of goods and services, including many on which we depend, being produced and transported to this city. And they will arrive not because it is traditional that certain tribes or families send them here, or because some central authority has decreed that they are to arrive. They are being brought here, to use Adam Smith's mysterious metaphor, as if by an invisible hand. And none of you, cognizant that your toothpaste or orange juice supplies are running low, or aware that you need new shoelaces or new panty hose, will lose any sleep thinking that these items will not be on the store shelves tomorrow. The invisible hand will see to it that they are."

After about thirty minutes, Spearman drew the first Cubbage lecture to a close. He paused as his eyes scanned the auditorium from left to right. The words he chose to conclude his remarks came to him afresh; they were not drawn from the remarks he had prepared.

"When Adam Smith wrote *The Wealth of Nations*, the experience of most people over the whole span of mankind's existence was one of grinding, hopeless poverty—poverty with no relief, poverty with no hope of improvement. Smith decided to explore and explain the rare aberrations: why and how some nations had escaped this fate and become wealthy. Hence the full title of Smith's masterpiece: *An Inquiry into the Nature and the Causes of the Wealth of Nations*. What a remarkable title.

"His name was equally remarkable. Adam Smith. How fitting is that? *Adam*, the name of the first man, gets paired with *Smith*, the most common surname in the English language. God put a man named Adam in a garden, so the Bible story tells us, that he might flourish. We are told that particular episode didn't go so well. We know that wealth became the province of royalty, potentates, religious, and military leaders, while poverty was the plight of everyone else.

"But after countless generations of hardship came an Adam who wrote a book...a book that tells us how even the Smiths of the world—the ordinary people, the little guys—might flourish, enjoying goods and services that leaders of old could not have imagined.

"We sometimes hear the question: what's in a name? In the case of Adam Smith, there's a great deal in the name." Spearman smiled as he again scanned his audience, left to right, before remarking, "And on that remarkable name, ladies and gentlemen, I shall close my remarks, thanking you for your courtesy this evening and for the warm welcome my wife and I have received at Monte Vista University."

•

When Spearman's lecture had concluded, it was time for questions from the audience. Professor Abraham went to the lectern to announce the format. Questioners were to raise their hand, he would select some, and then they were to stand, give their name, and ask a question. "And please *do not* give a speech yourself," Abraham said with a smile. "Remember, we all came here to listen to our speaker. Nobody came to Mason Auditorium to hear you!" Mild laughter and a smattering of applause came from the audience. "Professor Spearman will take questions for fifteen minutes. Who would like to be first?"

Henry Spearman sipped water and waited. He knew from experience that, for many in the audience, a speaker's prepared remarks were like the appetizer of a meal. Q&A was the main course. That experience also led him to expect two things to happen during the question and answer period.

First, Spearman knew that the initial question from the audience would be the same one that was always put to him. It never failed.

Second, he had come to realize that most of the questions put to him would bear little relation to his prepared remarks. Many people in an audience used this opportunity to ask what was really on their mind, regardless of whether their question had any connection to the talk they had just heard. This did not bother Spearman. Just as focus groups were useful to marketing executives to find out what consumers actually thought, so the Q&A period informed Spearman as to what was on his audience's mind.

For the first question, Abraham pointed to a gentleman in the second row. A heavyset man struggled against the forces of gravity to rise from his seat. "My name's Wilson Berry and I'm with Charter Bank and Trust here in San Antonio. This here's my question. If economics truly offers what you call a 'transcendent power of economic logic,' tell me what's going to happen to interest rates in the next year?"

Inwardly Spearman chuckled, but he looked at Mr. Berry with a stone-cold seriousness. "That's a great question," were the first words out of his mouth. Everyone in the crowded auditorium stared at Spearman as he took a long pause and then replied. "And yes, I do know what will happen to interest rates." Spearman again took a long pause. Everyone in the audience who invested in stocks and bonds waited in anticipation. "They will fluctuate," Spearman said confidently. "Next question."

Spearman beamed at the laugh-out-loud response that his reply brought forth from the audience. Thankfully, the laughter was as much of a sure thing as the question.

Abraham noticed a young woman near the front of the auditorium vigorously motioning with her hand. "Let's take this question from the front," he said. A tall, slender brunette who did not have to battle the forces of gravity popped up from her seat.

"Hi, my name is Della Katassan." There was a murmur in the crowd. "No, it really is," she said. "I'm a senior at Monte Vista majoring in international relations. I want to come back to what you said about trade. Aren't we in danger of losing out to Chinese if we keep trading with them? We won't have anybody making anything in this country. They'll make it all."

"I appreciate the concern behind the question. I can remember awhile back when people had that concern about the Japanese taking over. Recently people expressed the same concern about Europe. The insight from Adam Smith and economists ever since is that 'we'—the United States—are not 'competing' with China. We are *trading* with them. There's a big difference. Trading is more about cooperation than it is about competition." Spearman paused to gather his thoughts. He walked to the very front of the stage. The podium was now behind him.

"The collapse of communism, the technological breakthrough of containerized shipping, the reduction of tariffs and quotas by many governments, all this has extended what Adam Smith called 'specialization and division of labor.' That phenomenon is now global. A smartphone may be assembled in China, because China currently has labor costs that favor the final assembly of goods. To the naïve, it may appear that the device is 'made' in China. But in the sale of that smartphone, most of the value added goes to entrepreneurs who may be in the USA, bankers who may be in London, and design engineers who may be in Germany or Israel.

"When I was a young man, I could look at an item and it would have 'Made in USA' or 'Made in Japan' printed on it. And it was. But for my students today, that statement makes no economic sense. The product may have been made through the efforts of inputs in a dozen different countries."

Spearman returned to the podium. One hand rubbed his chin while his brow was furrowed in thought.

"Here's another example: say you drove a new car to get to the auditorium today. By naming just one country, you can't tell me where the vehicle was made. Sure, you *might* be able to tell me where it was *assembled*. Maybe, though I would not bet the farm on that. But you could not tell me where the entire vehicle was made.

"If you want to speak of competition today, think of competition between brands and technologies that are global in their character—not between countries. If it didn't sound flippant, I would say think of something as 'Made on Earth' rather than 'Made in the USA' or 'Made in China.' "

As the fifteen-minute time period came to an end, Abraham announced that the next question would be the last one. In the case of a dull speaker, announcing that "this will be last question" usually meant there would be no more questions. No one wanted to prolong the agony. But in Spearman's case, many hands went up, each held high by someone hoping to be the final questioner.

Abraham selected a young man who had stood through the entire lecture, leaning against the east wall of the auditorium. When the young man was recognized, he stood up straight and bellowed out his question so everyone in the auditorium could hear. "I'm proud to say my name's also Smith. But it's Sam Smith, and I'm a junior at Monte Vista. I have a question for Professor Spearman. Does economics teach that money buys happiness? Is that what you and Adam Smith are really saying?"

Spearman looked earnestly at the young man. "Economics doesn't teach that money buys happiness, nor is that what I've been saying. Economics teaches us three things about money. First, that money is a medium of exchange. Most of the time, it beats bartering. Second, that money is a store of value. So are a lot of other things, but they don't fit as well in your backpack. And third, that too much money causes inflation, though lots of governments will tell you otherwise."

Spearman paused and got on his tiptoes for a better view over the podium, then gave up and stepped to the side. "As to buying happiness, every major religion that I know of, and every parent that I've ever met, teaches that money does not buy happiness. What economics teaches is that having money expands your choice set. This means compassionate and generous people are better off having more money than less money, because they have more money to give away. Selfish people also are better off having more money because they can buy more things. Even misers are better off having more money because they can hoard more.

"I cannot tell you the number of times when I've taught a course called 'Money and Banking' that I have had students protest the subject matter and tell me the Bible says that 'money is the root of all evil.' And I tell them, no, no, they're distorting the quote. And I refer them not to *The Wealth of Nations* but to the Bible, where we are told, 'the *love* of money is the root of all evil.' "

As he spoke, Henry had retrieved his wallet from his back pocket. "Can you see this from a distance?" Henry held up a hundred-dollar bill. "This piece of currency with Franklin's picture on it is not evil. It's an economic fallacy to contend it is. If I were to exchange it with you for goods or services worth more to me than a hundred dollars and which you owned but valued at less than a hundred dollars, I would suggest we have put it to a good use. We both benefit. We each can say 'thank you' to the other. If you love the hundred dollars so much that you would steal it from me, or wish I did not have it, then it is your love of money that is evil."

Spearman stopped speaking and put the bill back in his wallet. He was deep in thought, almost oblivious to the fact that there were several hundred people looking at him. He spoke directly to Sam Smith.

"I like the way Adam Smith put it. He described happiness as 'tranquility of mind' and he could not have been more clear that neither money nor what it could command would bring happiness. I can still recall Smith's words: 'power and riches . . . produce a few trifling conveniences . . . which in spite of all our care, are ready every moment to burst into pieces, and to crush in their ruins their unfortunate possessor.'

"That's pretty strong language from the father of economics, claiming that money isn't the objective. When Adam Smith asserted that possessions can crush and burst the human spirit, the founder of economics anticipated the 'hedonic treadmill' long before modern psychology gave us the term for it."

•

Pidge and Henry walked back from Mason Auditorium after speaking to President Quinn, Annelle Cubbage, and several student interlocutors.

"You were reflective in your closing answer tonight," Pidge said. "Usually you end with a quip."

"The question merited the response I gave," Henry replied. "It was a deep question, very much unlike what I think will happen to interest rates."

"Do you think the lecture went well?" Pidge knew her husband never took public appearances casually. Unlike prima donna academics, he cared about his audience and took seriously the opportunity cost of their time.

"That's always hard to say," Henry replied. "Monte Vista is very different from Harvard. It strikes me as being more like a community, what Thomas Jefferson called an 'academical village.'"

Pidge nodded in agreement. "It does seem more like a community.... Perhaps that's why the suicide of that artist has cast such a pall over the school."

Henry Spearman held his wife's hand and walked along in silence.

17

OFFICE HOURS: IN THREE ACTS

It is the maxim of every prudent master of a family, never to attempt to make at home what it will cost him more to make than to buy.... What is prudence in the conduct of every private family, can scarce be folly in that of a great kingdom.

—ADAM SMITH

The knock on the door could barely be heard. Spearman listened—it seemed almost more like a scratch than a knock. But there it was again. "Come in," he said in a firm voice, not really sure whether anyone was outside in the hallway or not. But the door opened to reveal a young man standing in the entrance to the office.

"Professor Spearman?" a voice inquired hesitantly.

"Yes, come in, have a seat," Spearman replied. He did not recognize the visitor as a member of his Art and Economics class, though he appeared young enough to be a student.

"I'm Sean . . . Sean Daniels that is. I'm an assistant in the Art Department. I know I'm not a student in your class, and I see on your door that your office hours haven't begun just yet. But . . . I wonder if you might be able to help me with something. Are your hours only for people in your class?"

Students knew they could tell a lot about a professor's accessibility by the office hours posted on the office door. "Friday morning, 8–9" meant the professor was not excited about seeing students. If the note on the office door simply read "Office Hours by Appointment Only," forget it.

Spearman always posted a sign on his office door indicating when he would be there. But over the years he had come to realize that he could not predict what he was going to be asked. He'd had students come by his office at Harvard to ask for help filling out their income tax forms. He'd had students ask him to tell them which job they should take when they had multiple offers. He'd even had students ask about girlfriend-boyfriend problems. After receiving the Nobel Prize, this "aura of omniscience" had only increased. He had finally learned to laugh at it, once noting wryly that "Pidge is the only person in the continental United States who doesn't think I got smarter when I got the prize."

Daniels initially seemed hesitant to take a seat, notwithstanding the unoccupied chairs in the office obviously meant for visitors. Henry gestured with an open hand and pointed to the one closest to Daniels. "Please," he said. As Daniels sat down, Spearman looked his visitor over. The young man was dressed in standard Monte Vista uniform: jeans and a maroon tee shirt. The look on his face was one of anguish. He sat stiffly.

"I don't have a question about economics, Professor. I graduated from Monte Vista last year and never took an economics course. But I heard that you could solve crimes."

After Tuesday's class, Spearman was not totally taken aback. Here was someone else who had learned of his extra-economics exploits. His guess as to how proved correct. Daniels smiled sheepishly. "I heard on campus that you were a detective, or something. And then I Googled you." The smile quickly faded.

"I came to you because of the police, Professor Spearman. They think I killed Tristan Wheeler. Wheeler was your neighbor . . . sort of . . . but I guess you never had a chance to meet him, because he died. At least I suppose you know he's dead? It was in the news. But if you didn't know that he's dead, he is." Sean was no longer reticent. He began to speak rapidly. "You're in the Monte Vista guest house. Well, Wheeler lived just two doors over from you. I go past your place on the way to my work. Or, I used to. I guess I forgot to say, I was Wheeler's assistant. I'm the one who found him dead. I wish I hadn't gone to work that day. But I did. But I didn't *kill* him. Or did I already say that?" Daniels looked confused as the words poured forth. Perspiration had beaded on his forehead.

Spearman looked at his watch. It was one forty p.m. He then looked kindly at the young man and smiled, "I may have students coming by at two, and I usually try to give my students priority. But it's only one forty, so consider yourself at the front of the queue. There might not even be a queue today because it's early in the semester." He leaned back in his chair. "And in any event, no one is here yet . . . so why don't you take a minute to compose yourself."

Sean Daniels exhaled audibly, but Spearman could see that his visitor was still wound up.

"Let me ask you this, Mr. Daniels. . . ."

"*Sean*," the student implored, "please call me Sean."

"Sean it is, then." Henry replied. "You say the police think you killed Wheeler, but I don't see any handcuffs on your wrists." Daniels stared dumbly at Spearman and Henry realized that his attempt at levity had been a lame one. He tried another tack. "Maybe you're misreading what the police think. Have you actually been charged with a crime?"

"Well, not exactly. I'm told that I'm a 'person of interest' and that I shouldn't leave town—as if I'm going to be charged with murder at some point. That's what has me scared. If the police are looking at me as a suspect, I need advice. I'm hoping you can help me out. I can't afford to hire a private investigator to look into my boss's death, and I can't afford to hire an attorney either. I don't have a dad, my mom lives alone, and she's scared too. I don't even know if I'll have a job tomorrow. And I think my mom will die if I end up in jail—not literally, mind you, but my going to jail would just about kill her. So you can see why I came to you."

"Not really," Henry replied. "I'm not a lawyer and I'm not a detective. It sounds as though you could benefit from the labor services of both. But let's assume for the moment that they're outside your budget constraint, and go over what we know with the resources we have."

Spearman turned his head slightly and looked out the office window instead of at Daniels. "Economics is a study of causation, not coincidences. That's not to say coincidences don't occur. They do, all the time. But economics is not helpful in explaining them. What economic analysis is good at is explaining the hidden logic between events that are linked by economic incentives. It may or may not explain why someone died."

At this point, Spearman picked up a yellow pad on the office table in front of him. He then reached into his pocket and took out his pen—as if he were going to take notes on the conversation. "I told my wife yesterday how odd it seemed that while I'm preparing a class on art and economics, a prominent artist who lived just two doors down, turns up dead. I also learned that in the house right next door, artwork had been stolen only weeks before we arrived. And not only that, the stolen art was by the very artist who turned up dead. Then you show up at my office with a demand for help."

"Please don't get me wrong, Professor Spearman. You're kind just to see me. I'm not *demanding* anything."

"I apologize, Sean," Spearman responded. "I know you're not 'demanding' anything of me. 'Demand' is a buzzword in my world of economics. For us it means you have a preference for something. You have a preference for me to help you. I'll try."

"Would you, Professor? I would have enrolled in your Art and Economics class if you were here before I took my degree. I don't know anything about economics, but I love art. That was my major. My mom, on the other hand, would have loved it if I'd taken an econ course. She always wanted me to study something more practical than art. She doesn't think it's practical enough."

Spearman grinned and looked kindly at Daniels. "I think the economic way of thinking is very, very practical. So your mother and I are in agreement on that. But I'm afraid not everyone agrees with your mom and me. Many people think that economics is too theoretical and that economists never agree on anything."

Spearman began to jot on the pad in his lap and endeavored to console his visitor by explaining, "Sean, simply because you found Wheeler's body is enough to make the police want to question you about his death. You would be questioned by the police if you had witnessed an automobile collision in which someone was killed— even if you just happened to be driving by at the time." He paused. "You say that the police have informed you that you are a 'person of interest.' That simply means that your input will be useful in clearing up the case. It is not a synonym for 'murder suspect.' "

"But the police know my boss had become kind of weird, angry. They learned somehow that he used to take it out on me. I think some of the art professors knew about it, and it got out. So the police want to know if I was angry enough in return to want him dead."

"And . . . ?"

"I didn't like being yelled at by Wheeler—I mean who would?—but I also reckoned that my boss was going through something that I didn't know about and if I waited, he'd come back to being the way he used to be." Sean paused and added, "The police also asked me questions as though they think I might have killed Canvas and Frame."

"Canvas and Frame?" Spearman's look of miscomprehension faded quickly. "You mean his two parrots?"

"Yes. Technically they're African greys. Tristan always corrected people in his studio who would say, 'ohh, what beautiful parrots.' 'They're African greys, not parrots,' he'd say. He used to worry when people came to his studio, whether they'd like his birds or not. I told him it didn't really matter. What mattered was whether they liked *him*. Because everyone who liked Tristan knew how much Canvas and Frame meant to him, so they'd be nice to his birds."

Spearman interrupted Daniels. "That's actually thinking like an economist, Sean. Incentives matter. Maybe you don't need to enroll in an econ class." But Spearman's attempt at cheering the young man up failed. Sean looked down at the floor, then back up to Spearman. "I didn't tell the police about the birds because I wasn't sure how it would be interpreted. Just between us, I didn't like them very much. I was the one who had to clean their cages. I even had to supply bird food in the studio. When I took the job, I was told I was to make sure that Wheeler had the paints and brushes he needed. No one told me about scooping up bird poop." He shook his head in disgust. "And I learned early on that cleaning out their cage didn't make me their friend. Tristan could take them out and they would nibble on his fingers. But whenever I tried that, they bit me so hard they'd draw blood. Both of them had beaks like chisels."

"So what's the connection between Wheeler and Linus Torvalds?" Spearman asked. "The newspaper account made reference to it but with no explanation."

"I'm not a geek, but I know that Torvalds is the Linux guru. Microsoft supposedly hated Torvalds because he set Linux up so it could be downloaded for free. Wheeler admired Torvalds for that very reason. He disliked Microsoft—thought it was a monopoly. But Wheeler went further. He thought art should also be free, free to everybody, everywhere, anytime."

Sean Daniels caught his breath. "I know it sounds crazy, and it probably is. But Wheeler had a knack for looking into the future and he thought laser printers someday could print in 3D. As soon as that could happen, Wheeler thought any abstract painting he did could be replicated exactly, producing a painting that had exactly the same texture and dimensionality of paint, but available all over the world. Wheeler hoped it would be so like the original that nobody could tell the difference."

Daniels was nervously drumming his fingers on the tabletop. "You should know, professor, that everyone who already had bought Wheeler's paintings thought this was nuts. Like killin' the golden goose. Tristan's lawyer tried to talk him out of this as well—told Wheeler that even if he believed it, he needed to stop talking about it."

"Did you have any incentive to have Wheeler dead rather than alive?"

"Well, that's what's so weird. Two weeks ago, I would have said no. But . . . I'm a freakin' beneficiary in his will!" Sean buried his face in his hands. Then he looked up again. "I only heard about it a couple days before he died. I showed up at his place, just to get the list I used to work from, and he was sitting in his studio with a drink in one hand. He turns around and says 'Hey, Sean, I'm sorry for the way I've been treating you. But I want you to know—I'm gonna make it up to you. You'll be in my will.' I thought he was just kidding, and said so, but he went on: 'Nope—NOT kidding. I've even talked to Bruce about it.' He was the attorney I mentioned."

"Did Wheeler drink a lot?"

"Not normally, no. He'd drink when he was painting—he called it his 'creative crucible.' He'd lock himself up in his studio and not come out for two to three days. It was drink—think—paint—repeat. Anything he ate, he'd cook on a funky old gas stove he had in the corner. Wouldn't even answer the phone . . . but in a few days, he'd come out with a new masterpiece and things would get better. The bottle would get put away till next time." He paused. "That's why I thought he was kidding when he said that. Maybe he'd been drinking too much." Daniels ran his fingers through his hair and then clenched his fist. "Man, I wish I'd never mentioned that to the police. I swear, I *swear* I have no idea what the will says."

"How much time did you spend in Wheeler's house?"

"Quite a bit. I'm assigned to him for twenty-five hours a week, and because Wheeler's main studio was in the house, I was often there when I wasn't running errands for him, or doing things on campus for him at the art building. So I was there a lot. I tried to explain to the police that it wasn't odd that I was in the house. I'm paid to be there."

"How did you know the attorney who drew up the will?"

"The police asked me that. Wheeler didn't like to go downtown. So his attorney always came to see him. Sort of like a 'studio call' instead of a 'house call.' Sometimes I was there when the attorney came, sometimes I wasn't." He shifted uneasily. "But I never heard them talking about wills. Honest. The only thing I know about the guy is his name. It's Goolsby, Bruce Goolsby."

Daniels watched as Spearman jotted down a note.

"Why do you suppose Mr. Goolsby came to the studio on multiple occasions?"

"He'd help Wheeler arrange the contracts for their sale, either to a person or to a gallery. And there were other business details: like who was going to pay for shipping, or whether Tristan would be there for an opening. Good painters can make money selling their art, they can make money talking about art. But Tristan was getting away from all that what with the whole open art movement. He and Goolsby would argue over that, Goolsby said 'open' was a code word for 'free', and if his paintings were going to be free, then Tristan wouldn't need a lawyer to help him with contracts. He'd need a lawyer to help him with bankruptcy."

As Spearman jotted down the word "bankruptcy," there was a knock at the door. It was precisely two o'clock.

"Sean," Spearman said, as he got up to answer the door, "let's plan to meet again after I have given some thought to our conversation. I suspect there are students here to see me now."

Daniels nodded. He then stood, smiled, and extended his hand, which Henry shook. His step seemed lighter as Spearman took him to the door.

•

As Daniels exited, Spearman saw ten students waiting in the hallway. He noticed that they clustered in two groups of five. Study groups, he predicted. And he was right.

"We were here first," said a tall young man whose name Spearman remembered was Walter. "We want to talk with you about our class project."

"What makes you think that *first come first served* is the allocation method I use for office hours, instead of drawing straws or flipping a coin?" Spearman asked, giving the students pause before they saw the smile that followed.

The four economics majors in the group immediately began to discuss the topic. The lone art major—"Dan the Man," as Spearman recalled—said simply, "Because that's what's fair. Whoever gets here first gets to see you first."

"Okay, we'll consider first come first served as fair," Spearman responded, inviting the first group in. The second group in the hall made no objection. He invited them over to the small conference table, motioning to the four chairs. "I'm afraid one of you will have to stand or sit on the floor," Spearman said, as the group began peeling their backpacks off and strewing them about. Dan took the floor in order to preempt any debate among the economics students about chair allocation.

As the students settled in Walter repeated, "We're here to talk to you about our class project. We think we know what we want to do." The group's intention, he said, was to study the *cost* of producing a painting: getting data on the cost of an artist canvas, the paints, the frame, the marketing. If the market price was really at the intersection of supply and demand, they reasoned, they wanted to study the cost of supply.

As the discussion ranged back and forth, Spearman was pleased to observe that the quality and caliber of the questions were not unlike what he would have expected from his students at Harvard. The accents were different, to be sure: he could not detect one New England intonation. And every now and then a "y'all" would surface. But this, he observed, promoted a rather congenial degree of familiarity.

"The only thing I'd add," Spearman told the group as their time together began to wind down, "is be careful not to forget the cost of the artist's time. Creating a painting is usually very labor-intensive. What might be tricky in your project is imputing the cost of the artist's time at its true economic cost: which is the artist's highest valued opportunity foregone."

Before Spearman could wrap up his time with this group, a loud rap sounded from the door. It was the exact opposite of Sean Daniel's timid attempt to gain entry. Then the door opened, and before Spearman could even respond, Annelle Cubbage came into view. Dan the Man knew who she was. She was a stranger to the others.

"May I see you?" she asked, oblivious to the other students' place in line.

"Ms. Cubbage . . ." Henry began.

"I thought we had agreed on 'Annelle,'" Cubbage interrupted.

"Of course, I do recall . . . Annelle. And we can meet, but I'm afraid this group of students sitting in the hall has priority." Spearman looked over at the group who had been waiting patiently, and then back to Cubbage. "But if you don't mind waiting. . . ."

"Not at all," Cubbage responded. Spearman could see the look of pleasant surprise on the students' faces. But he welcomed the incident. He knew from experience how modest was the cost of information transmitted among the student body—what some called the "student grapevine." Spearman had commented to colleagues that the information network among undergraduates at Harvard was analogous to what economists called the efficient market hypothesis in financial markets. He knew that within a matter of minutes, most of the student body at Monte Vista would have heard that the visiting Nobel Prize winner had stood up a member of the Board of Trustees in order to meet with ordinary students. Spearman could not speak for Monte Vista, but he knew that at Harvard such an incident would have a shelf life of up to five years and would affect student evaluations for that amount of time.

As the previous group picked up their gear and exited, Spearman invited the next five students in, turning to Cubbage as he did so. "Annelle, why don't you sit in while I talk with these students? They're all in my Art and Economics class, and you're as responsible for their being in the hallway as I am." Everyone traipsed into Spearman's office, Annelle Cubbage among them, with two of the students graciously opting to sit on the carpet.

This group's proposal was a study of the demand for French impressionists, comparing the prices of these paintings over time with the share prices in the S&P 500 Index. One student named Terry had done an internship on Wall Street and had data on publically traded stocks. Another student in the group, whose name Spearman had not caught, said her mother was a hedge fund manager in Austin and could help in this regard as well. Spearman told the group, "The financial benchmark data shouldn't be the challenge. What will test your research skills will be getting the price data on the paintings."

As the group talked about how to tackle that endeavor, Annelle Cubbage offered to help through contacts she had at Christie's. Spearman was all the more glad that he had invited the trustee into the discussion.

"What's your hypothesis?" Spearman asked the group. "Do you have one? You should, before you forge ahead in collecting data."

No one responded at first. Then Donnie, legs folded like a pretzel on the floor, piped up. "I think the rate of return on art will be less than the rate of return on stocks. That's what I want to test, anyway. If paintings generate utility because of their looks, people should be willing to hold them with the expectation of a lower rate of return than that of a stock. Nobody puts a document showing they have two hundred shares of Apple stock on their wall for art's sake."

Soon discussion wrapped up and Spearman ushered the students out of the office. As his students took their leave, Henry wondered what might lie in store as he faced his visitor from the Board of Trustees.

●

Annelle Cubbage looked around the office, shook her head, and said, "I was there for your public lecture—and not just because I was picking up the tab. I have a lot of money, so I need to understand economics. But I'll confess I'd rather be riding or hunting. And if I have to read a book about something, I'd rather read a book about art than the *Wall Street Journal.* But in your lecture you talked about the invisible hand and how markets can help business...."

Spearman quickly held up his hands. "Let me stop you there, Annelle. I didn't say that markets help business.

Markets help *consumers*. Being pro-business is not the same as being pro-market." He paused and looked his office guest in the eye. "In fact, some of the most effective enemies of the market system are business leaders. Many of them want free markets for everyone else, but not for themselves. They preach free enterprise, but then subvert it by seeking tariffs and regulations that favor them over other sources of supply. You may have heard that it was Lenin who said 'Capitalists will sell us the rope with which we will hang them.' " Spearman paused, waiting for the objection he knew would be forthcoming.

Cubbage obliged. "But free enterprise needs *some* restrictions. I can remember my daddy saying that cheap oil flooding in from the Middle East would cripple Texas crude production. Quotas, my daddy said, would enable a level playing field."

"A level playing field sounds great in athletics," Spearman replied. "Less so in economics." Spearman would have preferred not to discuss international trade with Annelle Cubbage. Though he was unabashedly enthused about teaching economics, he had to confess that the basic economic principles of international trade, upon which virtually all economists agreed, were nevertheless difficult to teach to those not tutored in the field.

"Athletics provides many useful metaphors for life, but it's limited in helping us understand trade between nations." He searched for a Texas example. "If the Dallas Cowboys play the Chicago Bears, one team will win and another team will lose. But there can be trade between nations, and both sides can win; that's what economists call 'gains from trade.' My friend at Harvard, Alan Vanderveen, grew up in Iowa. There's not a lot of oil in Iowa, unlike Texas. Do you think people in Iowa would be better off not buying crude oil from Texas, because there's not a level playing field? Would your father have thought it unfair for Texans to have to buy corn from Iowa for the same reason?" Henry hoped that Cubbage would see that these were rhetorical questions. He continued.

"One of the myths that economists from Adam Smith to the present have been unable to demystify is that exports benefit a nation and imports harm a nation." Henry raised his hands in frustration. "Actually, it is just the opposite." He paused again. Cubbage had a look of skepticism written across her face. Undaunted he continued.

"Just the opposite. One of my teachers at Columbia had us memorize a funny statement by Frank Knight, who had been his professor at Chicago. I think I still remember it. '*The man from Mars reading the typical pronouncement of our best financial writers or statesmen could hardly avoid the conclusion that a nation's prosperity depends on getting rid of the greatest possible amount of goods and avoiding the receipt of anything tangible in payment for them*.' Yes, that's how it went. Everyone in my class was asked to commit that to memory—so we might not fall for the fallacy that imports are bad for a nation.

"Smith's brilliant understanding of international trade is one that many policy makers still do not appreciate. In fact, if you took the words of some politicians seriously, you'd think exports were good and imports bad. Adam Smith exposed the fallacy of mercantilism, explained the benefits from international trade, and taught us that exports were the 'cost' of imports."

Spearman stopped just long enough to let Cubbage digest what he was saying. "Put yourself in the position of living outside the USA. No rational trader in another country wants to send valuable goods and services to the United States, unless the United States in turn exports goods to them. Exports equal the cost of imports. There are lots of footnotes one could make to that proposition, but it's important that those footnotes not obscure the basic truth about the gains from trade."

Now it was Annelle's turn. "Henry, when I was a little girl my daddy always made me attend vacation Bible school. There wasn't but one little church. Anyways, I remember when the Apostle Paul was trying to get King Agrippa to convert to Christianity. And the king said—how did the Bible verse put it?—'*Almost* thou persuadeth me...' I'll leave it like that, Henry. I'm not persuaded, but you came close. Awful close."

Cubbage smiled at Spearman as she said this. "I'm starting to see firsthand what I'm getting for my investment. I try to be above board with people who want my money, and there's a *lot* of people who do, and I tell them that it's really my daddy's money they're after. I tell 'em I simply managed to get born into the right family and the family lived in the right location. Troup, Texas: a place that somehow just happened to have a lot of valuable minerals under the ground."

"I've heard from others that you've been a shrewd steward over those resources, Annelle. That didn't come from being born into the right family. But," Spearman sat back in his chair, "I doubt you came to my office today for a lecture on international trade. To what do I owe the pleasure?"

"Sean Daniels."

"Really." Spearman's eyebrows shot up. "If you'd been here forty minutes earlier, you'd have bumped into him in the hall. He was just in my office."

"Well, I actually saw him as I was leaving the president's office. I guessed that he'd been by to see you. I wanted to let you know that I don't think Sean Daniels killed Tristan Wheeler. If the police think that, they're wrong."

"So why do you say that?" Spearman's brain worked overtime as he tried to understand this unexpected turn of conversation, with the person economically responsible for his presence in San Antonio. Which had led to his knowing about Tristan Wheeler. Which had *then* led to his knowing that there even was a young man named Sean Daniels. The chain of connected events that led to their conversation was as humanly inexplicable as it was complex.

"Why? Because I think Tristan Wheeler killed himself, the damn fool."

"What's the reason? I thought Wheeler was on a career trajectory of considerable success. And I understand that you deserve partial credit for that. Am I mistaken?"

"You ask me, it was the birds. I grew up on a ranch. On a ranch, you see animals live and you see them die. I've had to put down horses that I loved. I've seen cattle die giving birth. I've lost some of my best dogs to rabies, snakebite, you name it. Some of 'em just disappeared. Life on a ranch isn't easy. But you have to grow up." She snorted. "Tristan lived in the city all his life. City life is artificial. It isn't real. He lost his two birds—and he couldn't handle it."

She sighed. "I loved Tristan. Loved his paintings too—both before and after the sabbatical, if a little less than

Lewis Martin over at the Travis, who's apparently nuts over 'em. But Tristan never grew up. He couldn't handle life."

Annelle paused, and then picked up her purse from the floor and put it in her lap. "I have a connection with Sean Daniels. It's one the police don't know. It's one that even *he* doesn't know." She looked away for a moment and then looked back. "I paid some money to Monte Vista to finance his job as Tristan's helper. I did it because he didn't have a daddy. Now, he's never to know this. In fact, I don't think the boy even knows who I am. But I don't want him to pay the price of Tristan's death. If you can help make that happen, I'll consider the Cubbage Chair to be my daddy's money well spent." She got up to leave.

•

As Spearman walked Cubbage to the door, they both saw a student seated in the hall just outside the doorway. It was the young woman in the Art and Economics class that Spearman thought of as Miss Cowgirl. "Let me introduce you to Annelle Cubbage, Cookie. I didn't know you were in the hall. You should have knocked."

"Oh my gosh, you know my name? I'm impressed." She shook hands with the trustee. "Nice to meet you Ms. Cubbage." She then turned her attention back to Spearman. "I didn't knock, Professor, because I heard that you were meeting with a trustee. But that's okay. I got some work done while I was waiting."

Spearman shook his head again at the speed of the student grapevine, and bade goodbye to Cubbage. He then followed the young woman into his office. Cookie replaced Cubbage in the office chair.

"Thanks for seeing me, Professor Spearman. You remembered my name, so you probably remember that I compete in rodeo shows. Well, there's a local show in New Braunfels this Saturday, that's in the Hill Country outside of town. I'd like to invite you to come watch me compete. Your wife is welcome too. I can get you tickets for free."

Spearman could not resist: "Cookie, economists have always maintained that 'there's no such thing as a free lunch.' Are you now telling me that there's such a thing as a free rodeo?"

Cookie's face had the look of a little girl caught stealing a cookie—out of the cookie jar. "No, no. You're right. I'm an econ major at Monte Vista. I should have known better. So let me reframe my invitation. Hmmm." She closed her eyes. "It takes an hour to get to New Braunfels, if there's no traffic, and an hour back. And the rodeo lasts about two hours. So figure four hours." She opened one eye, as if to calibrate her calculations. "The opportunity cost of your time is probably high: I'm going to estimate five hundred dollars an hour. So figure the total cost is two thousand, plus gas and a couple hot dogs for you and your wife. That takes it up to two thousand thirty. But at least you won't have to add two tickets of ten dollars each on top of the two thousand thirty, which would bring it up to two thousand fifty. I'll grant that two thousand fifty makes for a very costly rodeo. But two thousand thirty isn't too bad, is it?" Cookie looked at Spearman with a sly grin on her face.

Spearman was a charmed by Cookie's economic analysis as he was by her earnestness in having the Spearmans see her compete. As he gathered more information about the date and location, there was another knock at the door. It was Pidge.

Spearman introduced the two, as Pidge apologized to Cookie for the interruption. She then turned to Henry, "I happened to be on campus with Madelyn Howell . . . do you remember her? The provost's wife. She invited me to a Zumba class at the field house. I thought you might be wrapping up office hours and we could walk home together. But if you're still occupied. . . ?" She looked at Cookie and then back at her husband.

"No," Cookie said. "I'm just on my way out. I'm in your husband's Art and Economics class—one of the lucky ones to get in. Did you know that two hundred students wanted to enroll? And actually, I'm glad to see you. I came by to invite you and your husband to see me ride in a local rodeo. I gave him two tickets . . . at zero price. I hope you both can make it!" With that, Cookie slipped on her backpack and made her way down the hallway.

As the Spearmans were walking down Oakmont to their home, Pidge said to her husband, "Henry, do you ever notice how pretty the coeds are at Monte Vista?

"What do you mean, Pidge?"

"Well, like Cookie, the girl you introduced me to. Or like the young woman that just walked by."

"Do you mean the girl with the cute bobbed hair? And the pouty lips? The one who was wearing the blue and white shorts?"

"Yes, *that* girl."

"I can't say I even noticed her," Spearman said to Pidge, with mock seriousness in his voice.

"Henry Spearman!" Pidge said with feigned indignation, acting as if she were going to swing her purse at her husband.

"It's a joke, Pidge. One of the oldest jokes in Vaudeville." He looked at her and smiled. "I think we'd make a pretty good act."

18

THE HIRING SQUAD

Price is a crazy and incalculable thing, while *Value* is an intrinsic and indestructible thing.

—G. K. CHESTERTON

Danishes, doughnuts, and coffee in a Starbucks box had been set out to fuel a morning meeting of the Department of Economics' faculty hiring committee. The "silverware" was plastic and the cups were Styrofoam. The committee members were not at the meeting because of the quantity or the quality of the food and drink.

The membership of the committee was diversified vertically. Herbert Abraham represented the old guard in the department: expected to be experienced and trustworthy, a member who would prevent any serious mistakes from being made. Matthew Battles represented the young Turks, inserted on the committee to signal that Monte Vista cared about the views of its junior faculty. Hannah Talsma's presence was important because she was hampered by neither youthful inexperience nor the jaded indifference that sometimes came from years of professorial incumbency. As an associate professor, Talsma was the porridge that was neither too hot nor too cold. She also brought gender diversity to the committee.

There was likewise a faculty representative from another department on each hiring committee whose job, it was surmised, was to inform the dean or the provost if members of the department were behaving like a cabal—or not taking their hiring task seriously. Michael Cavanaugh from the Department of Art was the odd man out at this meeting. He possessed no particular expertise in evaluating the scholarly potential of economists, but he would serve as the eyes and ears for the administration, alerting them if the Department of Economics at any time failed to follow proper procedure. By the time Spearman joined the committee, the time to invite candidates for an on-campus visit had arrived.

As the meeting commenced the committee's usual chatter was noticeably absent. Short stacks of curriculum vitae, recommendation letters, and interview notes lay on the table before them, but no one dared to speak up. They were all waiting for Spearman to offer his counsel and ranking. His answer surprised them.

"The three of you who were engaged in the interviews have the comparative advantage over Professor Cavanaugh and me. We can get a good idea from the written data, but you've seen them in the flesh. I think you should take the lead, and then the two of us," Spearman nodded to Michael Cavanaugh, "will give our thoughts." This broke the silence, and Abraham, Talsma, and Battle went through their rankings for the assistant professor position, the only slot that the committee was considering on that day.

Henry reflected as the committee deliberated. When Alabama or Michigan State offered an athletic scholarship to an outstanding high school football player, it had a pretty good idea the young man would be a top-notch athlete. What was often less clear was whether he would make the grade academically. The hiring committee at Monte Vista faced a similar dilemma. The research potential of a new Ph.D. candidate in economics was more predictable than future teaching prowess. This worked to the advantage of schools like Harvard, who hired junior faculty that prized research. But for a school like Monte Vista, where teaching really counted, it was harder to know beforehand how a newly minted Ph.D. would fare in the classroom. The search costs were higher.

Further complicating the task was the labor market for newly minted Ph.D.s in the field of economics. There were multiple sources of demand in addition to higher education: think tanks, government agencies, banks, corporations, and consulting firms all sought the services of economists. Even if the committee could sort out applicants by the attributes the department sought, it realized that any offer the school made would not necessarily be accepted.

The committee's choice set eventually narrowed to two candidates. One had impressive letters from his professors about his dissertation: an extension of Truman Bewley's work on competitive equilibrium models with an infinite number of commodities. Battle favored this person. "Bewley models are hot," he said several times. The other candidate was an econometrician whose dissertation involved non-Gaussian nonlinear time series. Her specialty was kernel estimation in time series contexts. She also delved into wavelet methods. Talsma had made the case that the department needed to beef up the teaching of econometrics to its majors.

"I think you need to look for stronger signals about teaching skills," Spearman said, when the time came for his own input. "Hiring a colleague is a major investment. You don't want to invest in someone who's not likely to survive Monte Vista's teaching filter. So look for signals as to what teaching experience the applicant had in graduate school. If you haven't done so, read their doctoral dissertations. You can learn a lot there about whether candidates can write clearly. If they can't, chances are they can't teach clearly. And I'd ignore much of what you read in the letters of recommendation."

"Why do you say that about the rec letters?" Cavanaugh asked. "I've always thought they were important."

"I have read hundreds of these letters," Spearman said. "Most of them are full of glowing encomia: *'Best student I've had in years,' 'One of the finest students I've ever taught,'* et cetera. I see that over and again. So I go back to first principles: remember the economic incentives at play. Professors want to help their students get jobs; their own prestige is affected by this. And the market for junior faculty is not one with repeat purchases. Promoting a graduate student is a lot like selling a new car: the dealer knows you're unlikely to come back soon and make another purchase, and so plays his cards accordingly." Spearman looked around the table at the other committee members. "If Monte Vista hires an economist just out of a major university, it isn't going to be back buying dozens more in the next couple years. This is the kind of market that cries out for caution—and the shouldering of sizable search costs."

Cavanaugh admitted to being ill at ease with both candidates. "I know I'm the outsider here, but it seems to me that these candidates are more . . ." he paused to find the right words ". . . more like technicians than anything else. Neither has a dissertation topic on how to help the Hispanics who are doing yard work get better jobs. Isn't that economics? Neither has written about how to get the homeless in San Antonio into good public housing. I would think these would be important things for an economist to figure out. And I know this sounds self-serving, but the candidates you're considering haven't written one word about how we need to do more to support the arts. The money wasted on sports and the military in this country is almost obscene, while the arts are being starved."

The ticking sound of the wall clock was clearly discernible in the silence that ensued.

●

The committee members completed their deliberations in the late morning and elected to have lunch together at the faculty club. The food at the club would trump the doughnuts that had passed for breakfast. As the group walked across campus, they passed one of the university's largest buildings. A granite sign in front of the entrance read "Andrew Crampton Library."

"So, I wonder who Andrew Crampton was?" Battles asked. There was no immediate reply to his question. As the faculty member with the longest tenure, Abraham felt obliged to at least respond to Battles, even though he was mildly embarrassed by the only thing he could offer. "I'm not sure," he said, looking back at the building as if another glance at the familiar structure might give him a clue about its provenance. Turning again to Battles and the others he admitted, "I don't know, even though I've been at Monte Vista for years and been in that building hundreds of times."

"I think *I* can answer that question," Spearman volunteered. The group looked at him in surprise. Clearly enjoying the moment, he continued. "I realize I'm a newcomer to campus, but I believe Crampton was a writer."

"A *writer*, you say?" Cavanaugh queried. "I don't pretend to know all of the English canon, but I've never heard of a writer named Crampton. What on earth did he write?"

Spearman paused before answering and then said, "He wrote a check."

Cavanaugh looked puzzled. "Crampton wrote a *check*, you say?" Watching both the twinkle in Spearman's eyes and the frown on Cavanaugh's forehead, the other committee members struggled not to laugh out loud.

"Yes. I suspect he wrote a check to Monte Vista University—and I imagine that what Crampton wrote got great reviews here."

Cavanaugh had walked several paces when a smile replaced his puzzled frown. "Oh, yes, yes. I see. The man wrote a check, you say. You mean Crampton gave money to the *school*!" Cavanaugh beamed, seemingly pleased to have made the deduction.

"A large amount, I predict," Spearman said. "I can't speak for Monte Vista, but at Harvard, if you can write a large check the administration will consider you a great writer."

As they entered the building's doors Spearman added, "I've never understood why so many professors have a dislike for capitalists. Capitalists give lots of money to colleges and universities. But the colleges and universities don't honor these people for their business skills. They honor them because of their *writing*! Professors of English should admire people with such skills in writing."

•

Lunch at the faculty club was buffet style. As Spearman observed each of his colleagues departing with a different choice—Abraham with the soup of the day and a tossed salad, Talsma with a protein shake and a large bowl of steamed vegetables, Battles with a giant pastrami sandwich, Cavanaugh with broiled sole—he thought of his hero Adam Smith. No central planner could ever have anticipated that on this day, at this location, these individuals would demand these particular items for lunch. They themselves could not have predicted what they were about to consume even a week ago. And yet all of the five seemed to enjoy their luncheon preferences that day, met—as Adam Smith put it—"as if by an invisible hand."

Spearman meditated once again on the quotation by Bastiat he had recited at his public lecture. He realized that there were many products that the residents of San Antonio needed to have tomorrow. Some of them, such as auto parts, groceries, medicines, and fuel, could be classified as vital. And yet as he looked around at the professors in the faculty club at Monte Vista University, he saw a great paradox. Many of these professors were anti-market. But their anti-market leanings were not hindered for a single moment by the knowledge that their daily necessities were being made available, both tomorrow and into the future, courtesy of that self-same free market.

Spearman had forewarned his colleagues that he would have to eat and run, in order to make a twelve-thirty appointment for a television interview in Coppock Hall. Two of the others likewise had commitments at that time. This would not be a leisurely lunch.

Midway through their meal, Cavanaugh turned to those at the table and said, "After reading about the candidates and listening to you talk, I think I better understand why so many of us in the humanities are uncomfortable around economists."

"Because of our salaries?" Battle asked.

"Matt, a question like that probably only ratifies what we're about to hear," Abraham chided his junior colleague.

"No, I'm serious," Battles replied. "If you believe in a Marxist labor theory of value, that's a legitimate gripe. Economists don't work any harder than professors in the humanities and yet we get paid more."

"No, it isn't that," Cavanaugh went on. "Marxists may still live in English Departments, but not so many in Art Departments. My discomfort really goes back to Plato. Plato compared the soul to a chariot, drawn by two horses. One horse is emotion, or the heart. The other is reason, or the mind. All I see in the young scholars I've read, all I see in your discipline generally, is *one* horse: reason, what you call the rational actor. So where's the other horse? Surely you don't deny that it exists?"

Everyone at the table looked to Spearman, whose supply of words always seemed to meet demand. He thought for a moment before replying. When he did, his tone was gracious. "We don't deny the other horse, Michael. We really don't. What we think is that economists bring a special talent to the marketplace of ideas . . . a special asset, as it were. Against the chance that other disciplines put too many chips on the horse of emotion and passion, we put our chips on the role of reason and rationality." Spearman put his eating utensils on the table and clasped his hands as he thought.

"One of the most brilliant economists in the United States has a name like mine, as I'm sometimes teasingly reminded. I'm 'Spearman,' his name is 'Arrow.' Kenneth Arrow from Stanford. He was awarded a Nobel Prize years before me, and deservedly so. And he put it this way: '*An economist by training thinks of himself as the guardian of rationality, the ascriber of rationality to others, and the prescriber of rationality to the social world.*' " Spearman pointed a finger at Cavanaugh. "Please note the word Arrow chose: *guardian.* Guardians play an important social role. They preserve things that otherwise might be lost. If you want, think of us this way: when you decide to go and smell the roses, economists are the kind of people who will cover for you at the office."

Cavanaugh could not decide if he was being looked up to or talked down to. Sensing the tension, Spearman eliminated it in one swoop: "Michael, serving on the Econ Department's hiring committee is one of those thankless tasks which universities seem to have in abundance. So let me, on behalf of all of us rational actors, thank you for agreeing to offer your views to the committee and put up with us. We are in your debt."

Cavanaugh's shoulders shrugged off Spearman's words of appreciation but his expression softened.

•

"Mind if I walk back with you?" Spearman said to Cavanaugh as the lunch was breaking up. "The studio for my interview is in your building."

"I can lead you right there."

As the two men walked briskly across campus, Spearman turned to Cavanaugh and said, "I'm afraid none of us gave you a satisfactory response to your concern about the focus of my discipline. That's an occupational hazard for us all."

Cavanaugh's countenance was grave as he looked at Spearman. "To my mind, it isn't just the technical nature of your subject that is disconcerting. The economic perspective is deeply pernicious, perhaps especially in the field of art. And now I observe, at my own school, a course being offered on the economics of art. Can you imagine how troubling that is to those of us who feel called to 'guard' the arts?"

"In what way? I can't imagine that my course is a threat to the arts."

"Oh, but it is. It *is*," Cavanaugh repeated. "We might agree that it's harmless to put a price on things like wheat and steel. But economists don't stop there. You put a price on human endeavors like the arts."

"Where's the harm?" Spearman found himself starting to fall behind the taller man, and began walking faster.

"You really don't see it, do you Professor Spearman? Let me put it to you in a way you might understand. People used to go to a museum to appreciate the art. But these days when they flock to see something like Picasso's *Garçon à la Pipe*, they gawk and exclaim, 'that cost a hundred and four million dollars!' People talk more about the price tag these days than the art. I blame economics for that."

"Don't blame economics," Spearman said. "Blame demand and supply, or blame the market—that's where the hundred and four million dollars came from."

"But don't you *see* . . . ?" The professor's pace increased. "The discipline of economics has given a ratification to those prices. And the explanation, ever so subtly, soon becomes a justification. I don't hold you personally responsible of course. Although," he lifted an eyebrow slightly, "lawyers might call it a case of 'contributory negligence.' But regardless . . . once the wheels of economics commodify something, in the public's present state of mind its value has been set. You may have a price, I'll grant you that. But you don't have a value."

•

Spearman, puffing, walked on in silence. He realized that he did not have conversations like this with his econ colleagues at Harvard. As the two men turned the corner that led to their destination, Spearman surprised Cavanaugh by saying, "May I ask you something that has nothing to do with economics?"

"Of course. I might then have something worthwhile to contribute," Cavanaugh said with mock self-derision.

"You were at the dinner that President Quinn hosted for my wife and me shortly after we got to campus. You and I didn't get to chat, but you did talk with my wife Pidge. She told me about your conversation."

"Oh yes, I did meet your wife that night, and I remember you sitting next to President Quinn. I was not myself that evening, I fear."

"Yes. That dinner was right on the heels of the death of Tristan Wheeler. My wife told me that she was surprised you were up to attending the dinner, given your relationship with Wheeler."

"It was a difficult evening," Cavanaugh responded. "I hope I didn't embarrass myself in front of your wife. I found her charming."

"Oh no, not at all. It was gracious of you to even be there. But I'd like to ask you about something you said to my wife—that Tristan Wheeler didn't commit suicide. My understanding is that his body was found hanging from the ceiling in his own house, with a stool lying on its side beneath him. What do *you* think happened to him?"

"I know it wasn't suicide."

"But how do you know?" Spearman repeated.

Cavanaugh stopped suddenly, turning to face his companion. "How do you know you love your wife, Professor Spearman? You just know you do. I understood Tristan. We were colleagues. I watched the transformation of his artistic expression. I dealt with the same setbacks. I had the same sensitivities he had. 'Sensitivity'—that's a word you don't use in economics. But it means a lot to artists." He began to walk again, his face set like a flint toward the Art Department building. "We are sensitive to truths that you cannot understand with Bewley models or measure with wavelet methods. I don't need what you call a 'general equilibrium model' to know that Tristan Wheeler did *not* commit suicide."

"How did he die, then?"

"I'm not sure, but someone's responsible. And it wasn't Tristan."

"Maybe this is a question out of the blue," Spearman said. "But do you know Sean Daniels?"

"Of course, everyone in my department does. Young Daniels was Wheeler's assistant. Before that, he was a student of mine. Interesting young man. Limited artistic talent, but no slouch. He has a keen eye for color. Too heavy with the brush, though."

"Do you think Daniels could have been involved in Wheeler's death?"

"Oh, he's involved, alright. He found Wheeler dead. You can explain how he came to be in Wheeler's house, that I'll grant—he worked for Wheeler after all. But why he was there at *that time?*" Cavanaugh shrugged.

"You knew both Wheeler and Daniels. Was there a reason Daniels might want Wheeler dead?"

"The talk in the department is that Daniels did have a motive, maybe even two, depending on how you count. One is that Wheeler had become so difficult to work for. But has there ever been a professor who at some point hasn't had a difficult dean or chairman? You don't observe professors routinely killing their deans and departmental chairs." Cavanaugh glanced about to see if anyone was within hearing range.

"The other possibility getting around is that Daniels is in Wheeler's will. In that scenario, Sean killed Wheeler to collect a big inheritance. Wheeler was still a young man . . . maybe he was asking Daniels to wait too long a time. I gather some of the family members feel this might be the case. Although they don't care about Tristan: they simply don't want their inheritance diluted."

Several students waved at Cavanaugh as the two approached Coppock Hall, but their gestures went unacknowledged. Spearman spoke next. "As you may know, Monte Vista has us staying at the university's guest house on Oakmont. We're just two doors down from Wheeler's house and studio."

"I know the house you're in. I've been in it on a couple occasions. Actually your neighbor right next door was quite close to Wheeler. Raul Ramos, a surgeon. Did you know that?

"He and I met recently, not in the most pleasant manner I'm afraid. Do you know him well?"

"Oh, of course. He's a real poobah in the art community in San Antonio. Good eye for art, canny eye for rising talent. Serves on the board of the Travis. He doesn't do a lot for our department at Monte Vista—more apt to give to the Travis than to us. But he's been an asset to Wheeler's career. I wager Ramos wouldn't be well known in New York, but around here he's definitely connected and a player."

The two professors walked in a side entrance and stopped outside of Cavanaugh's office. Guessing his opportunity for conversation was closing, Spearman threw in one last query. "I understand his Wheeler paintings were stolen. Any idea who took them?"

"There must be a million theories out there. Some people think the caterers. They had to take things in and out of the house, and they had a van right there. Some people think one of Dr. Ramos's guests scoped out the house, maybe left a window or door unlatched, and came back after everyone was asleep. Some people say no, it had to have been professional art thieves—real pros, on behalf of a reclusive collector—because there's never been a ransom request. I've even heard it advanced that the housekeeper stole the paintings." Cavanaugh's face took on a look of skepticism. "Sort of like in an Agatha Christie mystery, but instead of the very proper, very loyal butler committing the crime, it's the sweet, hard-working Mexican housemaid. Rubbish, in my view." He opened his office door, bade Spearman good day, and walked inside, closing the door behind him.

19

SURPRISE AT SOTHEBY'S

FRIDAY–SATURDAY, JANUARY 20TH–21ST

It is not that pearls fetch a high price because men have dived for them; but on the contrary, men dive for them because they fetch a high price.

—RICHARD WHATELY

Like most prominent academicians, Henry Spearman was a frequent flyer. While not racking up quite as many miles as the marketing VP of a major corporation, he was not far behind, especially after winning the Nobel Prize. Departing from Boston had offered him numerous direct flights to major cities around the world. But there was a smaller choice set out of San Antonio. Because of its proximity to the giant Dallas–Fort Worth hub, travelers nearly always had to go through DFW to get where they wanted to go.

Today, however, Spearman could avoid DFW. He would be flying to New York City with Annelle and Jack Cubbage, and the Cubbages did not fly commercial. They leased a Dassault Falcon 900EX, which meant goodbye to check-in lines and waiting for luggage. The spacious cabin of the private jet was like First Class Plus. For Henry, the marginal benefit was not that great. Because he was so short, legroom on a commercial flight was always plentiful—even flying coach.

White Plains, the favored terminal for many business jets going into New York, was their destination. Attending an art auction at Sotheby's was their objective. A week earlier Annelle had told Henry that if he were going to teach about art and economics, he should go where art and economics intersected most starkly: an auction for high class *objets d'art*. "There's a Wheeler on the block," Annelle told him. "Jack and I want to be there. There's room on our plane and the trip won't interfere with your teaching schedule—I already checked. So you won't even miss an opportunity to be carried out of the classroom."

Cubbage never let Spearman forget his metric for stellar classroom performance. "Been carried out of the classroom, yet?" she would ask whenever she encountered him.

Annelle Cubbage slept for most of the three-and-a-half-hour flight. Spearman occupied himself by reading scholarly journals: what economists in their professional lingo usually identified by initials. He had with him the QJE and the REStat, which is how economists referred to two journals published by Harvard, the *Quarterly Journal of Economics* and the *Review of Economics and Statistics*. His attaché case also held the latest issues of the AER—the *American Economic Review*—and the *Journal of Political Economy*, known as the JPE. The only major journal he had with him that did not have a slang abbreviation was *Econometrica*. Across the aisle, Jack Cubbage was stretched out reading *People* magazine.

Once in New York, a town car took the Cubbages to their apartment, dropping Spearman off at the Wyndham near Central Park. Checking into his room, Spearman caught up on emails and phone messages that his administrative assistant at Harvard had sent him. Without Gloria's filtering screen, he would have been overwhelmed with communications. She had a knack for separating wheat from chaff. This day her talents were especially appreciated as Spearman did not have a great deal of time. By six o'clock he had to be on the Upper East Side to join the Cubbages at Sotheby's.

Spearman took a cab from the hotel to the corner of York Avenue and East Seventy-Second, where the gleaming glass building that enclosed Sotheby's auction facility was located. For a person who had taught auction theory and who had students write term papers and dissertations on auctions, Spearman surprisingly had never attended an actual, real-world auction. His only visual exposure to an auction had been in his favorite movie, Alfred Hitchcock's *North by Northwest*. He and Pidge had enjoyed the classic together more than once.

Film critics often singled out the crop dusting scene with Cary Grant as one of the most brilliant set pieces in American cinema. Other fans preferred the opening act, in which foreign spies mistakenly identified Cary Grant's hapless Roger Thornhill as their target for assassination. But for Henry, the highlight of the entire movie was the art auction. There Grant called attention to himself by continuing to offer a *lower* bid than the last one tendered by someone else, much to the consternation of the auctioneer and the patrons. The auction in the movie presumably would offer little guidance for what he would encounter at Sotheby's, Henry mused, as the taxi moved over to the curb.

The Cubbages entered Sotheby's like the veterans they were, nodding to familiar faces. Like many of those present that evening, the Cubbages had been labeled UHNW (Ultra High Net Worth) by Sotheby's management. Their professor guest followed along more hesitantly. The auction room reminded Spearman of a large theater, except he had never seen a theater with so much standing room—or with such well-dressed patrons. The floors were all carpeted to keep sound down. The tony chairs augmented the theater-like appearance: each had a velour manchette and a contoured backrest. Annelle Cubbage whispered to Spearman, "Sotheby's only wants prospective bidders to be in the audience. But there's such drama in some art auctions that it's hard to separate those interested in buying from those who're just interested in watching."

This provoked Henry Spearman to look around the room at the people taking their seats. He wondered: *was* there a way to discriminate against the mere observers, and favor those with demand for the products being sold? He tucked this thought away as a good term paper topic for a student. Against the far wall Spearman thought he spotted a familiar face, but then someone else passed between and blocked his view. Being short made it difficult for him to see across any crowded room. When he did have an unmolested view, the person he thought he'd recognized was not to be seen.

At Sotheby's, the art object being sold had the lead role. The staging, the lighting, the presentation worked in unison to frame and highlight the star. But the role of best supporting actor clearly went to Hovey Lansing, the auctioneer. Whenever the audience was not looking at the work of art that was up for sale, they would be looking at Lansing. He was rail thin but with broad shoulders, and his V-shaped frame emphasized the exquisite cut of his tailored suit. His face was youthful from the front, but rugged from any other angle. His posture at the rostrum was one of commanding understatement. And the voice! Deeper than one would expect from someone so lean, it brought forth an enunciation and diction that was impeccable. The tone never came off as pleading. Rather, Lansing's overall demeanor left bidders not wanting to disappoint him by the amount of the bid. To top it off, he was an aesthete. Whatever was on the block at the time— paintings, manuscripts, furniture, jewelry, porcelain—he didn't just hawk it. Hovey Lansing *knew* it.

Spearman settled into his seat next to the Cubbages. As the auction began, he contemplated the business model of the premier auction houses like Sotheby's and Christie's. What news accounts of famous sales did not reveal was the underlying economic equilibrium that was at demand and supply's confluence. When a major piece of art was sold for, say, a million dollars, there was a "buyer's premium" to be paid by the successful bidder. This figure was around 10 percent of the sales price. In addition, there was a seller's commission, also a percentage of the bid price that was paid to the auction house by the owner of the painting that was sold. This figure was often around 5 percent. So the seller got less than the bid price, and the buyer paid more than the bid price. The auction house pocketed the difference.

Just a few years earlier, it had been discovered that Sotheby's and Christie's were not content to compete for that differential. The two firms had formed a cartel to rig these rates. This action caused a major brouhaha in the world of art. In Spearman's world, economists were interested to understand why a duopoly of Sotheby's and Christie's could not squelch active price competition between them through oligopolistic interdependence. Instead they used a clumsy and illegal price-fixing conspiracy. Had they not done so, the executives might still be spending time in tony salons instead of a federal penitentiary.

Game theory suggested why the two firms turned to outright collusion. The art being auctioned off was so heterogeneous that what economists called repeat games were difficult. Tit for tat did not work across disparate items of value. When an especially large collection was up for grabs between the two firms, there were several different ways to compete. One firm could waive the consignor's fee. The other could respond by rebating the buyer's premium back to the seller. This could in turn provoke a response to fly the collection to prospective buyers for personal inspection. The two firms could also compete by offering higher guarantees—even fine-tuning the competition by the elegance of the collection's catalog. Spearman grinned as he imagined the temptation of top management to say, *"Enough of this! Let's just rig the game."*

Several works of art had been hammered down when Annelle nudged Henry. "Here we go" was all she said.

"We will now have lot number nine, a painting by Tristan Wheeler." Hovey Lansing made this announcement with just the right amount of pizzazz in his voice. A polite murmur moved through the room as patrons spoke to those seated next them. Spearman's pulse quickened.

For the fans and admirers of Wheeler's art, this was the main event—with everything else merely an interesting undercard. In just a few minutes, someone would be adding a valuable and timeless prize to their collection and subtracting accordingly from their bank account. For those who did not plan to bid on the Wheeler painting, there would still be keen interest in the sale. Watching the drama of dashed hopes was irresistible to some. Even regular customers at Sotheby's still enjoyed catching the look on the face of the winning bidder. The expression was difficult to describe no matter how often it was seen. It reflected a curious blend of joy and relief mixed with a look of dread.

Spearman had picked up on this look during the earlier sales. As an economist, he had a theory that explained exactly what was happening. On display was the facial expression of what economists had named "the winner's curse," the dread behind the question, "if there are so many savvy buyers in the room, why am I the only one willing to pay this much?"

Sotheby's had spared no expense to make sure that the acoustics and the audio system were perfect. Lansing's soothing yet authoritative voice could be heard clearly throughout the room. "Our next painting, ladies and gentleman, is Tristan Wheeler's *Challenge*. There is quite a bit of interest in this. Who will start the bidding at five hundred thousand dollars? Do I hear five hundred thousand?

"The gentleman on my right. Thank you sir. Do I hear six hundred?" Spearman looked over to the gentleman on Lansing's right who had bid five hundred thousand.

"Six hundred it is." A portly gentleman in a tailored pinstripe suit had nodded to Lansing.

"Seven hundred?" Lansing asked.

"Yes, I got you madam. Seven hundred is the bid." Lansing pointed to a woman bidding from the center of the auditorium. Spearman jumped when he realized the bid was from the chair next to him. "Who will give eight hundred?"

Henry turned his head and his eyes confirmed what his ears had heard. The current bid had indeed been made by Annelle Cubbage. Her husband Jack was somewhat less intrigued by the bidding: his eyes looking straight ahead, his expression nonchalant.

"Eight hundred? Is that a bid sir? Don't be shy. Yes, thank you. Do I have nine hundred?" Spearman did not catch who had pushed the price up to eight hundred thousand.

"Nine hundred over at the center." Annelle Cubbage had raised her bid.

"One million?"

"Not yours, madam. I have one million from my right." Lansing looked directly at an elderly, silver-haired lady who had bid a million dollars, indicating that he had seen someone else signal a million before Cubbage did. One million was the prevailing bid. Lansing had moved the price of the Wheeler painting another hundred thousand dollars closer to the price that eventually would bring his gavel down.

Spearman was like a puppy with a soup bone. He was accustomed to markets clearing as demand and supply engaged in the process of *tâtonnement*. But what he enjoyed even more was *hearing* the market move to equilibrium where demand and supply would come to rest. This was music to his ears. The bidding reached a million five.

"A million six anyone?" Lansing asked. "Do you want back in sir, is that a yes?" The pin stripe suit was back in.

"Thank you sir. I have a million six." The bidding went up another two hundred thousand.

"Do I have a million nine?" Spearman looked over again at Annelle Cubbage, whose hand cupped her mouth as she spoke with her husband. He then scanned the crowd, trying to pick out in each instance who had offered the current bid.

From his seat he had noticed a tall brunette standing against the wall, listening to a cell phone and occasionally speaking into it. As the bidding progressed Lansing had looked over at her after each bid, as if expecting a response or signal from her.

Spearman asked Annelle who the woman was. "Harriett Evans," she said, sotto voce. "She's an employee of Sotheby's. Very professional. Harriett's probably talking to someone she's authorized to bid for. Could be a buyer who wants to be anonymous. Could be someone in Beijing, or Berlin—anywhere in the world these days. Keep an eye on her. She knows her business."

Cubbage raised her hand to signal her new bid. No one could tell whether her husband concurred or not.

"A million nine! I see you madam. I have one million nine hundred thousand bid for lot nine." There was an anxious look on Annelle's face.

Spearman's head swiveled as he watched the bids, groping through the process of recontracting to some as yet undetermined market clearing level. No actual exchange would take place until this precise level was attained.

As the bidding process entered what Lansing thought to be the final phase, he cautioned the crowd. "I have a bid of one million nine hundred thousand for the Wheeler painting. Let me remind you that no more Wheelers will ever be painted."

While speaking, the auctioneer thought through his strategy. His goal was to maximize the price paid: that being the desire of both the principal—that is, the seller—and the agent—Sotheby's. The highest bid would maximize Sotheby's return on the sale so the principal-agent incentives were aligned. Lansing had the bidding going up in hundred-thousand increments. It might be time, he realized, to change the bidding to fifty-thousand increments. Lansing would not want to lose a bidder who was willing to pay one point nine five million but who would not go two million. He paused to give the final bidders a chance to reassess their positions.

"One million nine hundred fifty thousand for the Wheeler, anyone? Yes, on the right, I have you sir at that amount." A gentleman in the back, his face flushed, barely had raised his hand—just enough to signal his new bid.

Lansing's years of experience paid off. He had squeezed out another fifty thousand. Could he bring the bid to two million dollars? This would be a remarkable accomplishment. The Sotheby's catalog had placed an estimate of a million and a half for the Wheeler painting.

"I have one million nine fifty. Who will make it two million? Are you in, sir?" Lansing looked at the pin stripe suit. The man shook his head back and forth. He had been priced out.

"It may be down to the two of you." Lansing looked at Cubbage and the gentleman in the back. "I have one million nine fifty. Do I hear two million?"

"Do I have two million?" Lansing again asked. There was not a whisper from the crowd. Spearman looked back and forth between the auctioneer and Annelle Cubbage.

"Two million, anyone." Lansing paused again, to give both parties a moment to rethink their bidding posture. The interval seemed like minutes to the final bidders, but it was only about ten seconds on the clock.

"All right then," Lansing said, "fair warning . . ." but before he could say "sold" a new bidder exclaimed, "Two million dollars." Her bid could be heard throughout the room. Spearman quickly glanced to his right. Annelle's face was a study in frustration.

"I have two million dollars for lot number nine. Do I hear two million one?" Lansing decided to return to the hundred-thousand increment. Spearman saw a man with his back to the wall, a cell phone at his ear. Henry then gave a darting glance to Harriett Evans, who was whispering into her cell phone.

"Three million."

The room went momentarily silent. Then an audible, excited buzz filled the air. Everyone had begun talking at once. Hovey Lansing looked at the person who'd just voiced the three-million-dollar bid. Years of experience had taught him to never, *ever* look surprised. If the fiery Hand of God were to write a figure on the wall, a pro like Lansing could be counted on to take the bid in stride, giving it no more attention than the invisible hand of Adam Smith that determined the prices. His training held him in good stead.

"I have three million bid. Am I correct, three million?" The bidder nodded affirmatively.

"Three million is the bid. Do I hear three million one?"
It would have been hard for Lansing to hear a higher bid,
as the room continued to hum and throb. To say the experienced crowd had been surprised would have been an
understatement. But among the dozens of savvy veterans,
there was one witness more surprised at the seemingly
outlandish bid than anyone. That would have been Henry
Spearman, who turned slowly to stare at the bidder sitting
calmly beside him.

Annelle Cubbage's arms were tightly folded. After con-
firming her bid she looked straight ahead, oblivious both
to the glances darted surreptitiously in her direction and
to the stunned silence of Henry Spearman. Jack Cubbage
looked bored. Spearman looked away, scanning the crowd
while trying to make sense of what he had just witnessed.

"Lot number nine at three million dollars." Hovey Lansing tapped his gavel on the podium. "We now turn to lot
ten, a very nice Matisse. . . ."

But Spearman was no longer listening to the swirl of
words around him. Had he just witnessed a Hitchcock
movie in reverse? he wondered.

•

The private jet returned to SAT on Saturday afternoon, its
flashing lights reflecting on the runway's wet tarmac as
it touched down. During the flight back, talk among the
passengers was in small supply. Jack Cubbage reclined his
seat and almost immediately started to snore. Spearman
attempted to engage Annelle Cubbage regarding the ra-
tionale behind her seemingly irrational bid, only to be

tersely rebuffed. "Professor, I don't tell you how to teach economics, and you don't tell me how to bid on paintings. Let's just say I had my reasons and leave it at that." Following this conversation stopper Cubbage reclined her seat and closed her eyes as well, leaving the professor to his thoughts.

A few hours later, as the trio trudged through the private terminal at the San Antonio airport, the heading of an *Express-News* story caught Henry's eye: "Wheeler Death Ruled Suicide."

20

TRIP TO THE TRAVIS

Political economy is in no sense the highest study of mind—there are others which are much higher, for they are concerned with things much nobler than wealth or money....

—WALTER BAGEHOT

"Isn't this a lot like middle school?" Haden complained. "I mean, we're going on a *field trip* to a museum. For this, my folks are paying fifty grand a year?"

"Hey man, I don't know where you went to school, but I doubt if there were Nobel Prize winners taking you on guided tours," Donnie responded. "The present value of Dr. Spearman's income stream is in the millions. If he wants me to go with him to Wal-Mart, I'll go along for the experience."

"Or put it on your résumé," Anita added. "That's what I'm going to do." She made a motion with her hands as if framing a headline. "I can see it now: 'Collaborated with Nobel Prize Winner on the Economics of Art Museums.' That's a pretty good line item to have when I go on the job market."

After considerable bantering of this sort, the students in the Art and Economics class boarded a school bus at eight thirty a.m. for the short trip to the Travis Museum of Art. Jennifer Kim and Henry Spearman occupied the two seats behind the driver. Cookie and Anita sat in the shotgun seats across from the two faculty members. Far from sharing the cynicism of some of their classmates, the two were visibly excited about the trip, conversing with both animation and laughter.

Non-Texans associated the names Davy Crockett and Jim Bowie with the Alamo. But Texans accorded greater honor to the name *William B. Travis*. Travis was the commander of the Texas militia who fought to his death at the Spanish mission. For Texans, Travis occupied the same pantheon as Paul Revere for a Massachusetts resident like Spearman.

To prepare for the trip, the students had been asked to research the museum business. They now knew that there were supermuseums, such as the Louvre, MoMA, the Metropolitan, the Getty, and the Rijksmuseum, whose brands were as recognizable as those of Ferrari and Patek Philippe. They'd also learned that most of the supermuseums had one superstar painting anchoring their identity. For the Louvre, it was the *Mona Lisa*. For the Rijksmuseum, it was *The Night Watch*.

The Travis was not in this league. There were not thousands of people at its door each day waiting to get in. While important regionally, it was still a second tier museum with aspirations of someday becoming a destination museum for people outside the city's footprint. The Board of Trustees hoped that in the future San Antonio would be a go-to place because of the River Walk, the Alamo, and the museum named after the Alamo's hero. The fact that the Travis held more Wheeler paintings than any other museum had proven an increasing plus for the place ... with the artist's death no doubt adding a macabre attraction.

Michael Cavanaugh had persuaded Lewis Martin, the Travis's curator, to act as guide for Spearman's students and be a respondent to any questions they might have. As the students unloaded from the bus, Martin met them at the entrance. Spearman had guessed that the curator of a museum named "Travis" might dress western. But Martin was wearing a light blue linen suit. No bolo tie. His shoes were black loafers with tassels. No lizard-skin boots. Martin dressed nothing like his employer's namesake.

As the group assembled Spearman thanked Martin again for hosting his students, while at the same time reminding him of the class purpose: the Monte Vista students were interested particularly in the museum as an economic enterprise. He then told the curator that some of the students would no doubt have questions along the way.

Martin began the tour without preamble as they walked into the museum's lobby. He addressed them in clipped tones, his hands clasped behind his back. "I understand that you're mostly interested in the business side of the museum. Just so. But above all else the Travis is an aesthetic enterprise, and I don't want you to leave without seeing the true DNA of the place: our art. So as you're all from Monte Vista, let's head first into the gallery and begin with the paintings we hold by Tristan Wheeler— who, as you know, until recently graced your faculty."

Martin turned and walked briskly to a staircase as the group hurried to follow. Without breaking his pace or making eye contact the curator led the students up the stairs, speaking all the time with flawless diction—never an "uhh" or "umm" in his remarks. "Wheeler's paintings have been more popular than ever since his lamentable death. It's good that you arrived in the morning, before the museum opens. Otherwise you would have had to compete with the crowds around our display."

He slowed as he entered the main gallery. Spearman and Kim walked at his side, while the students fanned out and began to talk. Sensing and resenting even this slight dispersion of focus the curator raised his voice. "There they are: the Wheelers," he announced, pointing to the paintings on the south wall of the spacious room. The works had been hung against a gray plaster wall. Their colors, accented by the museum's state-of-the-art track lighting, were accordingly all the more vibrant and seemed to leap out at the viewer. Martin's voice took on the tone of a schoolmaster. "You can trace here . . . and here . . . and *here* Wheeler's evolution as an artist. The first era shows him to be a competent draftsman with oils. The second era shows him to be a creative genius with oils."

Spearman and Kim, standing off to the side, noticed a change in the curator's expression which was hidden from the class. It had become beatified, almost reverent. His voice lowered as he continued. "I have studied these paintings countless times, standing before them even as you do now. And I tell you frankly that I believe they have few equals in brilliance, in daring, or in demonstrated syncope of idea and action. Only a handful of contemporary artists have risen to this level."

The class went silent. Spearman shot Kim a raised eyebrow, which was returned. Dan the Man seemed to be in awe. Miss Cookie thought, *I think even I could do the abstract stuff—drizzling and spraying paint on a canvas. It's the other work I couldn't do. Painting a ship sailing on the ocean, it'd be hard to get the waves just right.*

Martin shook himself from his reverie and went on. "Of course, a great museum cannot be based on a single artist's work, though there are some exceptions to that rule. Our collection includes art from Ancient Rome, from Asia and from Africa. We're especially proud of our Latin American holdings, particularly the Frida Kahlo and Diego Rivera pieces. We even have Aboriginal art from Australia, on loan to us from the Kluge collection in Virginia. At the Travis we want our guests to sample the best of art, from all schools and eras."

"How come you call them 'guests'?" Cookie interjected.

"I beg your pardon?" Martin said, peering to pick out the questioner from among the group.

Cookie raised her hand to attract his attention. "You just said you want to offer your 'guests' different schools of art. And I wondered why you call them guests."

"Well, simply because we see those who come to view our art as our guests."

"But don't you charge admission?" Cookie asked.

"Yes, of course." Martin seemed mildly irritated. "Like almost all museums, we have a nominal admission fee."

"Well, I just never head of charging a *guest* a *fee*, that's all," Cookie said. Other students nodded.

The curator was momentarily at a loss for words. But he recovered quickly. "In the museum business, 'guest' is a term, shall we say, of *art*." Proud of his pun, he turned his attention back to the larger group. "I'm now going to lead you through some other parts of the Travis. Later we'll retire to one of the lecture rooms downstairs where you'll find some seats and we can continue our discussion. When you leave, I'll take you back up through the museum's gift shop, as I expect you'll want to get something to remember your visit. By that time the shop should be open for business."

•

The group spent the next hour strolling through the various rooms of the Travis. After the students had taken in most of the museum's offerings, Martin motioned them over to a side door marked "Employees Only." "I'm now going to escort you into our 'inner sanctum,' as it were: that part of our facility that most guests never see." He pointed theatrically at their feet. "That's where our preservationists work their wonder. It's where the air handling equipment that keeps all the art at optimal temperature and humidity is located. And, as you'll notice," he said with a conspiratorially arched eyebrow, "it's *also* where we store the wonders that not everyone gets a chance to see."

Over the course of the next thirty minutes the class was exposed to a sizable inventory of art—paintings, manuscripts, furniture, jewelry, and other artifacts—that were not exhibited in the galleries above. Spearman estimated that at least five thousand square feet of space had been devoted to storage. Martin's face beamed as he swung around, pointing to various treasures among the array that the Travis held in its permanent collection. He then guided the students through the double doors of still one more basement anteroom. Tiny black track lights illuminated both its meeting space and the variety of prints that adorned its walls. The chairs, the students gratefully found, were more comfortable than anything on campus.

Once they all were seated, Martin stood before them, a thin wooden lectern at his side. His face bore a similarly thin smile. "So, let's talk about the economics of running a museum. You might well be surprised"—the smile widened a bit, deprecatingly—"to find that the majority of us curators are not exactly MBA types. We are artist wannabes. But we came to realize that we were more talented in the business aspects of art than in being artists. And so we ended up running museums. Had you asked me when I was your age what I would be doing when I was fifty, I can assure you that the very last job I would have guessed would have been curator." Martin hesitated just a moment before continuing. "Right now you are planning for some particular career or job. But by the time you are my age, I can almost promise—and statistics back me up on this— that three-quarters of you will be doing something else, something that you never would have predicted."

Spearman and Kim both noticed how quickly this "promise" got their students' attention. And well it should, Spearman thought. He'd had students whose careers bounced around like the steelie in an old-fashioned pinball machine.

"So what's involved in running a museum? Hmmm." Martin joined his fingers together, bent them outward and cracked his knuckles. "Well, we get money from four main sources. As you just heard, we charge our 'guests' for admission to the museum. If you like, you can call them customers, though I prefer 'guests.'" He fixed Cookie with a disapproving smirk.

"Most people think that museums support themselves by selling tickets. Actually, admission revenue accounts for only a fraction of our revenue base, perhaps 30 percent. As for the other 70 percent? Well . . . we also get money from individuals. 'Patrons' or 'Friends of the Travis,' we call them." Martin paused and looked at the students. "Maybe someday you will decide to be one of these."

The curator then went behind the lectern and leaned on it with his elbows. Surprisingly it held. He rambled on: "Our other revenue 'streams,' as I think you would call them, are relatively shallow and slow-moving. One comes from foundations that support the arts . . . and another from sales at the gift shop. And then," he sighed, "there are the trickles. Very tiny sources of money, like royalties on reproductions of some of our art . . . and people who pay us to hold wedding receptions or social gatherings at the Travis after hours. We've actually found that we can charge quite a bit for those." Martin looked around the room. "But that's it. Questions so far?"

Two hands went up. Martin pointed first to Kelvin. "Mr. Martin, what about art that's given to the Travis? Isn't that a source of revenue?"

The curator looked puzzled. "No," he responded. "When somebody gives us a painting or a sculpture, that's a gift. We don't get any money from it."

"But the art has economic value," Kelvin replied. "So shouldn't it be booked as revenue, just as if someone had given the museum a cash gift? After all, the painting could be turned into cash if you sold it."

"We just wouldn't do it that way," Martin responded. "A gift isn't the same as cash, because like most museums, we don't deaccession our art. We retain possession, even if we don't display it."

Kelvin was not satisfied. "Professor Kim taught us that all gifts have a cash equivalent," he said, leaving his question open. But the curator moved on. Spearman wondered if Martin was dodging the question or whether that really was his answer.

"If there are no further questions on the revenue side of running a museum, let me make a few remarks about what it costs to operate the place. 'It ain't cheap,' as they say. Every curator of every museum in the United States, with the possible exceptions of the Getty in Los Angeles and the government museums in D.C., worries about costs. There's the cost of keeping the lights on; every building has that. Then there are the costs for security, and trust me, they are over and above what other businesses incur. There's wear and tear on the building. And finally, there's the incremental effect of time on the art itself, which we go to great lengths to forestall or avoid. The 'below the iceberg' part of a museum houses the preservationists and equipment that keep our art from deteriorating. The people who can do this are dedicated. But they're also expensive."

Martin stole a quick, surreptitious glance at his watch. The museum would be opening for visitors soon. "Let me see . . . other labor costs are for staff, from the curator like me down to the custodians who keep the place clean. And finally, just like commercial businesses, the Travis needs to hire accountants, lawyers, and HR personnel. All this adds up."

"So how does it finally come out?" Haiyang asked. "Do the revenues exceed the costs for your museum or are you in the hole?"

"We barely scrape by, and many years we *are* in the hole," Martin responded, continuing to lean on the lectern which by appearance seemed to offer little support. "That is the fate of museums in America. We often go begging, hat in hand, to wealthy individuals to make up the difference between what money we take in versus all the expenses we have to shoulder."

"In our field of study, we'd call that an example of Baumol's disease," Kim noted.

"I'm sorry?" Martin said. "What disease?"

"Baumol's disease. William Baumol is a well-known economist who predicted that the performing arts, like symphonies and Shakespeare companies, would be economically stressed in a growing economy—because while overall wages would be rising with the economy, it'd be difficult for performer productivity to increase in similar fashion. A piece of music written for a string quartet requires hiring four musicians, and it always will. There's no way to substitute capital for labor. Baumol's observations about this led to the problem being called Baumol's disease."

"I've heard of Bell's palsy disease, but Baumol's disease is a new one to me. But yes, it sounds as though we are afflicted with a case of it." The curator's face was bland, but his shifting feet indicated that for him, soon, the tour would be over.

At this point Spearman raised his hand. "You mentioned security as an expense of running a museum. Has the cost of this input changed over the years?"

"Yes, very much so. We spend perhaps a million dollars a year for security. It's a huge portion of our budget. The theft of *The Scream* was a wake-up call, even though it took place in Europe. And it isn't just paintings you have to guard these days." Martin looked directly at Spearman. "I believe you're from Harvard, Professor? The Fogg Museum on your campus had a fortune in antique coins stolen from its vault one night. How?"

Martin looked back at the group. "A visitor checked a brown paper bag with security during the day—which happens all the time. He then called just after five p.m. and said he'd forgotten to pick up his bag, that he'd be back in the evening. He came back, rang the night bell to pick up his package and a guard let him in—only to find himself facing the business end of a pistol. Four more men entered, five men left with a priceless collection in their pockets. Every museum director in the country thought: that could have been me. Our guards, just trying to be helpful, might have fallen for that."

"Were the collectors ever caught?" Seth asked.

"Collectors? They weren't *collectors*. They were thieves." Martin's tone of voice allowed for no argument.

"Well yes, that too," Seth responded. "I only meant they were collectors of other people's possessions."

Spearman quickly turned the conversation back to Harvard. "The theft to which you refer took place before I joined the faculty, but I've certainly heard about it. I'm glad to report that the thieves were eventually caught, and that Harvard got most of the coins back. But it wasn't easy." Without pausing he moved to a related topic. "What about the theft of art locally? I read that several Wheeler paintings were stolen from a home near campus last fall. When something like that happens, do you worry about your Wheelers being more at risk and make a response?"

"We do—and we did. That particular theft was at a private residence . . . . one of our board members, as a matter of fact. Cognizant of the demand for Wheeler paintings in the market today, we beefed up security as soon as we heard of the theft. We don't want to lose any of our paintings—to thieves, or collectors, or whatever you care to call them."

At this point, Cookie raised her hand.

"Yes?" Martin said, pointing to Miss Cowgirl.

"What about losing them to other buyers? I mean, what's wrong with selling off some of the art we saw in the basement as a source of revenue?"

Martin's face had a look of annoyance. "That wouldn't be appropriate, Miss. That would be like the queen of England selling the crown jewels."

"But why's that?" Cookie persevered. "You aren't showing the paintings or other stuff we saw stored there. Why not sell some of it off, if the museum is so strapped? That's sure what *I'd* do." She looked around for support. Several heads nodded as the group's attention switched back to Martin.

"It just isn't done," the curator responded stiffly. "There are some things you just don't do." He looked over to Spearman. "Professor, the museum is about to open to the public—to our 'guests'—and I'll need to be upstairs for an appointment with a couple who are prospective donors. Maybe they'll help us find a cure for Baumol's disease. So if you don't mind, I'll take you back to the main floor and leave you at the gift shop."

As they followed Martin upstairs, Spearman turned conversationally to Jennifer Kim. "Did you notice the sign by the door when we came in?" he remarked. "I was struck by the degree of discrimination practiced by the museum."

Martin overheard the comment and, stopping short, whirled to look down at the surprised economists. "I'm afraid I must register a protest, Professor—a vigorous one. The Travis doesn't discriminate." Martin paused for just a moment. "Now I'll grant you, maybe at one time we didn't have the best history of encouraging Latinos to visit the Travis. But those days are over. We're open to all races. I think it would be against the law for us to discriminate—but in any event, we don't." He was frowning at both Henry and Jennifer.

It took Spearman a couple of moments to see through Martin's confusion. "No, no, you misunderstand. We're talking about *price* discrimination, not racial discrimination."

"I don't think we discriminate at all, at least not since I've been the curator here," Martin responded icily, not to be deterred. "I'm opposed to discrimination of any form."

"Well if you are opposed to discrimination of any form, you'll need to take down the sign at the front door."

"I beg your pardon. Which sign?"

Spearman's voice took on its classroom timbre. "We all passed it coming in. I remember the numbers. The sign said the admission price for an adult was six dollars, but for anyone over sixty-five, the price was only three dollars. I presume the marginal cost of having a fifty-year-old customer and a sixty-five-year-old customer is about the same. When a seller of a good or service is charging prices disproportional to marginal costs, there is discrimination going on: price discrimination, that is."

Martin looked both befuddled and annoyed. Spearman continued. "As I recall, the sign at the entrance says the museum also discriminates in price between adults and students, adults and children, and adults and military. So you see, the Travis engages in a lot of discrimination. I was simply telling my colleague that I was struck by the *degree* of discrimination between adults and senior citizens: 100 percent. That seemed large to me. But I assume you and your staff know better than I the relevant demand elasticities that provide the optimal degree of price discrimination. You have more incentive to get it right, certainly."

"Now wait a minute," Martin said. "There's nothing wrong in charging lower prices to senior citizens. That's only fair."

Spearman smiled at Martin and held up his hands in a placating gesture. "I never meant to suggest that there is anything wrong with engaging in discriminatory pricing. You misunderstand me here. But I don't think you discriminate in order to be fair."

"Well, why then? We've always given our senior citizen customers a discount to get into the Travis."

"I suspect you engage in price discrimination because it allows the Travis to capture more revenue than if you charged all visitors the same price. In language most of the students trailing along behind us would use, you're exploiting different demand elasticities in your customer base, and in order to pull it off you are counting on a lack of arbitrage."

"Arbitrage?"

"Resale. You don't expect elderly people to buy blocks of the relatively cheap tickets and stand out front, selling them to adults who haven't yet reached the age of sixty-five."

"We wouldn't want that to happen."

"Precisely," Spearman said. "Arbitrage is the economic death of discrimination. The Travis is fortunate in that arbitrage isn't much of a threat to your pricing strategy. But that's in part because of the amount of discrimination. Imagine what would happen if tickets for senior citizens were available at zero price—and you charged regular adults fifty dollars admission. Then you'd observe an active secondary market in tickets, with some older folks buying them and trying to resell them to younger adults."

Martin frowned. "What you call discriminating in price—I still think it seems fair."

"Again, Mr. Martin, what you're doing may well be fair. I don't have an opinion on that. I'm saying that your pricing strategy is *efficient*. Engaging in price discrimination means that the Travis has a greater output, and you serve more customers than if you charged everyone the same price. And I've no doubt that the Travis makes more money as a result."

Lewis Martin was glad that no one on his Board of Trustees had challenged the museum's practice of price discrimination. If someone did, at this point, he was uncertain whether to disown the practice or defend it.

•

Upstairs in the museum's spacious gift shop, the students were confronted by shelves and counters stocked with books about art, prints, jewelry, apparel and postcards, as well as calendars bearing the images of famous works of art. There were numerous replications of art objects found in the Travis, some quite expensive, others at trinket price points. There were even umbrellas with an artsy theme.

Jennifer Kim turned to Spearman as their students mingled among the aisles and shelves. "Europeans may love to sit alongside boulevards, drink coffee, and talk about the affairs of the world. But one thing you have to say about Americans: they get out and shop."

Spearman responded, "Yes, they do." He looked at the line of students already waiting their turn at the cash register. "In America, we know how to turn going to a museum into the equivalent of going to the mall. To quote Yakov Smirnoff: 'What a country!'"

•

Having waived the usual admission fee, the Travis Museum of Art had nonetheless made a good investment hosting the Monte Vista field trip. By the time Spearman's students got on the bus for the trip back to campus, the gift shop had taken in several hundred dollars of additional revenue. *Nice*, Henry thought. *But not enough to cure Baumol's disease.*

During their ride to campus the two professors sat at the front of the bus. Rather than talk to each other, they attempted to catch what they could of the students' chatter. Spearman could not pick up what was being said at the back, but behind him he heard Dan in conversation with Cookie. "You know what I think? I think Martin's museum had a bullet fly by."

"Why's that?" Cookie asked.

"Because the Travis depends a lot on admissions revenue. And Martin wants to make the Wheeler paintings the big draw."

"So . . . what bullet flew by?"

Dan leaned forward, raising his voice slightly for the benefit of heads that were turning around. "Wheeler had this thing for open art—where his paintings would one day be reproduced, I mean reproduced *exactly*, by some kind of computer technology. Let's say you wanted a Wheeler painting. You'd download it and go to someplace like Kinko's and get it printed by a three dimensional printer. What you'd walk out with would be just like the real thing.

"So if Wheeler had had his way, and everyone could get what they wanted at Kinko's, like who'd go to the museum? Right?" He looked around. There were obviously no light bulbs appearing anywhere above his listeners. He tried again. "It would be like what's happening to Crampton. Who goes to the main library to do research for a paper anymore? You just pull off the stuff you need online and print it. I still go to the library because it's a good place to hang out with friends. But nobody's going to go to the Travis just to meet their buds."

"So where's the printer that can print in three dimensions?" Cookie asked.

"It doesn't exist—yet. But Wheeler was weird. He saw all this happening. He said that someday soon they'd be painting paintings not with brushes and canvas, but by having the artist's vision actually coded and integrated within some laser machining fabricator. It would be like, you know, the replicators in *Star Trek*. And he thought this would revolutionize how people viewed art. I heard Wheeler and Martin fight about it when Martin visited our class. That guy's pretty old-school, as you could tell. He thought reproducing fine art would debase it. Called it 'commodification' and told Wheeler he needed to understand that great art was *never* mass produced. Said it was absurd to think it could be, or ever should be."

The students' discussion soon turned to other technological frontiers, and the ripple effects their crossing would generate. But Spearman was no longer following the conversation.

He was thinking.

21

CLASS ACTION

THURSDAY, JANUARY 26ᵀᴴ

Economics should come back into the conversation of
mankind. It is an extraordinarily clever way of speaking,
and can do a lot of good. The way to bring it back is to
persuade economists that they are not so very different
from poets and novelists.

—DEIRDRE MCCLOSKEY

Spearman walked into the classroom promptly at nine
a.m. and put his attaché case on the table. He wasted no
time on preliminaries. "Today we have three topics to
cover. We're going to cover the pricing of art, the distribution of art, and the question of art and externalities.
That's a lot—so fasten your seat belts, okay?" Henry took
off his glasses and put them on the lectern. For a moment,
he appeared lost in thought. Twenty students sat before
him, some with expressions of anticipation, others with
apprehension.

"You've read some articles that claim the pricing of art
is different than the demand and supply model of price
formation" he began. "That art prices only go up, like a
ratchet. 'Ratchet,' that's the term that's used. What does
that mean?"

To Spearman, a price ratchet had no grounding in conventional economic analysis. He remembered how at times his father had to discount the price of his tailoring services to retain the patronage of certain customers. His father couldn't simply keep raising his price, as much as he might have liked to. What, Spearman wondered, would make the market for paintings any different? "And I'd like to hear from someone who has not spoken up much in class so far," he added.

Iso, a third-year student from Turkey, slowly raised his hand and got Spearman's nod. "The idea of the ratchet is that, say, a painting by some famous artist sells for twenty million. The buyer of the next painting by that artist would be willing to pay more than twenty million, because that gives the new buyer the bragging rights of having paid the most for that artist. So the ratchet begins. And the ratchet continues this way onward and upward, so art prices go up and up and up and never down."

Henry nodded. "Good. Iso, let me then ask you this: how is what you just described different from price determination in a competitive market?"

"Well, the demand and supply model predicts that prices are determined by both demand and supply, and they can go up and go down, not just up." Encouraged by Spearman's answering smile, the student continued, pointing out a peculiarity he'd noted in the assigned art magazines: they wrote only about *escalating* prices. They did not report how work by the same artist could be discounted if market forces were pushing prices down.

At this point class discussion began to revolve around the difference between a list price and a transaction price.

Several students pointed out that dealers and galleries could discount off list prices with slow moving items—leaving the art magazines either unaware of the transaction prices, or inclined against publishing them. If galleries were to report the actual transaction prices paid by their customers, the class noted, the data would soon draw the attention of economists.

Cookie pointed out that the work of artists often was sold to museums at heavily discounted prices, but that the prices were not made public—unlike transactions made at auction. "Take artists like Ed Ruscha and Sandro Chia, who were hot in the nineties but not anymore. The prices of their art didn't ratchet up when their art lost favor. Just the opposite: in demand and supply terms, demand shifted to the left and market prices fell. In some cases, the fall in price wasn't observed because there was no longer an active market for their art anymore."

After several minutes of back-and-forth Spearman summarized the class discussion: "I think we can all agree that dealers don't want to discount the paintings of the artists they represent. They make less money on the sales, and no doubt a fall in value upsets prior buyers who paid higher prices. But there is nothing in economic logic that enables dealers to predict and stem a decline in demand, simply because they don't like the ensuing economic unpleasantness it creates." Henry retrieved his glasses from the lectern, put them on, and addressed the class. "Now what did I say was next on the class agenda?" In fact he knew very well, but wanted to see if the class had been paying attention.

"Distribution," Walter responded.

"Yes, or what in B-school lingo would be called marketing. Let me start with a hypothetical question, and I'll put it to you, Walter." Walter sat up in his chair. "Assume you're a famous artist. You aren't Jasper Johns or Damien Hirst—not yet anyway. But you're very well known. And not only that, you think you have a long career ahead of you. Would you want your art distributed widely through a number of galleries, or just one?" Before Walter could respond, Spearman added, "The question I've put to you may seem to belong in a marketing class. But it's economic logic that supplies the answer." Spearman moved to the side of the classroom and hoisted himself up on the window ledge, his feet dangling above the floor, waiting for Walter's answer.

Walter hesitated before responding, "Well, I *think* I'd want lots of galleries selling my art, so customers would have wide access to my work. But I know from our readings that most artists have exclusive sales arrangements with just one gallery. So I reckon there's something wrong with my reasoning. But . . . I'm not sure what." He began to slouch back in his chair.

Spearman looked out over the class, and waited . . . and waited. He was not going to explain his own hypothetical. After what seemed a long time, Anita spoke up. "I can see what Walter's saying. I'm from Houston. Having lots of galleries in Houston selling Walter's paintings would seem like the best way to go. But there's an economic reason for giving an exclusive right to just one gallery. A gallery with an exclusive has a greater incentive to promote Walter's work, because that gallery knows that it, and it alone, will get the money from any demand increase generated by its own promotion."

Spearman gave a nod toward Anita but then turned back to Walter. "You're not off the hook just yet. What would happen if some dealer in Houston didn't have an exclusive on your art, but nonetheless spent a lot of resources promoting your work there?"

"Some other gallery that didn't incur all those costs could benefit from the increased demand, and might end up making more profit than the dealer who paid for the promotion."

Spearman kept his gaze on Walter: "What would we call that dealer?"

"'Clever,' maybe?" he said with a smile on his face. "Or maybe a pirate?"

"No, this is an economics class. Let's use the right lingo. What's the dealer called?"

"Free rider," Cookie spoke up. "That's the term we learned in our industrial organization class."

"And what's the term that describes a market shot through with free riding?," Spearman pressed.

"Market failure," Cookie responded. "Because consumers who want the kind of marketing services that the exclusive dealer offered won't be able to find them—the free-riding dealer makes it too unprofitable for the other dealer to survive. So the market doesn't do what consumers want." When Cookie had finished, Spearman thought to himself, "This is why I like teaching."

Dan the Man's hand shot up. "Of course, if art was all for free there'd be no free riders, right? Competition and pirating supposedly wouldn't happen. I've heard Tristan Wheeler tee off on that." He glanced over at Jennifer Kim. "But when Professor Kim heard him go on about free art, she set him straight. Do you remember that time?"

Before Kim could respond the student turned and grinned at the class. "I wish you all could have seen the sparks fly. Like, I was pulling for Tristan at first, but she nailed him. He was going on about freedom and art and the purpose of mankind, on and on, and then she just smiled, talked about costs and incentives, and *swept the legs.* The score ended up: 'Economic Analysis 1, Art for Free zip.'" Dan laughed again, oblivious to the unease that the mention of Wheeler's name brought into the room. "No offense to Tristan but it was a total smack."

Spearman glanced at Jennifer. He saw that her lips had compressed into a thin, tight line. She sat facing straight ahead, as immobile as a piece of cast sculpture. A moment's observation was all he needed. Quickly and smoothly he took back the floor. "Thank you Dan, for scoring it so highly for the economists." Turning his back to the class Spearman walked to the board at the front of the classroom, and pulled open a marker. "'EXTERNALITIES,'" he intoned, writing the word in block capitals. "Who can give me a definition?"

Virtually every hand went up. Spearman called on the one student who always seemed eager to speak in class. Pete did not disappoint. As though reading from an introductory textbook, the class clown turned pedantic: "A negative externality is when a private market transaction imposes costs on someone who isn't party to the transaction." He grinned and looked around. "Pause . . . for effect," he added. As the class laughed he continued. "If a transaction produces a benefit for some third party, on the other hand, then that's a positive externality."

Spearman welcomed the levity that diffused the tension. "And what does the economist's concept of externality have to do with the market for art?" he asked.

Several hands went up, but Pete continued, "Art supposedly confers positive externalities on the general public. So like, when someone buys a work of art and maintains it, I might get the benefit of it by being able to look at it sometime, or look at it in a book, or check it out digitally. That's not the case when someone buys, say, a toaster. There's no externality that affects me as a third party."

"Let's assume there is a positive externality in the production of art," Spearman continued the thread. "What does economics teach about positive externalities?" Class consensus held that if there was a positive externality from the production of art, then the government needed to step in and subsidize it—because the unfettered market mechanism alone would be incapable of generating sufficient supply . . . just as it tended to produce too little of any purely public good, such as national defense. Noting the general agreement that the supply of art had positive externalities, Spearman asked who then should decide what art, or artists, should be subsidized—and what art, or artists, shouldn't be?

"Ought elected politicians decide?" he asked. No one seemed inclined to defend the idea that congressmen, governors, or even mayors should hand out money to artists.

"The artists themselves?" Everyone agreed that the arts community would then have incentives to oversubsidize art, because the money went into their pockets.

"A government bureau that decides which artists get subsidized?" The class discussed what they had read about the National Endowment of the Arts, how it operated, and how its budget had been determined. No one seemed enthused about a government bureaucrat picking which artists conferred positive externalities, which ones got public funding, and which ones didn't.

As the discussion reached the point of diminishing returns, Kelvin spoke up. "I don't think there should be *any* subsidy. None at all. Not because we can't agree on who dishes out the money or how much . . . but because we know, empirically, that subsidies don't work. In the Netherlands the Dutch tried subsidizing artists. The government simply bought their art, so a great many artists sold their work only to the government—mainly because no one else was willing to pay much for it. Eventually, the Dutch government realized it was accumulating rooms full of art and ended the subsidy. The economic irony is that when the subsidy ended, and the government began selling off all this art, the increase in supply *depressed* art prices—which in turn harmed the artists who'd refused the subsidy, and who'd been putting their art out there to meet a market test."

Cookie, whom Henry and Jennifer both thought was the best read student in the class, had her hand up while Kelvin was speaking. As soon as her classmate finished she burst in. "Look, we have another market test. It's France. Here's the country that gives the world Renoir, Cezanne, Pissarro, Monet, Manet, Lautrec . . . I mean, the list goes on and on. But what about now?" Cookie's question was rhetorical. "Today the French Ministry of Culture subsidizes art. I mean, like the French government subsidizes art tons more than the National Endowment in the U.S. does. *Tons* more. But can anyone name a living French artist who would rank in the top twenty contemporary artists?" No one responded. "I rest my case," Cookie said with a look of pleasure on her face.

"Cookie," Spearman teased, "you may end up a rodeo star after you graduate, but if that doesn't work out there's a career waiting for you in law. For the rest of us, our class time is up. Let me remind you that I have office hours this afternoon."

As the students packed up their belongings, the buzz of conversation began to fill the air. Spearman pulled together his notes and inserted them in his briefcase. He then paused, looking for Jennifer Kim. He had sensed her discomfort during the class. But her seat was empty.

As one row exited, a student clapped a hand on Dan the Man's back. "Nice one, genius. They used to date, remember?" Sheepishly, Dan nodded and the two hitched up their backpacks and left the room, already laughing over other topics.

Spearman remained in the classroom for some time, leaning against the table, deep in thought. Then he snapped out of it. The class was over. Once again, he had not been carried out of the building on the shoulders of the students. But he returned to his office with a deep sense of satisfaction that this class period had come within shouting distance. Maybe someday, he smiled.

22

AN ARTIST'S EULOGY

Some are born weird, some achieve it, others have weirdness thrust upon them.

—DICK FRANCIS

After the Bexar County coroner's finding of suicide, Wheeler's body had been released and subsequently turned over to his family. An evening memorial service was soon organized, to be held in the Richman Chapel of Monte Vista University.

The chapel sat at the corner of the campus, a large red brick building with a copper cross attached to the front. Its construction had begun almost as soon as the university opened its doors, with blueprints that called for a sanctuary large enough to hold all of Monte Vista's students for a worship service. Those days had long since passed, however—leaving it as a venue for weddings, student groups, and special academic ceremonies. On Friday evening the 27th of January, it would be a place to honor the dead.

Annelle Cubbage and Charlotte Quinn stood at the entrance, greeting those who came to pay their last respects. Visitors were offered a chance to sign a guestbook before being diverted to their seats, where programs detailing the order of service had been laid. Inserts within the programs also offered an opportunity to make a contribution to the Travis Museum in Wheeler's memory.

The body of the deceased lay in a closed casket at the front of the sanctuary. Members of Wheeler's family occupied the front row, while the second seated the four faculty from the university's Department of Art. Michael Cavanaugh, the senior member of the department, sat on the aisle. This foursome had been asked by the parents to serve as pallbearers along with Tristan's brother and sister. In the third row were representatives of the two major art museums in San Antonio, the McNay and the Travis.

Henry had decided to attend the service. His decision had little to do with the fact that he lived on the same street. He and Pidge were "neighbors" of Tristan Wheeler only in the geographic sense of the term, and had never had the opportunity to be "neighborly." However, Henry was teaching about art and economics—and Wheeler was the local artist of fame and status. In addition, he realized it might prove his last opportunity to learn more about Wheeler himself. *Plus, the transaction costs of my attendance are low,* he reasoned. *The chapel is only a three-block walk from our home.* After being seated he looked around. The number of women present exceeded the number of men, that was evident. Jocelyn Abraham was present. Herbert was not.

Whispers subsided into silence as Lewis Martin left his seat in the third row to deliver the eulogy. From a lectern near the casket, glancing occasionally at a three by five card, Martin spoke softly: "We mourn here today the loss of Tristan Wheeler, an artist of great talent. Our friend chose not to display his skills for his own sake. Instead he presided over the creation of works that brought visual pleasure to those who love art.

"In Wheeler's earliest canvases he chose as subject matter representational works which drew and deserved much admiration from his peers: landscapes, vases of flowers, and bowls of fruit These serve today to remind us of that down-to-earth integrity which we all came to associate with his character.

"And yet even these early works, painted while he was yet in his twenties, have such an aura of tranquility and simplicity that they leave the observer speechless. They are aquiver with the vitality and certainty which we associate with the sublime. At the time they drew offers of one-man exhibitions from dealers throughout the country. While sales to the masses were few, people of artistic discernment were deeply impressed. Although evocative of a passing era of artistic temperament, these early paintings of Wheeler were powerfully predictive of an even richer future.

"In recent years Tristan became enamored by the potential marriage of art and digital technology. He considered Linux software to be a model for the free distribution of art, and he considered Linus Torvalds to be an artist himself. We shall never fully understand what influences took Wheeler down this peculiar path. But with his death we can forgive him this folly, surely. His aesthetic sensitivities overshadowed his business insensibility." As he warmed to his remarks, Martin's words took on the cadence of a revivalist preacher.

"Tristan Wheeler accepted the homage of his contemporaries but refused to submit to the aesthetic dictates of others. After an intense year reflecting on Pollock's oeuvre, Tristan abruptly changed his style to traverse a different path. He committed himself to the unbridled indulgence of his subconscious mind. Although only in his early thirties, Tristan immersed himself in an aesthetic revolution, out of which emerged those marvelous abstractions which rendered representational imagery as passé and obsolete as the cave paintings in Lascaux." Martin's voice rose and fell as he moved to his concluding remarks.

"These colorful paintings, which reveal the somber richness of his torrid, liquid hues are now visible on the walls of contemporary museums around the country: and not only in the Travis Museum of Art, I am gratified to report, but in the prescient homes of those happy few of keen discernment. Because of his all-too-early death, Wheeler's paintings in this style are few in number. But looked at in total, they have a transcendental quality that contains only intimations of what might have been . . . if Tristan Wheeler had lived to attain the biblical four score and ten." Martin dabbed at his eyes with a handkerchief. His voice had a slight quaver.

"Alas, it was not to be. Wheeler goes to his resting place with the secret of his artistic talent inviolate. He did not share it with others. Indeed, I suspect that even he only partly understood that secret himself. What remains are those glowing presences he left behind for us to enjoy, and from which we will take inspiration for the rest of our days."

•

The memorial service left Spearman dissatisfied. What he wanted to learn about Wheeler hadn't been illumined, had not even been mentioned. His facial expression showed respect for the sobriety of the occasion. But Pidge would have seen through it, and recognized that her husband had found Martin's remarks to be unctuous and vapid. Shakespeare's famous aside about life—"a tale told by an idiot, full of sound and fury, signifying nothing"—went through his mind.

As the funeral ended mourners milled about on the sidewalk outside the chapel. In muted tones, they exchanged greetings and grimly discussed the emotions they felt. But while others lingered in the courtyard, Spearman walked directly away from the chapel, his mouth without its usual smile, his eyes looking straight-ahead, without their usual twinkle. His breath showing in the cool night air, he drifted away from the crowd.

As he walked in the direction of Oakmont Court he heard a voice. "Mind if I join you, professor?" It was Detective Fuller. Without waiting for a response she sidled up next to Spearman. "My car's parked in front of your place, so it looks like we're going the same way."

"So it appears."

The two walked in silence until they turned onto Oakmont Court. Fuller then broke the ice. "I go to this service to see who shows up, Professor. Not to pay my respects. And what do you know, I see you." She glanced to see if Henry's face registered any emotion. It didn't. "Now I know you don't know Wheeler. You told me that when we first met. So I ask myself, is this guy here to pay his respects to someone he doesn't even know? And then I noticed your wife isn't with you, that you go all by yourself. And I wonder why that's the case, if you're going because that's the good neighbor thing to do. And *then* I notice

you don't talk to anybody after the service. So I'm thinking, maybe because he's new in town, he doesn't know
anyone else. But then I think—if he doesn't know anyone
else, and he doesn't know Wheeler, why show up?"

"Economists like to quote the old saying, detective: *de
gustibus non est disputandum*—it means there's no accounting for tastes. Maybe I just like memorial services."

Nonplussed, the detective continued. "There are people
like that in San Antonio. They show up at every funeral in
town. They usually don't cause any trouble, and there's
nothing we can do about it unless they do. But somehow
you don't strike me as a serial funeral attender."

"I'm teaching a course in art and economics this semester at Monte Vista. Wheeler was the BMOC when it came
to art. And as you can see, the transaction costs of attendance are low. Ah, here we are—almost back to my place."

As they passed the Wheeler residence, Fuller saw Spearman's house come into view, her unmarked car parked in
front. She tried to keep the conversation going. "When we
first met you'd just arrived. Bet you didn't know you were
moving into such a bad neighborhood, eh? I mean, last
semester there was a break-in at the house next door. Then
there's Wheeler's death—which was almost next door to
you on the other side. I mean, it must make you wonder,
doesn't it?"

Spearman did not respond immediately. "I thought
Wheeler's death was suicide," he finally said, as he approached the walkway to his home. "Is it a criminal matter
in Texas to take your own life?"

"I work homicide, professor, so that always makes me
suspicious about suicides. I know what the evidence says,

but I also know other things too. I know that Herbert Abraham threatened Tristan Wheeler in front of a crowd. I know Wheeler left a trail of emotional breakups behind him. I know that Sean Daniels was left a sizeable chunk of change in Wheeler's will. My gut tells me this wasn't suicide. What does your gut tell you?"

"I just do economics, Detective. Economics has a way of thinking about the world that's not based on instincts. We have a theory as to when it would be optimal to take your own life."

At that point, a muffled ring came from Fuller's pocket. She paused. "Hold on professor. I gotta call coming in." She held the phone to her ear for just a few seconds and then said, "Got it." The detective turned and began to walk away. "Have to go, professor. You may be hearing from me soon."

"What is it?" Henry asked.

As she walked off, Fuller turned back and smiled. "A piece of resistance."

●

"Is that you, Henry?" Pidge called from the den. "How was the service? Are you glad you went?"

"I'm afraid the candid answer is no," Spearman replied as he closed the front door behind him. He spoke briefly with Pidge about the service and his unexpected encounter with Detective Fuller. Then he retreated to his study—and paced. As he strode from one side of the room to the other, his thoughts turned to his religious faith—or, rather, its absence. In college he had abandoned the orthodoxy of his parents' Judaism. But because Spearman possessed an excellent memory, it had been difficult for him to shake the recollections of his time in Hebrew school when he was a boy growing up in Brooklyn. The memorial service had prompted Spearman to recall what the Talmud taught about suicide. He remembered the words, or at least a paraphrase of them: "For him who takes his own life with full knowledge of his action, no rites will be observed—no rending of clothes, no eulogy."

Did Wheeler take his life with "full knowledge"? Spearman thought that no one could prepare a noose for himself and stand on a chair without having full knowledge of his action. Wheeler was not Jewish, Spearman reasoned, at least from the sound of his name. But if he had been, would a rabbi today perform a rite of burial? Monte Vista University had permitted a eulogy to take place in the school's chapel. But the university was not a synagogue. And Lewis Martin, who gave the eulogy, was not a clergyman of any faith. He was a curator.

While acknowledging that religion was a source of comfort to many, Spearman had concluded that it was not for him. This had been a source of great disappointment to his parents, which had in turn caused discomfort to him. He sat down and began to scroll through his Harvard email account. He hoped this would rid his mind of Hebrew school memories . . . but just the opposite took place. As he read an email about changes in the Harvard health plan, up popped the memory of a neighborhood boy he had not thought about for years: Lenny Steinman, excitedly raising his hand in Hebrew school when the rabbi was teaching about suicide. "What about King Saul? What

about King Saul? When the Philistines defeated the Israel-
ites, the Bible says that King Saul fell on his sword. Wasn't
that suicide?" Lenny asked. Spearman recalled how Lenny
earnestly wanted to know the answer to such questions.
And Henry realized, with some sadness, that he had never
really cared what happened to King Saul.

Spearman viewed the world only through the lens of
economics. The rational actor model, to his mind, made
the most sense of human behavior. But where did suicide
fit in? Was it an exception that proved the cost-benefit rule?

As he stood up again to pace, Spearman tried to perform a cost-benefit metric of his own death by suicide.
The benefits? Suicide could mean the avoidance of possible debilitating disease, the pain of an incurable mental illness, or a terrorist attack on a plane. But these were
benefits that had to be discounted by very low probabil-
ities of occurrence. The costs of suicide? As he returned
to his desk, the opportunities that suicide would forego
flooded his mind: time with Pidge, time with their daughter, his research, his classroom experiences, his friendships
with colleagues like Henderson Ross, his opportunities to
teach the mystery of the invisible hand. For him, it would
be a bad deal. Had that been the case with Wheeler, he
wondered?

23

LOST & FOUND

Works of art, which represent the highest level of spiritual production, will find favor in the eyes of the bourgeois only if they are presented as being liable to directly generate material wealth.

—KARL MARX

Geographically speaking, the two men were very close: they lived right next door to each other. But at the personal level, they were not close at all. The relationship between Henry Spearman and Raul Ramos had gotten off to a bad start and had scarcely moved since, with the two men having little contact following their initial encounter shortly after the Spearmans' arrival. A few wooden hand waves were all that transpired between the two.

Pidge, on the other hand, had become well acquainted with Rosie Segura. She was helping Dr. Ramos's housekeeper complete her GED while Rosie, in exchange, helped Pidge improve her Spanish. As a consequence Henry was accustomed to seeing Pidge and Rosie together in the yard—or, when Rosie was not working, at the Spearmans' dining room table, while the two talked back and forth in Spanish.

Henry was therefore all the more surprised to see Dr. Ramos bound into his yard that Sunday morning, a broad smile on his face. "I want you to be one of the first to know, my paintings are back." It took Spearman a moment to grasp the meaning of the doctor's words. Ramos continued to exude. "They're back! The cattle are back in the corral," he laughed.

"You mean the Wheeler paintings, the ones stolen last fall?"

"Exactly! Yes, they're all back, with only one damaged, and even that isn't too bad."

"Really? When did this happen?" Henry's surprise was unfeigned. Like the police, he had assumed those cattle gone for good.

"Just last night. Late. I got them back. I'm about to call Detective Siegfried and give him the news. The police investigation isn't going anywhere, anymore, but I need to let him know that he can stop."

"You mean the police weren't involved in their return?" Henry queried.

"Oh no, no. It was because the police were *not* involved that I got them back. Five days ago I got this little white envelope in my mailbox—it wasn't mailed, mind you, no postage, no postmark, *nothing*—just put in the box, with a note inside telling me that if I had two hundred fifty thousand cash, I could get the paintings back. A quarter of a million. That's a lot of money, but way less than the value of the paintings. And a *lot* less than the million dollar reward I'd offered. But"—the doctor looked sideways at Henry, wagging his finger as if in warning—"the note *also* said if I got the police involved, the deal was off; that

I'd regret telling the police because the paintings would be destroyed."

"So what did you do?" Spearman asked.

"You can imagine what I was thinking. If I called the police, there was a chance they'd figure out who the thieves were based on the ransom note ... or maybe catch them when I turned over the money. And I'd have the paintings back.

"But then I thought—what if the thieves had it figured right? If I got the police involved, they'd make good on their promise and I'd *never* get the paintings back. A lot of stolen art is never seen again."

Ramos shook his head as if to clear it, and then looked back to Henry.

"And *then* I thought: what if I pay two hundred fifty grand, and this guy or these guys, whoever they are, don't even have the paintings? There was nothing special in the note, no inside stuff that only the thief would know. It could've been a scam from someone who read about it in the news. Then I'd be out all the ransom money, with my only reward feeling stupid for not calling the police. It was a real dilemma, I'm telling you." Henry withheld his condolences. The look of satisfaction on Ramos's face bespoke a dilemma that had been solved.

"So," he continued, "the next day—Tuesday—I got another envelope in my mailbox. A manila envelope, one of those big brown envelopes you can put a magazine in. The first envelope was more like a letter. I wish now I'd watched the mailbox, or put a surveillance camera on it. But, stupid me—what do I know? Anyway, this big envelope had a note inside that said *in case you're wondering whether we really have your paintings.* And stuck down inside the envelope beside it was a piece of canvas. When I shook it out I recognized it right away. It was the corner of one of Tristan's paintings. I tell you Professor, when I looked at the piece of canvas, *whew*. It may as well have been the kid's ear."

"The kid's ear?" Henry asked, trying to follow Ramos's rat-a-tat speaking speed.

"Don't you remember? It was in all the news awhile back. The grandson of John Paul Getty, one of the richest men in the world, was kidnapped in Italy. The kidnappers wanted millions to return the boy. The grandfather didn't believe it at first, reckoned it to be a hoax—until he got a package with part of the kid's ear inside. The note said that if the ransom wasn't paid, that was how Getty would get his grandson back: in pieces.

"I never forgot that story. Gave me the chills, maybe because I'm a surgeon and I know that ears don't just come off easily. I couldn't bear the thought of getting the Wheeler paintings back in bits and pieces. So that was it. I did what they asked. I didn't call the police, I swallowed hard and paid the two hundred fifty grand—in cash. I think they call it a drop."

"Where did you meet up?" Spearman asked.

Ramos winced. "Now, this is where it gets weird. It took place right where we're standing, in the driveway between our houses, in the middle of the night. Two guys came up to me in the dark, one of them waving a gun. I don't know if they had a car or not. They may have snuck through the alley behind our houses, maybe? But they showed me the paintings, I showed them the money, we swapped and they were gone . . . vanishing behind me while I faced forward and counted to fifty. It was so simple I didn't have time to be scared. And now I have the paintings back."

Spearman wanted to ask why he was being told all this. He got his answer.

"I'd like you and your wife—who's been great with Rosie, by the way—to come over and see the paintings. Just so you can tell me I'm not in a dream of some kind." Ramos chuckled again. "The paintings didn't even have the wires taken off, and I never took the hooks down from my walls. So I've hung them back right where they were."

Henry excused himself and went back inside, where he found Pidge making coffee in the kitchen. The two then accompanied Ramos across the yard and into his house. He led them directly to the living room wall, now ablaze with color as the early morning sun glanced across the returned paintings. "There they are! But at this point, I can't say for how long. I learned a lesson from all this: leave really valuable art in the hands of really wealthy collectors, or at least with those whose homes have better security systems than mine. It's either sell them, donate them, or ante up and get a foolproof security system."

"Do you know how they were stolen?" Pidge asked.

"Don't I wish," Ramos replied. "The notes didn't say and the guys in my driveway didn't slap me on the back, thank me for being a good sport, and tell me how they did it." He laughed at his own joke. "That's a mystery that may never be solved."

At that point Rosie entered the room. Dr. Ramos could see surprise, even fear, on her face. "It's okay, Rosie, I invited the Spearmans in. I wanted them to tell me if I was dreaming or not. They've assured me that the paintings are right here before our eyes and not my imagination. I also wanted Professor Spearman to see them himself. I know he teaches about art and economics. Perhaps there's been a lesson in all this that he can share with his students."

•

Pidge had returned from the Ramos house and was catching up on correspondence with friends and family, including a long phone conversation with Patricia. Meanwhile, Henry had decided to indulge in the time-honored American custom of taking a Sunday afternoon nap on the couch. He had risen from his sleep and was just beginning to head upstairs to work on a research paper when the phone rang. It was Detective Fuller.

"Hi Professor. Well . . . it looks like we were right." Before Spearman could respond she continued. "Something's come up that has turned things upside down. The case is going to be reopened, and they're dropping the finding of suicide. Lieutenant's on board with it, and so is the ME. And so am I." There was a pause. "You're close with the Daniels kid. Abraham too. So I thought I'd give you a head's up."

Her statement was met with silence. Fuller wondered if the phone connection had been broken. Finally Henry spoke. "Thank you. As you said, I'm not altogether surprised. May I ask what the new evidence is?"

"Sure. It's a letter Wheeler wrote, dated January 10th— the day before the body was found. Recipient was out of the country on some academic junket. No question it's

Wheeler's, either—beautiful flowing script, ink from his fancy pen—it's got everything but illuminated capitals."

There was a pause, while Fuller searched for the letter among the many papers on her desk. "Ah, here we are. Yep. One read kind of knocks the stuffing out of the suicide theory. Listen: 'Can't wait to see you when you get back from the Netherlands, you hidebound old gorilla. If I have to drag you and the entire art community kicking and screaming into the 21st century I'm ready and waiting . . . momentum for Free Art is gaining every day . . . I'm even scheduled to speak at a conference with Torvalds in 2 weeks. Yours, etc.'" She stopped. "Doesn't sound much like a guy who's ready to hang himself, does it?"

There was silence on both ends of the line. Spearman finally closed the conversation. "Nice of you to call, detective. That's certainly an interesting development." Without waiting for a response he hung up the phone and slowly, distractedly walked out of the room and up the stairs. A great many things were whirling through his mind.

24

AN ARRESTING DEVELOPMENT

The cops aren't exactly dumb, you know. We can get our own answers.

—MICKEY SPILLANE

Students at Monte Vista had been in trouble with the law before. The offenses were usually confined to disturbing the peace, public intoxication, or speeding; and because these illegalities almost always occurred on Saturday or Sunday, they generally stayed on the plate of the dean of students until Monday—when the university's Public Relations Office might have to deal with any consequences for the school's reputation.

On the Monday of January 30th the offense was far more serious than the adverse consequences of an intoxicated student. To be sure, the offense did not involve a *current* Monte Vista student; but the person involved was a recent graduate. In fact, he was currently employed as an assistant *by* Monte Vista. And perhaps most problematic of all for the school's public relations staff, the alleged criminal activity was murder.

It all began with a curt announcement on local radio and television affiliates: the Bexar County medical

277

examiner had withdrawn her ruling of suicide in the case of Tristan Wheeler, as a result of new evidence that indicated criminal conduct. At a hastily called press conference soon thereafter, Detective Sherry Fuller said that, yes, the police did have a suspect, and yes, steps had indeed been taken to arrest him.

The apprehension that followed was as quickly accomplished as it was impressively staged. Sean Daniels, bicycling to campus, found his path blocked by a police motorcycle and a squad car as he approached the north gate of the school. As dozens of students and a handful of faculty looked on, a second car—with flashing red and blue lights—pulled in behind him. Before he could turn around, two officers identified him and read him his rights. Within two minutes Daniels was handcuffed, stuffed head first into the back of the second squad car, and taken away.

If speed of information dissemination was an NCAA-sanctioned sport, Monte Vista University would have been a contender for a national championship. Before ninety minutes had passed, virtually every student on campus had become aware of Daniels's arrest. Only professors hidden away in offices or library carrels could have remained uninformed of the breaking news. For some, the arrest made was overdue. Others disagreed. For still others, their interest was propelled solely by curiosity. These were the people who got utility from gawking at a serious automobile accident.

One person who derived no utility from Daniels's arrest was a galvanized and furious Annelle Cubbage. She swung into action. Jim Bowie could not have been any faster with his knife. As soon as she learned of Daniels's arrest, a phone rang in the Washington, D.C., office of Williams and Connolly, the law firm of choice for many high-profile white-collar defendants.

Within a few hours, a representative of the firm had arrived at the jail and was requesting to meet with Daniels. Following arraignment, bail was set—and quickly paid. By the time the sun went down, Sean Daniels—complete with his bicycle, which had been retrieved from the impound—was sitting, dazed and exhausted, in the apartment where his day had begun. His pocket contained the signed copies of his arrest and release. By the following morning, newspapers across Texas had made front-page room for his photo above or below the fold.

A preliminary hearing was set for March 10. For those responsible for protecting and promoting the Monte Vista University brand, the press coverage was seen as a mini-disaster that had staffers scrambling. The Public Relations Office held out little hope that news of the arrest of Sean Daniels would have a short shelf life. They prepared for maximum damage control. But as the fourth estate began to puff the news about Daniels, Annelle Cubbage's efforts trumped the local media and helped kept a precarious lid on the story.

As for Sean Daniels, he was formally charged with the first degree murder of Tristan Wheeler. Date for trial was given as April 27th—which also happened to be end of the semester, and the final meeting of Henry Spearman's Art and Economics class. Weeks of legal maneuvering were to follow as Hill Country days got hot and class projects neared their completion.

25

THE DEATH EFFECT

THURSDAY, APRIL 20TH

Anything wrong leaves a kind of impression on the eye; brain trots along afterwards with the warning. I saw when I came in, only just grasped it.

—DOROTHY L. SAYERS

T. S. Eliot claimed that April was the cruelest month. Literary critics speculate that Eliot meant the weather. However, Spearman liked to joke that Eliot was complaining about federal income taxes being due on April 15. He often amused himself by imagining the celebrated poet struggling to complete his tax returns on the night of the fourteenth. *That*, Spearman thought, would be a cruel writing task for anyone. But there was nothing bad about the weather this April morning in San Antonio. The warm temperature and bright sunlight made their way into Henry's office, brightening it as he sat down at his desk.

This particular morning, Spearman was about to violate a cardinal rule. He not only followed it in his own career, but when asked would commend it to new faculty at Harvard. The rule was to never schedule anything—not a meeting, conference call, checking email, *anything*—an hour before teaching a class. That hour was to be allocated

to last-minute reviews and getting pumped for the task
of teaching. But this morning Henry had agreed to meet
with Detective Fuller.

Almost three months had passed since their last meeting—a shared, cryptic conversation following the Wheeler
memorial service. Much had changed in the meantime.
Wheeler's death had been ruled a murder. Monte Vista
University had been pulled, however unwillingly, into
a spotlight it didn't want. And Sean Daniels, the young
man who'd come to him for help, had been arrested on
the charge of murder—leaving his career, his future, even
his life hanging by the thread of a jury trial or a judge's
whim. Now the arresting officer had asked to meet with
Henry at eight a.m. in his office. He'd agreed, even though
he was to teach at nine.

Spearman nodded as Fuller opened the door to his office. "Good morning, Detective. What did you want to see
me about?"

Fuller sat herself down. Working from a notepad of
her own, she looked up at Spearman. "Two things, Professor. Last January, when we were walking back from
the memorial service you asked me whether I thought
the guy killed himself . . . and I said my instincts said
no. Then you said economics had a theory about suicide.
That's what you said, but the way you said it makes me
think your theory came out at the same place as my instincts. Am I right?"

Spearman sat forward in his office chair. When he did
this, his feet could touch the floor. "If I were giving you
a grade, I'd award partial credit. Economists often use a
principle called Occam's razor. If you have two hypotheses,

with one complicated and the other simple, our default mode is to the simpler hypothesis—until we're persuaded otherwise. When it comes to the hypotheses of suicide versus murder, Occam's razor points to murder. But you'd know better than I, one can't prove something by woodenly applying Occam's razor."

"There's another reason I wanted to see you," Fuller said, leaving Spearman's response hanging. "In poking around Monte Vista, I've heard from several different people that you helped solve some murder cases as a professor. So I did some checking on you. I'm not ready to offer you a job, but I'm impressed." Fuller also leaned forward in her chair, her face now very close to Spearman's.

"Everyone knows they're about to try Sean Daniels on a charge of murder." Spearman nodded, saying nothing. "You know I was never convinced Wheeler's death was a suicide. There were too many reasons otherwise—one of them was your colleague sitting across the hallway from us right now. Another one headed up a local museum. And that wasn't the whole list. This guy wasn't exactly into making friends and influencing people the last few months of his life."

Fuller reviewed the case as she saw it, making the same points she had made in Siegfried's office three months earlier. Spearman listened intently but made no response, neither agreeing nor disagreeing with her conclusions. "So that's it," Fuller said, flipping shut her notepad. "You can see why I made the arrest. But maybe you can also see I'm not completely convinced we got the right guy. One of my colleagues, name of Siegfried, keeps telling me to let it go. That's easy for him to say. He got a monkey off his back when Ramos got his paintings back. Now he wants me to lose the monkey too. But . . . I dunno."

Spearman looked at his watch. It was approaching nine. "I think I need to begin packing up and making my way to class." He began to rise from his chair.

Fuller rose as well, but for her the interview had not yet ended. "Dr. Spearman, there's no longer a doubt in my mind that we have a very strong case for murder here. And Sean Daniels is the best suspect I've got. If you've got a better one, get him for me." Henry paused and nodded, making no further eye contact as he packed his teaching materials into the briefcase.

"Mind if I tag along?" Fuller said.

"Are you serious?" Spearman replied, arching an eyebrow in surprise.

"Deadly serious." The detective smiled tightly at the irony of her response. "Who knows, I might learn some economics."

•

The air conditioning system was on the blink. At Harvard Spearman would have thrown open the classroom windows. But it was Monte Vista University, the building was new, and the windows were designed to let in light, not air. And even if the windows could have been opened it would not have helped—the campus had already begun to swelter and there was no hint of a breeze. Henry sighed. Because he found the "art of teaching" to be physically demanding, he knew that before the class was over he would have worked up a sweat.

If the students cared about the temperature in the classroom, it didn't show. They enjoyed an advantage. While Spearman always taught in a coat and tie, and was wearing his usual leather shoes and knee-high socks, his students were wearing shorts and sandals, tee shirts, and tank tops. His teaching colleague Jennifer Kim looked smart, if warm, in a blue denim skirt, orange linen blouse, and light tan suede leather vest.

As usual, these students were on time and in their seats when the class was set to begin. This had been the pattern for three months and over two dozen classes. Even now, approaching the semester's end, Henry was still attempting to put a finger on this group. How could such an eclectic gathering of young people look so casual in their appearance, and yet be so attentive in their demeanor? To Jennifer Kim it was obvious: she knew the students were captivated by Spearman. His diminutive stature belied his professional status, while his impish humor was winsome cover for the way he brought economic reasoning into every situation.

Before the class began, Spearman introduced Fuller to Jennifer Kim. Kim had not forgotten the detective's insensitivity toward Abraham in the office hallway, months earlier, nor the anger it had produced. But she resisted letting this translate into a visible dislike for Fuller. The students for their part paid the guest no notice. Fuller might as well have been a potted plant that had been added to the room.

Today's class would be the first in which the students reported on their research. Two of the four teams of five—headed by Cookie and Dan, respectively—would present to Spearman, Kim, and their classmates the preliminary fruits of their labors. In accord with Adam Smith's principles, Spearman had instructed the teams to adopt a pedagogical specialization and division of labor: one student would present the problem that the group was addressing; a second, the results thus far; and the third, what research remained to be done. The other two would respond to questions and criticisms from the rest of the class.

As laptops and notebooks opened and chairs squeaked across the floor, a palpable tension filled the air that Spearman knew was not connected to the room temperature. Most college and university students, even the most talented, fretted about making class presentations. Students were concerned about making errors in front of Spearman, or looking foolish before their classmates. Professors generally were empathetic about these jitters, and Spearman was no exception. Still fresh in his memory was how nervous he'd been early in his own career about making mistakes in front of his students. Many of his colleagues, he knew, never fully overcame this fear.

First up was the quintet that included Miss Cowgirl. Spearman and Kim swapped sideways glances. Neither was surprised that Cookie was the leadoff batter. "We've been exploring the revenue model of art museums," she began, "especially art museums that are in financial difficulty. We've learned that most museums don't sell off any of their assets, even when things begin to go downhill." She looked at Spearman and Kim, and then quickly turned back to the class. "By their assets, we mean their paintings and sculpture. They don't sell off their paintings for the money. If they did, it would be called deaccessioning. But art museums hardly ever engage in deaccessioning."

Miss Cowgirl paused and looked at her notes. "This is the case even with paintings that aren't being exhibited. Those are kept in the basement in storage; they stay there and aren't sold, even when they could bring in revenue ... in some cases pretty sizable revenue. We're trying to figure out why." She went to the board and drew a three dimensional box, labeling it "farm supply store." "Let's assume there's a farm supply store like this one outside San Antonio, and that business is bad. Say the store had a couple English saddles in stock that nobody seemed to want. You'd expect the store to reduce the price, put the saddles on sale, and get rid of them ... liquidate some of their assets. Like why wouldn't they? The very last thing you'd expect them to say, with creditors' bills piling up in the office, would be 'no, we aren't interested in selling those English saddles at any price.' But that's just what an art museum does. It will hold on to the equivalent of its English saddles, even if they're worth millions, even when the museum is in dire financial straits."

Finished with her description, Cookie sat down, effectively handing the baton over to Haden who took Cookie's place at the podium. Haden explained that the group was going to use the Travis as the empirical locus of its work. "Last January we all heard Lewis Martin say the museum wouldn't sell off its art work. Everyone knows the Travis is in financial trouble, and that it's always begging for money. But Martin never sells a painting. We think deaccessioning would be economically rational to save the Travis."

Before Haden could proceed further, several hands went up. Jennifer Kim's passive face masked her amused take on the situation. *"There's blood in the water,"* she thought as she looked across the room at Spearman. Henry caught her glance and slightly, imperceptibly shook his head. "Maybe it's against the law for a museum to sell a painting that's been given to it," Anita proposed. "Have you checked into whether the museum holds transferable property rights?"

Orley asked a related question: "Your farm store example doesn't do anything for me. Everyone knows the store can sell the saddle. But what if the painting had been *given* to the museum by some wealthy donor? And then this donor picks up the paper one day and learns the museum sold it? He's going to think, 'that sucks' and raise holy. . . ." He looked at Spearman and Kim, cleared his throat and began again. "I mean, he's going to be really upset. Maybe even sue the museum to get the painting back for himself."

Susan suggested that reputational effects would disincentivize a museum from selling off paintings from its inventory. "Nobody would want to be associated with giving money to a museum that was getting rid of its paintings," she argued. "It would be like pouring their money down a hole." To this Donnie responded, "Hey, maybe it's just the opposite: if more financially strapped museums like the Travis were known to be selling paintings to survive, it would signal they really were in economic distress—and attract donors to come to the rescue."

A student in the back row named Tye, who rarely spoke in class, questioned the basic premise of the research project. "How sure are you that museums don't sell their paintings? I read somewhere that the art museum at Brandeis University sold off everything. Maybe there are lots of sales being made, all over the world, but museums don't want us to know." Gaining confidence from the attention of classmates and professors, he continued. "Maybe what you need to do is look at the museums that *have* sold some of their assets, instead of looking at the museums that haven't. That is, er, if you want to know what I think." Smiling nervously, he looked back down at his laptop.

After a little more back-and-forth Spearman held up his hands. "We've had a heated discussion on this first research question, but that may be because of the temperature in the room." Half the class smiled; the others didn't pick up on what he said. "But let me ask a closing question to anyone in the group." Walking over to the board, he began erasing Cookie's farm supply store. "A museum is not a typical commercial establishment. It isn't established or chartered to sell its goods—in this case, paintings. Galleries, private collectors, even some framing establishments of course are. But not museums. Museums are set up to *exhibit* paintings." He turned to face the group. "So my question to you is: why do you model the museum as a firm to begin with?" Spearman's forehead had beads of perspiration, but he had a sly grin on his face.

Miss Cowgirl stood to return the volley. "Because this is an *economics* class," she said. "And so we use economic theory. A museum like the Travis fits the bill: it makes money by selling admission tickets, selling items in its gift shop, and renting out parts of its building for receptions and parties. And it also takes in money from donors and patrons. As for galleries. . . ." She got up from her chair and walked over to the whiteboard. "A museum has a lot of the same expenses as a gallery: acquiring and maintaining land and buildings, acquiring and selling items in the gift shop. And acquiring paintings."

She looked at Spearman, glanced back at her group and then wrote "cost of painting" on the whiteboard, with the word "Fryer" beside it. Turning, she continued. "Professor Fryer, who teaches accounting, would say that the cost of a painting given to the Travis Museum is zero. It's a gift. No strings attached, no invoice issued, no check cut, no electronic transfer of funds made. From his perspective, there's seemingly no cost to the museum. But *we* know"— here she grinned at Spearman—"'there's no such thing as a free lunch.' And correspondingly there's no such thing as a free painting. The economic cost of a painting is the highest valued opportunity foregone of holding the painting, no matter what the accounting cost is. So the cost to the Travis Museum of any painting in its portfolio is the highest price someone else would pay Mr. Martin, the curator, for the painting. *That's* the cost. *Not* zero."

Triumphantly, she wrote a big zero on the whiteboard then drew a line through the middle of it. It now looked like the Greek letter theta to her sorority and fraternity classmates.

Leaning back in his chair, Spearman smiled, put one hand under his chin, and raised his eyebrows. He nodded slowly. "But," he queried, "if you are modeling a museum on the economic theory of the manufacturing firm, are the paintings to be considered the equivalent of the firm's capital equipment?" Cookie considered Spearman's query for some time. There was no indication that anyone in her group wanted in on the question. Finally she said, "Yes, our group would think of the paintings that way . . . that is, as being like the capital equipment of a manufacturing plant. Except paintings can have very long depreciation rates, unlike machines that can wear out in a couple decades."

•

As the next quintet moved to the front of the humid classroom, Spearman wiped his brow. One student, upon noticing Spearman's discomfort, spoke up and asked if anyone wanted to move the class outside. Spearman looked to Kim for advice. "I don't think so," she replied. "If anything, it's hotter outside in the sun than it is in here."

"And our group needs the whiteboard," piped another student, as she and four others moved to the front of the class.

As the five sat down before their classmates, Spearman noted how each one was symmetrically aligned with the others, almost as if by design. Five pairs of elbows rested side by side on the table, with five pairs of hands crossed in front of them. For some reason the effect was disorienting, almost bizarre. Dan the Man, the group's chosen spokesman, stood up—glanced quickly at his note cards—and took the lead. "We're exploring the effect of the death of an artist on the price of the artist's paintings," he began.

"Gross," interjected Mark. "Why don't we call our class the economics of death, instead of the economics of art?"

"Because it's been done," Pete called out. "There's a play called *Death of an Artist*."

"No, you're thinking of *Death of a Salesman*," the first student shot back.

"Guys, guys . . . c'mon." Jennifer interjected, noticing that Spearman seemed distracted by the heat. "Let's at least allow Dan to get started before we start piling on, okay?"

Dan cleared his throat and began again. "We've been thinking about this problem with demand and supply analysis. And what we've come up with we think is kinda cool." He hesitated, before flashing a cheek-to-cheek smile that would make an orthodontist proud. "Even if it *does* involve death. In fact, we call the effect this has on price the 'death effect.'" He looked down at the three by five cards in his hand, paused, looked up and continued. "So here's our theory. Obviously if the artist dies, that ends supply. So as a matter of theory, with supply restricted, the death effect ... should cause the prices for the stock of the artist's paintings to go up ... all other things being equal." Dan went to the whiteboard, wrote "DEATH" in block letters, then drew a large arrow pointing up. He also wrote "CETERIS PARIBUS" in block letters.

He then turned back to the class, looked over at Spearman and Kim, glanced at the foursome with whom he was working and then at the other fifteen students whose attention he now commanded. "But we know *ceteris paribus* conditions—'all other things being equal'—don't always apply. Here we know what's up with supply: no more art from this artist, unless a pretty awesome forger comes along. But what about demand?" He pointed at Spearman. "Professor Spearman taught us we can't just look at supply *or* demand. It's like with scissors. You need both blades to do the cutting, not just one or the other. So here's what we're thinking." He held out his left hand, thumb and forefinger connected to form a zero. "If the artist is old, our hypothesis is that the death effect would be zero, or close to zero. I mean, if you think of it from an actuarial perspective, if the artist is pretty old, the death effect, whatever it might be for him, would already be embedded in the market price of his work. On the other hand," he held out his right hand in identical fashion, "if the artist dies young, there's *no* death effect because there's no big demand for an artist with no reputation. It's when the artist is midcareer and death is *unexpected* that we think there'd be a spike. Then the death effect might be measurable—and profitable." Dan rubbed his fingers and thumbs together, smiling.

As he sat down he said, "I'm now going to turn the discussion of our project over to Haiyang, who'll talk about the empirical side of our research."

Haiyang got up, reached for the dry erase marker and—motioning with it in the air—began to talk numbers and database. "The library has helped us access a huge database on art prices called 'Hislop's Art Sales Index'. It has thousands of data points on the price of paintings, linked to the specific artists that painted them, which we then used to identify the artists' date of death." He turned to the board and began writing. "Obviously other things might affect the value of paintings when the artist dies, such as the state of the economy at the time . . . whether the art market is booming or stable . . . and whether the painting is signed or not. But we think we can gather data to allow us to control for these variables." He listed each variable on the board, heading them with a dash.

As Haiyang continued to speak of databases and research methodology, Spearman found himself becoming increasingly uncomfortable. He was perspiring noticeably and in response loosened his tie. Throughout his teaching career at Harvard, Spearman had never taught a class without a coat and tie. But now, as classroom discussion continued to drone in the background, he stood and—unobtrusively, he hoped—took off his jacket, hanging it on the back of his chair.

By the time Haiyang had handed off his baton to Kelvin, Kim's attention was divided between the students, to whom she sought to listen, and Spearman, whose disconnect with the class was becoming increasingly evident. Those sitting nearest couldn't help but notice that his mind seemed elsewhere. Some wondered if the talk of death had disturbed the (in their eyes) elderly professor. Henry shifted again in his chair. Cookie worried that he was ill, and wondered if she should say something.

The presentation continued. Spearman struggled to bring his attention back to Kelvin and his colleagues. Then, to the surprise of both the class and Professor Kim, Spearman got up from his chair, crossed in front of the students, and opened the classroom door. Turning back to the puzzled class, he said softly, "If you would excuse me for a moment. Please continue without me."

The hallway was abandoned. Unsurprising—it was the middle of the morning class period, and all students and faculty were either in class or elsewhere on campus. Spearman walked down the hallway, his footsteps echoing behind him. As he did so the image of another hallway came to mind. This one was not empty. It was bustling, and in the middle of the bustle was a Boston accent. Blake Bailey was asking a question about land prices. Henderson Ross's face suddenly swam before Spearman's mind's eye. His pace quickened.

When he came to the end of the hallway, he opened the door to the men's bathroom and went in. It too was empty.

Putting his glasses on the sink, Henry turned on the faucet. He waited until the water in the sink was very cold. Then cupping his hands he splashed it onto his face. His shirt collar, already moist with perspiration, was now even wetter.

The bracing water was a relief, but did little to slow the stream of images racing through his mind. He thought of Lord Duveen bidding on Houdon busts . . . Annelle Cubbage's bidding strategy at Sotheby's . . . why was *that* coming so suddenly to mind? Then his memory went back to Bailey and Henderson, and their puzzle over the Coase conjecture . . . the talk of possessions, prices, monopoly . . . before jumping again to Detective Fuller and her questions over the death of Tristan Wheeler. Images began to flash before him. The first were grainy, black-and-white newspaper photos of Wheeler's paintings, the ones that he had seen referenced in the *Boston Globe* article months earlier. Then Henry saw the African greys. "The two pet birds," he said quietly to himself. Three months earlier, he had gone online to learn about African greys. Now he struggled to get their image out of his mind.

He had visited Sean Daniels several times over the past weeks, both to cheer up the anxious young man and to offer support. Now he heard Sean's voice describing Wheeler's "creative cocoon." Finally came a fearful image of something he'd seen only in cowboy movies: a man twisting at the end of a rope, dead. He thought of Wheeler's body slowly turning as his life expired and his career ended. The heavily accented voice of his Hebrew school rabbi echoed eerily over forty years of time, space, and experience . . . *"for him who takes his own life, no eulogy, no rending of clothes. . . ."*

Spearman steadied himself at the bathroom sink. He looked at his image in the mirror and wondered out loud, "What in the world is going on?" He was supposed to be in a classroom teaching twenty undergraduates, but instead he was in a bathroom, his face dripping with water and perspiration. He took a batch of paper towels from the dispenser and began patting his head.

Then, as he stood before the sink, he looked once more into the mirror. This time he did not see his reflection. Instead before his mind's eye was a number: Wheeler's age. Then that number was replaced with a diagram. A very simple diagram. On the horizontal axis was age. On the vertical axis were dollars. Inside the quadrant was a bell curve.

"Got it." His quiet voice barely echoed off the tiled floor and walls.

Spearman no longer needed to steady himself at the sink. He no longer needed to splash cold water on this face. Straightening up, he adjusted his tie and retrieved his glasses. The only problem he now faced was whether to go back to his students and finish the class . . . or go to the police and tell them who had killed Tristan Wheeler.

As Spearman began walking down the hall to his classroom, he realized that he did not have to go to the police. The police were already in his classroom. Without another thought, he decided to do "art and economics" in a way he never could have anticipated when he first decided to teach about economics and art. He would use economics to solve a crime involving art.

26

THE BELL CURVE

Men must have profits proportional to their expense and hazard.

—DAVID HUME

As he walked back to the classroom, Henry was anything but self-assured. He had been an economist long enough to know that economic analysis was not like a soft drink machine that ejected easy answers when money was dropped in. For years Spearman had headlined every syllabus with the words of John Maynard Keynes, the twentieth century's most influential economist. Keynes had written,

> The theory of economics does not furnish a body of settled conclusions.... It is a method rather than a doctrine, an apparatus of the mind, a technique of thinking which helps its possessor to draw correct conclusions.

Now his students, along with their visitor, would see how much help this "apparatus of the mind" truly provided. He paused before the classroom door, took a deep breath, opened it, and walked inside.

"I apologize for the sudden departure." The students looked relieved by their professor's return as he stood front and center. "The class discussion, perhaps fueled by the temperature in the room, caused me to have what might be described as an epiphany—an economic epiphany of sorts. But I needed to leave the room to get my head around it." He removed his glasses and began polishing the lenses as he looked out the classroom window. Putting them back on, he faced the class. "I've decided to share this epiphany with you." The students noticed that Spearman was not smiling as he spoke. Even his eyes were dead serious. "I've pushed you this semester to get the economics right. The tables have turned. Now you get to push me to see if *I've* got the economics right." He walked to the whiteboard, picked up a marker, and began to write.

"Though you're too young to remember the original broadcasts, some of you may have watched episodes of the old *Twilight Zone* television show." Several heads nodded. "Do you remember how the show invariably began? The show's creator—Rod Serling, I think his name was—would face his audience with a smile, say 'Submitted for your approval,' and then lay out a fantastic story for them." Henry glanced around the room. His gaze ended with Detective Fuller. "Submitted for your approval, then. . . ." He turned and faced the class. On the board were written the words "THEFT," "VALUABLE," "NO INSURANCE," and "SUICIDE"—all in block capitals.

"A private home is burglarized, and several paintings of a talented artist are stolen. The owner, when interviewed afterward by the police, says that he never insured the paintings and that he considers his considerable financial loss a total one." Spearman paused and then continued. "Months later the artist who created the paintings—just beginning to enjoy a national and even international spotlight—seemingly commits suicide." Henry looked down at the floor and then back at his students.

"It would seem as though these events were unrelated. They took place at different times; one involved a theft, one involved a death. But as a famous economist named Paul Samuelson once put it, 'in economics, things are not always as they seem.' That's true here." At this, Fuller sat up straight and reached for her notepad and pen.

Henry went on. "Let's first address the *alleged* suicide." He circled the word on the board. "What do we know about suicide from economic analysis?" Spearman intended the question to be rhetorical. The class received it as such. No one said a peep.

"Suicide occurs when the expected value of the stream of future utility is negative. According to economic theory, that's when someone takes his or her own life. But in this particular case it didn't fit. This artist was not only a painter but a professor of art, with a skyrocketing career. He was a campus celebrity and a speaker in great demand. His paintings were selling for big bucks, and he had scheduled speaking engagements for months in advance." Spearman cocked his head and smiled ironically. "And you can add to these another not inconsequential fact: he was extremely popular with members of the opposite sex.

"What of the down side? We know the artist was despondent over the loss of two pets that were precious to him. 'Precious.' Interesting word: it means they were of high value. So let's ask ourselves: were the pets irreplace-able? In a sense yes. But in a sense no. There would be any number of pet stores, not to mention many options on the Internet, who would gladly provide the artist with replacements. Thus the case for suicide would seem irra-tional from an economic standpoint."

Henry turned back to the whiteboard. "That leaves open the question of how this artist died. What could ac-count for a death if not suicide?"

"An accident?" Kelvin hesitatingly offered.

"In some situations, yes, but not this one," Spearman said, first writing the word accident on the board and then drawing a line through it. "He was found with a rope around his neck. That doesn't happen by accident." Spear-man looked around the room. "Other hypotheses?"

Dan the Man raised his hand, looked quickly at his classmates and whispered theatrically, "*Murder!*"

Spearman acknowledged the student with a slight nod. "A verdict, as it turns out, that the medical examiner and the police department also reached. Which brings us to the next question: motive." Henry smiled slightly. "Is there a motive that might be discovered through analyzing art and the marketplace?"

Cookie was the first to raise her hand. "Passion? Jeal-ousy??" Her heart was in her throat. Miss Cowgirl thought she had a grasp on what was happening, and where Spear-man was going. She had heard the rumors on campus and yet Herbert Abraham was one of her favorite professors at Monte Vista.

"Possibly," replied Spearman. "But only if the benefits exceeded the costs. If the jealous person had reclaimed that which was lost, or thought to be lost, that changes the cost-benefit equation a great deal."

Jennifer Kim raised her hand. Henry caught her eyes and nodded in her direction. "Jennifer?"

She spoke quietly. "I wanted to say . . . I think Professor Spearman's analysis is correct." Kim looked out at the class. "Sometimes passion can be blinding. It can make us think we've lost goods that at first glance seem irreplaceable, irretrievable. But then we step back and see that the goods were never really lost in the first place, and that they were indeed durable goods"—she smiled at Henry—"so the benefits of lashing out dissipate. And the cost becomes much, much higher."

Henry smiled, "Well said, Professor." He turned to the rest of the class. "Other possibilities?" He scanned the room. Students were beginning to shoot glances of recognition and understanding at one another.

It was Anjali Vitali's turn. "What if this artist had a plan, say . . . to make his art free to everyone?" Spearman gave Vitali an approving look. Encouraged, Anjali continued. "What if this artist was trying to find a way to reproduce his art and make it available to everybody for free? That would devalue the art for museums and collectors, maybe force museums out of business and ruin the investments of collectors. When *all* paintings can be reproduced and distributed, who wants to pay to see them?" Vitali had been listening to the conversation on the bus after all. "Making sure that didn't happen could be a powerful economic motive to do something about it."

Henry nodded, looked away for a moment collecting his thoughts and then addressed not only Vitali but the whole class. "Here's the problem with that hypothesis. Even if the technology to reproduce paintings exactly *were* to come into existence, museums and private collectors of valuable paintings would not be adversely affected. We have a laboratory test of that with prints. Prints now offer nearly the same image that the original paintings provide. Yet the demand for paintings by museums and collectors continues unabated. People derive utility from seeing the originals. The original generates utils that a replica never can. Let me give you an example with which, I know, I may date myself.

"If I were a skilled craftsman, I might now—in my basement back in Cambridge—be able to make an exact duplicate of the ruby slippers that Judy Garland wore in *The Wizard of Oz*. If you don't know, the originals are on display at the Smithsonian in Washington, D.C. Thousands of people flock to see them every year. But nobody would flock to my basement to see the ones I made, even if admission were at zero price. In fact, even if I charged a negative price for tickets, and *paid* people to come to my basement, people would still stand in line to see the ones worn by Judy Garland—and not the ones made by Henry Spearman."

Spearman sighed. "There are few things in life we can know for sure. *Maybe* someone wanted to kill this artist because they were jealous of his talent. *Maybe* someone stood to inherit a lot of money from his death." Spearman looked directly at Detective Fuller in the back of the room. The class was absolutely silent, hanging on his every word. They knew there would never be another lecture like this in their lifetime.

"Do you recall the story of Lord Duveen?" Every head in the classroom nodded as one, except Detective Fuller's. She stopped her note-taking and blurted out, "Lord who?" The students all looked at the stranger in their class. Then Cookie responded, "The guy who paid a lot at the auction."

After relating the Duveen story again, Spearman continued. "As some of you know, I was recently at an art auction in New York City. The highlight of the evening was a seemingly irrational bid on a painting by a particular artist—as it turns out, the artist in our example." In the back of the room Fuller was trying to take notes without taking her eyes off Spearman.

"At first I thought I'd witnessed a modern-day Duveen strategy, designed to increase the value of the artist's paintings. There were a number of similarities between the bidding that evening and that of the famous arbitrageur of yesteryear. They were both wealthy and they both possessed an inventory of art whose value they might be inclined to increase. In short. . . ."

"*Bingo!*"

Startled, both class and professor turned to see Dan the Man rising halfway out of his seat, his face flushed and excited. "That's gotta be it. The motive for the murder. I mean . . ." he gulped. "I mean, if there *was* a murder. You would off the guy, make sure there were no more masterpieces coming down the assembly line . . . then make a big bid for one of the remaining paintings . . . and increase the value of your collection, like maybe a hundred times. It's foolproof."

Henry smiled, shook his head, and walked back to the front of the class. "I'm afraid I can only give you partial credit, Dan. In effect, Duveen tricked the market. But markets are not easily tricked. The bidder I saw in New York did not have the preeminence in the art market that Duveen had at the time and, as it turned out, was simply trying to acquire—quickly and authoritatively—a painting of great sentimental value. The Duveen similarities were just that—surface similarities, having nothing to do with the murder or the motive." Spearman turned around and erased everything off the whiteboard. "Duveen had his day, but even Duveen could not trick the market if he frequently adopted this bidding strategy. It is not that easy to trick any market on a sustained basis. No . . ." he put down the eraser and paused. "No, your hypothesis about Duveen will not hold up, but you were right about something else . . . something that, as a matter of economic logic, pointed to the real murderer." Spearman picked up a red marker from the table at the front of the classroom.

"When Dan's group was making its presentation, he called the effect that death has on the value of the artist's work 'the death effect.' That term was prescient." Spearman faced the whiteboard and drew a quadrant. On the horizontal axis he put age: from twenty to ninety. On the vertical axis he wrote a dollar symbol. Inside he drew a bell curve. Spearman then pointed to the left tail of the curve. "When the artist is young, the death effect generally would be small, because the artist does not yet have a reputation. There is no great demand for the artist's work so the death effect falls here." Spearman then pointed to the right tail of the curve where the dollar value on the vertical axis also was low. "When the artist is elderly, the market recognizes that the future supply of work from this artist is limited."

He then faced the class directly. "The market will, as if by an invisible hand, reflect the expectation that future supply of work by this artist will be limited. So the death effect is small for the young and the old. But what if there's an unexpected death of a well-known artist in midcareer?"

"The death effect maxes out," Haiyang responded.

"Yes. The implications of that curve triggered my leaving the classroom twenty minutes ago. I left . . . because I needed to gather my thoughts in private." Spearman walked over by the classroom door, close to where Fuller was seated.

"So who would benefit the most by having a well-known artist in this middle-range age cohort 'fling down the curtain'?" Spearman scanned the class for hands. Dan hesitated but Haiyang did not. "Someone who had a large inventory of his paintings."

"Indeed. Well done, gentlemen," he nodded to Dan and Haiyang. He then caught Fuller's eye. "Let's return to 'the Case of the Purloined Paintings,' if you will. The owner of paintings by a newly deceased artist would have stood to gain a great deal by the death effect—*if* the owner had still possessed the paintings." Spearman paused for almost a full minute. "The paintings were returned to the owner in the dead of night, as suddenly and as mysteriously as they were taken, only days after the death of the artist. Your thoughts?"

Cookie's hand shot up, but she began speaking even before Spearman's acknowledgment. "I'd say that there was definitely something fishy going on. Paintings showing up right after the guy is dead? And just after they've multiplied in price? C'mon!"

Spearman nodded. "And then there's the matter of the insurance, which for me 'sealed the deal' as they say.

"Shortly before leaving Cambridge I read a story in the *Boston Globe*, which I then had clipped and filed to take here. A few days ago I reread the article, which was about an art theft in San Antonio. I saved that article for two reasons. First, it involved the art scene in San Antonio, and at the time I was planning to teach this very course at Monte Vista. Second, I was puzzled by the article. It referenced an anomaly that made no economic sense to me at the time. In fact, I even had the story filed away as 'the barking dog.'"

At this, Spearman drew blank stares from the class. He continued.

"My curiosity was piqued by the owner of the stolen art. He said that he had not insured the missing paintings. But he then offered a sizable reward. I thought at the time, why would a rational person refuse to pay a relatively small amount to protect his assets, but then be willing to pay an amount many times greater to have those same assets returned? Interesting question isn't it? Anybody see the answer?"

Several hands shot up. "Kelvin?"

"If you planned to have something stolen, there'd be no reason to spend money on insurance or security. You could offer a big reward because no one would ever collect the money—you'd never have to come up with it."

Spearman beamed. "Kelvin, that's using Keynes's 'apparatus of the mind.'"

Now it was Jennifer Kim's turn to speak. She did not even bother raising her hand. Of all the people in the classroom, she was the one most emotionally connected to the narrative. "But . . . how? How was he killed . . . ?" Her voice trailed off.

Spearman looked expressionlessly across the room at Fuller. His voice was hard. "The artist was found hanging by the end of a rope. Perhaps he was forced to do so at gunpoint. Or perhaps he was rendered unconscious by carbon monoxide, a byproduct formed by the same type of cooking stove this *particular* artist used while painting. If the air vents in his studio had been blocked off, such a gas could have rendered him unconscious and easy prey."

Spearman at this point was as exhausted as he had ever been from teaching a class. There was one hand in the air. It was Fuller's. "Why the barking dog? I don't get it."

"In the Sherlock Holmes story 'Silver Blaze,' a man broke into a home and committed a theft in full view of the family's dog. *But the dog didn't bark.* Why? Holmes deduced that the intruder was the dog's owner. We don't know from the story, but the dog was probably wagging her tail with her tongue out while the theft was being committed."

"I think I see where you're going . . ." Fuller murmured.

Henry nodded. "Exactly. In the story, Holmes went on to discover that the owner had the most to gain from the theft. And the crime was the same here. No potential thief had as much to gain from the disappearance of those paintings, as did the owner himself."

Fuller matter-of-factly clicked her pen, rose, and exited quietly out the door. The room was quiet. Everyone knew that something of consequence had just taken place, and that the woman who had just left their classroom was somehow involved. But the oddity of their professor's latest economic illustration was foremost on their minds. Finally Anita broke the silence. "What just happened here?"

Spearman replied, "If I were as much the detective as Dan made me out to be," he glanced at Dan and winked, "I might at this point take out a pipe, fill it with tobacco, and begin playing my Stradivarius. But Monte Vista doesn't allow smoking on campus and I can't play the violin."

A few students traded glances with each other, their brows knit in confusion. Cookie, Anjali, and the others waited until realization began to dawn, and then smiled broadly. Henry returned the grin. "I'm no Sherlock Holmes. I'm an econ professor. But if Holmes had been in our classroom today, I can hear him saying, 'Elementary, my dear students . . . elementary *economics*, that is.'"

27

A LATE NIGHT VISIT

When a doctor does go wrong he is the first of criminals.
He has nerve, and he has knowledge.
                                          —SIR ARTHUR CONAN DOYLE

It was Friday evening, and the heavens were punctuated
with stars as Pidge Spearman took a leisurely walk in the
Oakmont neighborhood. The April evenings in San Antonio were more like early summer in the New England
she had left behind. April in Massachusetts? *Brrrr*, she
shuddered. After turning into the yard of their temporary
Texas home, she began to push open the front door when
a voice came from behind her.

"Mrs. Spearman?"

Pidge switched on the porch light and turned back to
the street. Having been raised on a college campus, she was
accustomed to unexpected visitors and gave a welcoming
smile. "Yes? May I help you?"

"Well, yes ma'am, you can." A woman walked up the
driveway from a Crown Vic parked at the curb. "I'm Detective Fuller of the San Antonio Police Department. I was
wondering if your husband was available to chat for a few
minutes . . . unofficially, off the record so to speak."

"Yes, of course. I think Henry's upstairs in his study, so if you'll come in I'll call him down."

Henry descended the steps without hesitation when Pidge told him of Fuller's arrival. "Well, detective, it's good to see you again."

"Likewise. I've enjoyed our visits—heck, I've even learned some economics. But I'm guessing this might be our last visit for awhile. Which is why I'd like to tie things up a bit before we head our separate ways. Would you have a couple minutes that we could just sit and talk? Privately?"

"I certainly do. Let's go out on the veranda." Henry led the detective through the living room and out onto the back porch. The two settled into the wrought-iron lawn chairs that Monte Vista University had thoughtfully thrown in—along with salary, house, car, and office—when Spearman's deal had been arranged. The two of them sat side by side, looking out to the yard where the live oak trees formed a silhouette against the evening sky.

For some time neither spoke. Finally Fuller broke the silence. "You were right."

In the light coming from the living room behind them, Spearman's head could be seen to nod as he replied. "Yes. As a matter of fact, we both were. All along you said it never seemed like a suicide. You had your instincts. I had my theory."

"Want to know how it was done?"

"I think I can infer a good deal of it. And I saw my neighbor being led out of his house in handcuffs a few days ago—I think it's called the perp walk, isn't it? But I'd like to hear the whole story from you."

"Well, the question is where to start." She cocked her head and thought a minute. "I guess you could say it started ten years back, when Ramos began leaking money as a result of some bad investments. Normal run of bad luck, nothing he might not have recovered from in time. But then the dot-com bubble burst—and that hit him hard. About that same time his wife filed for divorce—and took home a major chunk of his change in the settlement. Then he hit the trifecta when he bought the Wheelers. Bad move." Fuller leaned back, stretched, and put her hands behind her head. Her voice became somber.

"What do you suppose makes someone go off the deep end, Professor? Decide to do away with another human being, I mean?" Before Henry could answer she continued. "In this case it was money. Ramos was nearly broke. He maintained the illusion of doing well, kept up his parties, continued to hobnob with the artsy types. But behind the scenes the bills were mounting. Creditors were starting to holler.

"Meanwhile, living almost next door was Tristan Wheeler. One of the hottest artists in the country . . . *and* the guy who happened to have painted five works that were hanging on Ramos's wall. Works that were valuable. And works that could be made even more valuable, *if* the artist were to be eliminated . . . as you pointed out in class.

"Stage one was to arrange what would look like the theft of the paintings. Which was pretty easy as it turns out. Ramos waited until the conclusion of a late night party, then quietly allowed one of the guests—he's singing like a bird now—to reenter the house after everyone else headed home. We think it was while Rosie was assisting the caterers in the kitchen. The guy then hid in the house until she went to bed.

"When Rosie was presumably in dreamland, the two guys met in the living room and got to work. They lifted the paintings off the walls and carried 'em right through the side door to the guy's car—Ramos having deactivated the security system beforehand. Trouble was, they managed to wake up Rosie after all . . . but Ramos heard her downstairs and was able to reset the alarm and lock the door before high-tailing it back to his room . . . where he was, when Rosie discovered the theft."

Here the detective shook her head. "I have to hand it to you, professor. The fact that the paintings weren't insured didn't set off any warning bells for our guys, or me either for that matter. In fact, it removed Ramos from the list of suspects, as far as I was concerned." Henry sat quietly, staring straight ahead into the dark.

"Getting rid of the art temporarily, removing himself as a suspect, that was easy. Now came stage two. Ramos had to eliminate the artist. And that was going to be the hard part. Ramos figured to make it look like suicide, because artists are notoriously temperamental. Everyone knows about how van Gogh checked himself out. That image would play right into Ramos's hand. But how? Ahh, 'there's the rub,' as Shakespeare used to say. The guy had to do it so that *no* clues were left, not a *trace* of foul play." She looked over at Henry, who through her story had continued to gaze into the darkness. "He found a way. And you mentioned it in class."

"Gas."

"Gas." She sighed. "Ramos knew Wheeler would stay in his studio for a couple days straight while creating a painting . . . drinking, sleeping on a cot, and cooking for himself on a gas stove. 'His creative cocoon' he called it. It was common knowledge—the guy's assistant, his lady friends, even his art students used to joke about it. So what better way to kill him than to simply wait until he was drunk and asleep—turn on the gas, seal the door, and let nature take her course? Stringing him up later would be child's play.

"Ramos had checked on the birds once so he knew where the spare house key was hidden. Then Ramos waited till Wheeler was away, cased the studio so he could be sure of plugging up all the possible air vents, and waited for his chance."

"Hence the abduction and destruction of the parrots," Henry said. He grimaced as the mental picture of the two dead birds flashed again across his mind's eye.

Fuller nodded. "The African greys could've blown the whole thing. If the birds were in the studio at the time of the gassing, they'd die—like canaries in a mine shaft—and if Wheeler rolled over and saw them dead, it was just conceivable they could wake him up enough to catch what was going on. Then, too"—she shifted in her seat—"even if they died beside their owner, their bodies would be a telltale sign that something wasn't on the up and up. So a month or two in advance—as it turns out, even before the phony theft of his paintings—Ramos entered the residence and grabbed the birds. Killed them and tossed them in a campus dumpster. Their bodies were never intended to surface—but we think stray cats dragged them out. A case of 'murder most fowl,' eh?"

Spearman could not bring himself to smile at the pun. Hearing Fuller describe in detail such despicable machinations weighed his normally cheerful spirit down. He felt ill.

"After that it was only a matter of time. Ramos waited until Wheeler had another painting in the pipeline, called to make sure he was good and liquored up, and then slipped in a few hours later. He turned on the gas stove and closed off the air vents. Then, when the poor guy was insensible from whiskey and carbon monoxide—Ramos and the accomplice stole in, carried Wheeler into the bathroom, threw the noose over the iron crossbar in the skylight and strung him up. The ME said that the guy was alive before he strangled to death. I'm guessing he must have tried to free himself, in the end ... tried to cry out for help. But no one was there to hear.

"Ramos had kept a thank-you letter signed by Wheeler that he'd gotten earlier. It couldn't have been simpler. He cut off the 'thanks' at the top, printed a suicide note on what was left, and kept Wheeler's John Hancock at the bottom. He then planted it in the bathroom.

"Then? Ramos wiped off and unblocked the air vents ... and used the fan to clear away the rest of the gas." Fuller turned in her chair. Her face, framed in the distant light of the living room lamp, became hard and when she spoke her voice followed suit. "Do you want to know what the saddest, most ironic part of this whole terrible business was? I mean, the *worst* part of it all?"

Fuller got up and paced the veranda floor. "There were actually *two* attempts on Wheeler's life. The first one failed. Ramos had neglected to check on the status of the gas in the stove, and it emptied before doing much more than make Wheeler ill. As a result, Wheeler staggered to his feet and—feeling all the telltale signs of carbon monoxide poisoning: dizziness, nausea, headache—he made for the only place he could think of where someone could help. The house of his friend, the doctor. He lurched through the door and in front of a room full of guests, begged Ramos—*the guy who was killing him*—to help him. Which Ramos had to do." She paused. Spearman barely made out the detective's shrug. "Of course, in retrospect that should've been the first clue that something was fishy. Ramos escorted the guy back in full view of a room of partiers, and told us later that he tucked Wheeler in, closed the door, and let himself out. But when our guys dusted for prints after the murder—two days later—the only ones we found were the victim's and Daniels's. Cleaning lady hadn't come by, and wasn't due for another three days. So where were the prints of the Good Samaritan? They had to have been wiped." She shook her head.

"I presume you've got enough proof to make your case stand up, Detective?" Henry wondered if this question might be offensive, after Fuller had described the crime so quickly and with such assurance. But he needn't have worried.

"That's always the million-dollar question, if I could borrow an economic turn of phrase." The detective smiled at Spearman. "But yeah, once you helped us know where to look we made out okay. Ramos thought pretty highly of himself, I guess. But while he was wiping off the air vents, the smartest guy in the room left prints all over the chair rail he was leaning against." The detective chuckled. "A doctor, who uses gloves practically every day of his life, leaves them off—and now is going to spend the rest of his life regretting it. I tell you professor, you couldn't make this stuff up."

"Oh, and the accomplice? He saw Ramos getting shoved head first into a police cruiser, and figured the doc would give him up. That made him our new best friend."

The two arose, and Fuller followed Spearman through the patio door and across the living room to the foyer. The detective extended her hand and Henry took it. "Well, thanks again Professor. I asked you to find me a better suspect, and darned if you didn't deliver. As far as I'm concerned you solved the case, not me. Let me know if you ever think of joining the department. We'll put you to work."

Spearman held open the front door. "I think my comparative advantage is doing economics, not police work. But it's nice to know other employment opportunities might be open if the market for econ professors turns sour." He watched as Fuller moved beyond the reach of the porch light. A moment later he heard a car engine start. Making a slow circuit throughout the house he turned off the lights one by one. Outside the dining room window, barely visible across the yard, he could just see a basement light coming from the Ramos house.

28

DOING GOOD BY DOING WELL

MONDAY, MAY 8TH

Ultimately the teaching of economics boils down to the telling of stories.

—DAVID COLANDER

The labor contract between Monte Vista University and the Cubbage Nobel Visiting Professorship had called for the recipient to present one public lecture, with a second at the discretion of the chair holder. Henry Spearman's first public lecture had been given early in the semester. As the time drew near for the Spearmans to return to Cambridge, Henry exercised his option to give a second public lecture.

Since he was a Nobel Prize winner in economics, a public lecture booked by Spearman's agent would have commanded an honorarium of thousands of dollars. But this one would be on the house. Or, as Spearman thought of it, the marginal revenue generated by the lecture would be zero.

As with Spearman's first public lecture, his second drew a packed house. The word was out among students that the Cubbage Chair holder was a good speaker, whose talks were interesting whether one was an economics student or not. Faculty members at Monte Vista University who valued having a Nobel Prize winner in their midst also turned out. Townspeople had heard positive reports from friends attending Spearman's first lecture, so this audience contingent was amply represented as well. Of course, the fact that the speaker had solved two of the more notorious crimes in San Antonio history—an art theft and a murder—did little to deter them. In fact, just about the only people who did not show up were those who thought a talk by a prominent economist should include tips on what stocks or bonds to buy. Spearman had disabused his first audience of that notion.

Annelle Cubbage had asked President Quinn if she could introduce the Cubbage Nobel Visiting Professor Public Lecture. It was a request Quinn could not refuse.

Whenever people pegged Annelle Cubbage as a bull-headed, wealthy rancher from Texas, her New York City sophistication would shine like the lights on Times Square and force them to reconsider. It was equally true that when people thought they were getting an urbane New York patron of the arts, what they got instead was an eyebrow-raising, tough-talking lady from the Texas Hill Country.

But then, Annelle Cubbage had that effect on people.

In her introduction of Spearman's lecture, Cubbage dropped the tough-talking Texas Hill Country pose. Instead she gave a brief recitation of Spearman's credentials, citing the two papers that the Nobel Committee had singled out as chiefly responsible for the speaker's award. Cubbage devoted even more time to praising Monte Vista University for its prescience in exposing students to the best minds from around the world. President Quinn and her staff in Development and Public Relations were button-bursting proud. Annelle made no mention of the benefactor who financed the Nobel laureate's time at Monte Vista University: but then, almost everyone in the audience drew the connection.

Spearman's second public appearance was in the same auditorium. But this time the Facilities Department at Monte Vista University had secured a shorter podium. As a consequence, when Henry stood to speak he was able to view the entire auditorium. Those attending the lecture could see that the speaker's bald, bespectacled head was actually attached to neck and shoulders, that part of his body now being visible even to the seats in the back rows. Spearman was relaxed and his voice clear as the evening's lecture began.

"I want to thank Monte Vista University for inviting me to be part of the school's educational mission this semester; also let me express my appreciation to Ms. Annelle Cubbage for her kind introduction." Spearman paused and looked at Cubbage, who had returned to her seat in the front row. "I'm both honored and humbled to be the first recipient of the Cubbage Nobel Visiting Professorship. Ms. Cubbage's father was an entrepreneur, every bit as creative as any poet, artist, or musician." Nodding once more to his benefactor, he then turned his gaze to the hundreds seated in the auditorium.

"The production function for a public speech requires a speaker. But that is not the only labor input required. A public speech also requires an audience. While I plan to supply the speech this evening, there can't be a public speech if there's no demand for my services. That's where you, the audience, come in. You complete the demand-supply interaction. Let's see if we can reach a congenial equilibrium between your demand for a speech and my supply of a speech."

Spearman sipped some water from a cup that was on the speaker's stand, before looking back at the audience arrayed before him. As he did so, he let his shoulders drop slightly and he placed his hands on the sides of the lectern. Spearman was settling in to begin the formal part of his talk. The audience settled in as well.

"'So, a man walks into a bar. . . .?'" Spearman stopped and let his gaze go from left to right, until he had made eye contact with the entire audience. "There must be ten thousand jokes in the English language that begin with that opening line. Here is a variation, but it is not a joke. It is a true story. A young woman walks, not into a bar, but into an econ professor's office. She is a student at Harvard University; the office she walks into is mine. We go through the basics of getting acquainted. I learn she is from Saint Louis, Missouri; her father owns a business that sells plumbing supplies; her mother is a homemaker. She wants to talk to me about careers." Spearman again looked from left to right across the audience. "There is nothing unusual about this story so far. Professors of economics are magnets for students with questions about careers.

"The student tells me that she wants to have a career where she can, as she puts it, 'help people.'" Spearman raised his hands to shoulder level and wiggled both his index fingers to give the "quotes" sign when he said "help people." International students in the audience wondered what he was doing. "She asks me about some nonprofit organizations and we talk about them. I inquire about her going into the family business: the plumbing supply company that her dad owns and operates. She says no, she isn't interested in joining the family business and reminds me she wants a career where she can 'help people,' rather than be engaged in 'making money.'" When Spearman said "help people" and when he said "making money," he again put up his hands and gave air quotes to emphasize that he was reciting the words of the student in his office. The international students in the audience now understood the gesture.

"'Helping people' and 'making money' are seen by many of my students at Harvard as antithetical. In their minds' eye, it would be as if an environmental activist decided to take up logging redwood forests as a hobby. In my student's case, she perceives a vocational fork in the road. One career path involves self-interest and the pursuit of money, and she perceives its operative words to be greed and self-interest. The other career path involves the nonprofit sector or government, where the operative words are public service and compassion.

"In my first talk, I mentioned the influence that Adam Smith had upon me during my student days. When students now come in my office with a question or problem, sometimes I think: what would Adam Smith do?" He paused, smiled and held up one wrist. "For the record, I am still undecided on whether to wear a wristband with the letters 'WWASD' on it."

As the audience chuckled Spearman continued. "What Adam Smith would tell this young woman from Saint Louis is a mystery to many. Smith called this mystery 'the invisible hand,' as if it were so elusive and nonintuitive that many people would never understand it." Spearman spread his hands out to the audience. "But I want you to understand Smith's metaphor, even though it may be a mystery to you initially. The truth here may be stranger than fiction.

"The mystery of the invisible hand is that the student who walked into my office might help people more, or help more people, if upon graduation from Harvard she returned to Saint Louis and ran the family business at a profit—rather than doing something different with the express purpose of 'helping people.'

"Adam Smith put it this way: 'It is not from the benevolence of the butcher, the brewer, or the baker that we expect our dinner, but from their regard to their own interest.' Put differently, we don't appeal to the good nature of those who make food and drink, we don't appeal to their sympathy, we don't appeal to their compassion, we don't even appeal to their desire to 'help other people' in order to get them to put food and drink on our table. The mystery of the invisible hand is that we appeal to their self-interest—and in the process, we will have more food and drink.

"To come back to the student who walked not into a bar, but an economist's office: the mystery of the invisible hand is that if this student were to 'make money' selling PVC pipe, a toilet, and a sink to a homeowner who is adding a new bathroom to a house, the student is making money. But she is also making the homeowner better off—in other words, 'helping people.'" Spearman again made the "quotes" sign with his fingers.

"The hidden economic logic here is that if this student wants to make others better off, she should endeavor to make herself better off by engaging in mutually advantageous transactions with her customers. Let me again paraphrase Adam Smith: it *is not from benevolence or compassion or pity* on the part of home improvement stores that a homeowner is able to add a new bathroom or repair a leaky toilet. It is from regard for their own interest. This *transformation* is what Adam Smith called 'the obvious and simple system of natural liberty.' One of the very few errors that Adam Smith made is that he failed to recognize that most people would not find his economic analysis 'obvious' or 'simple.'

"Now let me anticipate a question that many of you may have, and if you don't have this question, you should: Did Adam Smith contend that a system of market allocation would *always and invariably* promote the public good?

"Here's the answer: no, he did not. Nor do economists make that contention today. Adam Smith's obvious and simple system of natural liberty is not the same as utopia. If there is one thing that training in economics will *never* do, it is to turn someone into a utopianist. A realist? Yes. A pessimist? Maybe. A utopianist? Forget about it." Spearman paused, scanning the faces in the audience. "One of the most powerful principles of economic analysis is that pursuing one's self-interest could, as if by an invisible hand, bring about the public good. The claim is provocative; the idea is profound; but it is *not* Panglossian. Millions have died at the hand of totalitarianism. Not so by the invisible hand."

At this point, Spearman saw Sean Daniels in the audience. The young art assistant, now cleared of all charges, was seated between Annelle Cubbage and her husband. Sean looked sad. Spearman looked away, refusing to be distracted from the task at hand.

"Imagine a business firm that buys plumbing supplies from a manufacturer, and then shoulders the cost of holding these supplies in inventory: hoping against hope that someday a customer will want to purchase these products on terms that will sustain the continuing operation of the firm. Let me ask a rhetorical question. How can such a firm *ever* be an instrument of injustice or oppression? To *withhold* the supply of plumbing equipment might be unjust. But to supply these goods to willing and informed buyers cannot be unjust. That is why, in the case of a voluntary exchange between an informed buyer and an informed seller, each party, the seller and the buyer, can say 'thank you' to the other when the transaction is consummated.

"As you know, I have taught at Harvard for several years. On that campus are many organizations that offer students who want to help others an opportunity to band together and do so. I am pleased to see that Monte Vista University has a similar portfolio of student-led organizations. Perhaps only disciples of Friedrich Nietzsche would contend that these organizations do not contribute to the flourishing of the community. But the hidden economic logic of Adam Smith, and of economic analysis ever since, says that private enterprise and the pursuit of self-interest *also* contribute to the flourishing of a community. It follows as a matter of economic logic that to heavily tax and regulate private enterprise is to reduce the supply of this flourishing agent, not to expand its beneficial outreach. Through market exchange, one can do *good* by doing *well*.

"My good friend and colleague at Harvard, Henderson Ross, teaches psychology. Sometimes in his research he will throw out the name of a person or an object, and ask: 'what's the first thing that comes to your mind?' He then analyzes the responses that people give. Let me put on my Henderson Ross hat for a moment, and toss out a name: *John D. Rockefeller.* What is the first thing that comes into your mind?" He paused. Many in the audience had a puzzled look on their faces. "In my younger days the response would have been 'great wealth.' Even now, many of you probably have heard the expression 'rich as Rockefeller.' It is a bit antiquated, but it has a ring to it that 'rich as Gates' or 'rich as Buffett' does not have. But there are other possibilities.

"If you are a historian and you hear the name Rockefeller, you might think 'robber baron,' based on Matthew Josephson's book and its progeny. If you work in higher education, you might think of John D. Rockefeller as the man who put up the money to start the University of Chicago, one of the greatest academies of higher education in the world. If you are a scientist, you might think of Rockefeller University in New York, the first institution in the U.S. devoted only to biomedical research. If you are in economic development, you might think of the Rockefeller Foundation and all the money it has awarded to the governments of less developed countries. But if you think like an economist, you associate John D. Rockefeller with saving the whales."

Spearman stopped to let those last words sink in. He reckoned that very few people would know where he was going with that statement, and suspected that many in the audience were preparing themselves to disagree. But he knew, from his vantage point, that he had everyone's attention.

"Why is that, you wonder? Am I about to reveal that Rockefeller was a secret financier of Save the Whales or Greenpeace? No. But John D. Rockefeller did have a passion to produce petroleum products at low cost—so that he could make a lot of money through high volume operations. Economically he did very, very well doing just that. That's the source of the expression, so familiar to those of us with gray hair, or in my case very little hair, 'rich as Rockefeller.'

"And what has that to do with whales? Just this: as the innovations and economies of scale that Rockefeller pioneered became operational, the price of kerosene fell so low that whale oil was no longer competitive. The whaling industry in New England virtually disappeared. And the quality of life for whales around the world improved." He smiled at his audience. "Rockefeller's pursuit of self-interest may have saved more whales than dozens of individuals whose objective function was solely to save the whales." Some in the audience were persuaded, still others were thinking "that can't be right." Spearman left them no time for reflections. He went on.

"I think it was Robert Benchley who said the world is divided into two kinds of people: those who divide the world into two kinds of people and those who don't. I am in the first category. I think the world is divided into two kinds of people: those who think that complex systems work best with top-down control and those who think complex systems work best through decentralized cooperation. The first group actually has it backward. Simpler organizations, like a family or a small firm, need people called parents or managers to control the organization from the top down. Large organizations, like industries and economies, do not require top-down control. They function best without a central plan." By now Spearman was hitting on all cylinders as he spoke.

"Parents and dieticians tell us we can't have our cake and eat it too. But the principle of the invisible hand says you can. My student at Harvard can return to her home city upon graduation and simultaneously 'make money' and 'help people' by selling PVC pipe, sinks, and toilets. She can do good by doing well. Perhaps especially in her case, because some people think indoor plumbing is one of the most important indicators of human well-being. As a footnote on the mystery of the invisible hand: I suspect the local Habitat for Humanity benefits by having a well-run plumbing supply store in town. And if my student goes back to Saint Louis and does well by doing good, I suspect she will never run out of work or be unemployed."

Spearman gathered up his notes and looked out at his audience: "I thank you for your attention this evening. I believe there may be time for some questions." As he said this, Henry wondered inwardly if the questions would be about his economics or his sleuthing.

•

Herbert Abraham came on the stage and resumed the role he played in Spearman's first lecture: moderator and facilitator of a question and answer period. As he did earlier, Abraham explained the ground rules, emphasizing that this was a time for questions from the audience, not a time for speeches by members of the audience: "After all," he smiled, "we've already heard a speech."

He pointed to a student near the middle of the auditorium.

"My name is Sky Townsend and I'm a government major. I haven't taken an economics course. But I'll take one next year if you'll promise to stay at Monte Vista and not go back to Harvard." There was a smattering of applause heard in the auditorium. When it stopped, the student said, "So here's my question. My parents want me to take a job in the nonprofit sector. Part of this is because they think working in the nonprofit sector means I haven't sold out. My folks aren't here, but if they were, what would you tell them?" The young man sat down.

Spearman smiled at the student, realizing how different circumstances were today when compared with his own growing up. "I'm no expert in how you should deal with your parents, but let me make this suggestion. Tell them that the term 'nonprofit sector' is a *loaded one.*" Spearman emphasized his last two words. "Many of my students, and perhaps their parents, are attracted to the nonprofit sector because it sounds more winsome than the for-profit sector. But as a matter of language, it is just as accurate to describe the nonprofit sector as the *nontax sector.*" Spearman again placed emphasis on the last two words in the sentence. "Economic analysis, you see, doesn't draw a major distinction between those who are employed in the profit sector and those who are employed in the nonprofit sector. We start with a rational actor model in both. Workers in both sectors pursue their self-interest as they perceive it. The key distinction is that one sector pays taxes, the other does not."

Henry put his hands together as he continued: "And you can tell your parents what I am saying comes from someone who is employed in the so-called nonprofit sector. From an economic perspective, Harvard and Monte Vista are in the nontax sector. A school in the private sector that taught someone how to do computer programming would have to pay taxes on its revenues. But when Bill Gates was learning computer programming during his student days at Harvard, nobody paid any taxes on the transaction. A pretty sweet deal for Mr. Gates and Harvard."

Herbert Abraham next recognized a young man who was standing in the back against the wall of the auditorium. Henry had to strain to hear his question. "My name is Carlos and I am a sophomore from Mexico. I am here to learn economics. What I don't understand is why you say that doing good in the private sector is greater than doing good in the public sector. Is that what you mean?"

Spearman always endeavored to take questions seriously. From the perspective of his audience, it was their questions, not his prepared remarks, that brought the rubber to meet the road. Henry chose his words carefully, realizing not only that the question was profound but also that it would be heard in the student's second or even third language.

"Why do I say 'greater,' you ask? Why isn't it at least a wash? That's a very important question. The answer is that in order to have a flourishing sector of charities, churches, and other untaxed organizations, a flourishing

private sector of commerce is a necessity—if not a sufficient condition. I say this not for what you might think
is the reason: that people who 'make money' in the private sector often part with their assets to help finance the
nontax sector. That's true, but that is not the heart of the
matter. Here's what is." Spearman took off his glasses and
held them in his right hand.

"Without a flourishing private sector, there would be
no flourishing sector of charities, churches, and NGOs.
The contrast between Mexico and the USA is informative here. Americans support charities far more than do
the Mexicans. The reason is no doubt in part because the
USA is a more enterprise-oriented economy: Americans
do not yet think it is the role of the state to solve every
hardship. I'm not a student of the Mexican economy, but
I believe if free enterprise flourishes in Mexico as a substitute for state control, a flourishing sector of charities,
churches, and NGOs would almost certainly develop. But
whether that happens or not will be for your generation
to determine."

At this point, there were twenty hands in the audience beseeching Abraham for recognition. Herbert spotted among them a familiar face and pointed to Haiyang.
The young man stood up and spoke more to the crowd
than to the stage. "My name is Haiyang and I'm also an
international student. I'm from China. When I came to
this country to study, I had no idea that I would be in
a class with Professor Spearman who is such a famous
professor. And I had no idea I would observe one of my
professors solve a crime. But all this happened. Every student at Monte Vista University knows this. I want to ask

Professor Spearman a question about how he solved the crime. I hope that's okay."

The look of affirmation that swept across the auditorium was transparent. *Spearman as sleuth* was on everyone's mind. Indeed, everybody had seemingly been waiting for someone else to raise the topic. It took an undergraduate from another country to do so. Sensing the approval from the audience, and seeing a smile of encouragement from Herbert Abraham, Haiyang spoke directly to his art and econ teacher: "Professor Spearman, I was in class when you came to realize who killed our school's artist. You said the death effect helped you solve the crime. But what about the Coase conjecture?"

Spearman faced a dilemma. He was always reticent to "go public" about his endeavors at economic sleuthing. He worried that it could distract and detract from his scholarly work in economics. On the other hand, the local press had made a big deal of his role in bringing Dr. Ramos to justice. For many in the audience, this was a bigger deal than Spearman's academic accolades. He took a sip of water, buying a few more moments to think. What made answering Haiyang's question difficult was that most in the audience had never heard of Coase, much less the Coase conjecture, and were perfectly content to finish their lives in just such a condition. Henry cleared his throat.

"Let me say first to the audience that Haiyang is a student of mine and he's being modest: it was in part his research and that of his fellow students about what they called "the death effect" that helped me solve the crime. I have received far too much credit for bringing a murderer and a thief to justice. The city of San Antonio should be grateful to its police force and one of its members, Detective Fuller. And to my students."

Henry drained the last of the water in his cup and then looked directly at his student. "Haiyang, you and I both know there are people in the audience who do not want a sermon on the Coase conjecture. So let me answer your question with a confession: at first, I didn't see any connection between the Coase conjecture and the crime. In fact, the Coase conjecture almost kept me from seeing the hidden economic logic behind the crime. But then, in class with you and the other students one day, I fit it in properly."

Spearman's gaze swept across the audience as he said, "Coase spoke about durable goods—goods that don't wear out—and he conjectured that it is very difficult for a monopolist of a durable good to be able to charge a monopoly price for it."

Spearman then fixed his eyes back on Haiyang. "When I first had it in my head that art was the quintessential durable good, more durable than a washing machine or a refrigerator, I got sidetracked and thought there wouldn't be any monopoly gains from possessing all the works of an artist. An artist like Tristan Wheeler. So why try? But I was mistaken."

Spearman turned to the whole audience. "It was learning from my students about how art prices were determined that changed my thinking."

Spearman walked to the very front of the stage and directed his attention back to Haiyang: "Do you remember how in class we discussed the ratchet effect, or the fallacy of it?" Haiyang nodded. "Maybe you recall students offering evidence in class of the work of artists going up and down in response to market forces. That drove home to me that paintings, while durable, were not Coasian monopolies. Paintings are certainly durable goods. Remember Orley reminding us that the *Mona Lisa* is over five hundred years old? Miss Mona is a very durable gal. *Night Watch* by Rembrandt seems to be ageless."

Spearman took his eyes off Haiyang and spoke again to the crowd: "But my students helped me see that even if you had *all the works of art by one artist*, this was not the same as having a Coasian monopoly. To make that argument would be like arguing Colgate has a monopoly of Colgate toothpaste on the basis of it's being the only seller of Colgate toothpaste. We all know that Colgate is the only seller of Colgate toothpaste. But there are other brands competing with Colgate, like Crest, like Tom's, like dozens of store brands. These competitors prevent Colgate from having a monopoly, even though Colgate is the only seller of Colgate toothpaste. Okay, let's translate that to paintings.

"Imagine, just imagine, if you were fortunate enough to own *all* the Jackson Pollock paintings; every last one of them. That's like owning a brand name—but it's a brand with many competitors. Not so many that the market's perfectly competitive. Famous artists sell their paintings in a market of monopolistic competition. So each artist has some market power, some discretion over price. But not a lot. That's when I got the Coase conjecture right. In class that day it hit me, hit me so hard that I had to leave the classroom. I realized there were monopoly rents to be made if someone could get their hands on a bunch of paintings by a famous artist. Then this young man (here Spearman pointed to Haiyang) and his fellow students started talking about their research on the *death effect*—that's the exact term they used—how the death effect could affect the value of the paintings of an up-and-coming middle-aged artist."

Henry paused and his smile faded momentarily. "I'd like to be able to say this was a 'eureka' moment for me. Actually I became ill. But economic reasoning was the tonic I needed. When I made use of what Agatha Christie called the 'little gray cells' I was able to return to class and make sense of the situation." Spearman paused. "Now Haiyang, that's a very long-winded answer to your question, and I suspect I've tried the patience of our audience in answering."

If the intense attention of the audience was any barometer, Henry was wrong on this account.

•

Herbert Abraham returned to the podium and said, "Monte Vista University knew it was getting an economist when Professor Spearman joined our faculty. We didn't know we would be getting Sherlock Holmes as well. Henry, the community is in your debt for both reasons." Abraham gave a slight bow to Spearman and then announced, "This next question will be the last."

Several hands shot up hoping for attention. A young woman in the second row was the favored questioner. She rose from her seat. "Hi Professor Spearman. Thanks for talking to us tonight. And thanks for coming to Monte Vista. My name is Shelby Colby, I'm from Houston, and this is my question. I know it's the last one, so I'll try to make it good. First off, I'm an econ major at Monte Vista. I think I agree with everything you say. But when I talk with other students, and frankly a lot of my professors who aren't in my major, they just don't seem to get it. They don't like markets, they don't like international trade, and I can't talk them out of it. Do you know why that is?"

Spearman looked kindly at the young woman. He had become fond of Monte Vista's students. Their ratio of earnestness to cynicism was appealing. Henry stepped from behind the lectern as if to address the student more directly. "The question you raise is as much one of rhetoric as it is of economic analysis. And your difficulty is not unique. I mentioned my dear friend Henderson Ross earlier in my lecture. We have been friends for years. And I can tell you that he is very smart—in his field. But Professor Ross is tone deaf when it comes to economics. So what's going on here?

"The primary shortcoming of those who care about economic issues, but do not know economics, is that they view the world as a zero-sum game. In a zero-sum game, if there are three ice cream cones to be allocated, if this person gets one, that person gets another, and the person over there gets one, I do not get any." Spearman pointed to three students in the audience who were seated close to the front of the stage.

"Now a lot of things in the world *are* zero-sum games: chess, poker—when Mr. and Mrs. Jones argue who will drive the car to the grocery. But in a market economy, if someone opens a Chinese restaurant in Cambridge, Massachusetts, or San Antonio, Texas—or your hometown of Houston—and prospers in doing so, a zero-sum game is not being played out. If someone invents a ball point pen or an automatic transmission or a cell phone and makes money selling these products, a zero-sum game is not being played out.

"What economists call a positive sum game is played when people trade, when people innovate, when people exchange labor services for wages. Both sides of the transaction can be better off. It is the hidden logic of economics that makes this point. But the logic is indeed hidden to many, even to those who want to 'do good' but cannot imagine doing so while 'doing well.'"

Unlike the other questioners, Miss Colby had stood up to ask her question and remained standing during Spearman's response. When Henry had finished his answer, to the surprise of everyone, she then interjected, "Well, if so many people don't get it, don't get economics I mean, should my generation be optimistic or pessimistic about the future?"

Herbert Abraham started to tell the young woman that she already had asked the last question, but Spearman waved him off.

"No, no," he said to Abraham, "that is such an important question let me respond to it. We'll call it a footnote to Miss Colby's question, so technically it's part of the same inquiry on her part."

Nobody in the audience budged. Spearman left his place beside Abraham and walked to the very front of the stage in order to speak directly to his young questioner.

"One of the curses of being an economist is that we usually end up being optimists and pessimists, *at the same time*. Now how can that be? you ask. Here's how. Economists are *pessimists* when we look forward: we see politicians and corporations engage in rent seeking, enacting rules and regulations that subvert the operation of the invisible hand. We see bankers in bed with government leaders consensually distorting capital markets. We see the desire for more goods and services constrained by the production possibility frontier. We see no prospect around the corner for an end to the gut-wrenching poverty that affects so many people, particularly those who live outside of what Adam Smith called the 'obvious and simple system of natural liberty.' So we wallow in pessimism looking forward.

"But then, *then* economists look backward. And we observe the stunning increase in real per capita income that has been part of the West over the past two centuries, and now is affecting other parts of the globe. We see the technological changes that have come out of Silicon Valley connected with computerization and the Internet. We realize that it is no longer the few that own the majority of the world's stocks and bonds, but the many. We see the rise of global markets and the enhanced competition that international trade brings to consumers. We observe how those same markets afford opportunities to entrepreneurs around the world, not just in Silicon Valley but in Vietnam, and India, and I hope soon in Africa and the Middle East. And looking backward, we notice that almost all governments in the world now realize that communism is an empty economic promise. When

I look backward I am no longer gloomy about the future for my students."

•

After the lecture, Pidge and Henry walked back to their home on Oakmont Court, both of them realizing that there would be only a couple more nights at this address before they returned to Cambridge. They were quiet as they passed what had been Tristan Wheeler's home.

The Spearmans' time at Monte Vista had been congenial—though not at all what Pidge and Henry had anticipated. Their expectations did not include Henry being caught up in the detection of criminal activity. In addition, because Henry's Art and Economics class was an experiment, he did not have high expectations of its success. But the class turned out to be a hit, for him and the students—so much so that Henry planned to offer a similar course at Harvard when he returned. As they walked, the two looked up at the star-filled Texas sky.

"The stars at night are big and bright, deep in the heart of Texas." Pidge laughed as she sang a line from the song that had now become familiar to her. She turned her face to Henry, whose own countenance was hidden in the dark. "A penny for your thoughts."

"I think because of inflation, you should at least raise the offer to 'a dollar for your thoughts.' Maybe even two dollars."

"Henry, I'm serious. I thought you gave one of your best talks tonight. But our time here is winding down. Are you glad we came to Texas? I am, but you're the one who had to sing for our supper."

Henry's response to Pidge was brief. "The benefits exceeded the costs," he said, "so I'm glad we came." He took his wife's hand but he walked on in silence.

After more than thirty years of marriage, Pidge knew when to pursue an answer and when to leave it alone. This was one of those times to leave it alone. She knew her husband was reflecting on his answer—and he was.

Spearman thought about the farewell he would soon be saying to his colleagues in the Department of Economics. Because Spearman had gone directly from being a student at one Ivy League university to the faculty at another, he'd been uncertain what to expect from his economist colleagues at Monte Vista University. What drove his colleagues at Harvard was a zeal to be published in the top-five scholarly journals. This was the coin of the realm. One Harvard economist even added, "It is not enough that I succeed, others must fail."

At Monte Vista University, it was okay to be more enthused about the marginal productivity of Tim Duncan, the NBA star, than of Duncan Black, the economics scholar. After a semester in San Antonio, Spearman now knew the difference between the two Duncans and understood the comparative advantage of each. One was more highly paid—Spearman smiled at his own corny pun—because he was better at dunkin.'

Spearman could not imagine Duncan Black living up to his namesake on the basketball courts. And at his height, Henry knew that he would never experience a true baller's rush. He would leave it to others to ply that trade. Henry Spearman was content to play on the team of those who practiced the dismal science, which he knew to be anything but.

ACKNOWLEDGMENTS

Grateful acknowledgment is made for permission to reprint the following epigraphs.

PAGE VI from *The Limits of Organization* by Kenneth Arrow. Copyright © 1974 by the Fels Center of Government. Used by permission of W. W. Norton & Company, Inc.

PAGE VII from *The Simple Art* of Murder by Raymond Chandler, copyright © 1934, 1935, 1936, 1938, 1939, 1944, 1950 by Raymond Chandler, copyright © 1939 by The Curtis Publishing Company. Used by permission of Vintage Books, an imprint of the Knopf Doubleday Publishing Group, a division of Random House LLC, and the Estate of Raymond Chandler. All rights reserved.

PAGE 19 from *Rat Race* by Dick Francis. Copyright © 1970 by Dick Francis. Reprinted by permission of Harper-Collins Publishers, and SLL/Sterling Lord Literistic Inc.

PAGE 43 from *The Witness for the Prosecution and Other Stories* by Agatha Christie. Copyright © 1948 by Agatha Christie Limited. Reprinted by permission of Harper-Collins Publishers.